Robert Edric's previous novels include *Winter Garden* (1985 James Tait Black Prize winner), *A New Ice Age* (1986 runner-up for the Guardian Fiction Prize), *A Lunar Eclipse* (1989), *The Earth Made of Glass* (1994), *Elysium* (1995), *In Desolate Heaven* (1997) and *The Sword Cabinet* (1999). He lives in East Yorkshire.

D1017828

Critical acclaim for *The Book of the Heathen*:

'The best historical fiction has something to say about the present as well as the past. Edric has demonstrated this in his previous novels and does so again, with accomplishment, in this latest work . . . Edric, prolific and critically acclaimed since his prize-winning debut in 1985, has struck an especially rich vein of form of late . . . the writing is as clear and intelligent as ever, without being showy, and achieves the vital unities of theme and story, past and present, personal and political. Europe's colonial grip may have relaxed since Victorian times, but Edric offers a characteristically subtle counterpoint to the relationship between men, and between the strong and the weak in today's global economy'
Martyn Bedford, *Good Book Guide*

'Edric describes a compelling plot in fine, spare prose'
David Isaacson, *Daily Telegraph*

'Stunning . . . evocatively brings to life the stifling humidity and constant rainfall of the Congo'
John Cooper, *The Times*

'Edric is a prolific and highly talented writer whose books give historical fiction a good name. They are distinguished not only by their formal skill and wide-ranging subject matters, but by their hairless, unshowy prose. In *The Book of the Heathen*, he uses suspense and thriller techniques to telling effect. His linguistic minimalism can also be effective – his low-key description of a hanging is quite the most harrowing I've ever read'
Sukhdev Sandhu, *Guardian*

'Many respectable judges would put Edric in the top ten of British novelists currently at work . . . as a writer, he specialises in the delicate hint and the game not given away . . . the territory Edric colonises is very much his own'
D.J. Taylor, *Spectator*

'Relentless . . . an impressive and disturbing work of art'
Robert Nye, *Literary Review*

'More disturbing even than Conrad in his depection of the heart
of darkness . . . out of the pervading miasma of futility
– conjured up with Edric's usual atmospheric masterfulness –
loom cameos of savagery and heartlessness. Their subjects
sometimes recall George Orwell's writings. So does the terse,
trenchant unforgettableness with which they are conveyed . . .
rendered in prose whose steadiness and transparency throw the
dark turbulence of what is happening into damning relief.
Admirers of Conrad will soon spot affinities between this book
and *Heart of Darkness* . . . but where Conrad leaves "the horror"
at the centre of his story unspecific, Edric gives his a hideously
charred and screaming actuality that sears it into the memory. It
will be surprising if this year sees a more disturbing or haunting
novel'
Peter Kemp, *Sunday Times*

'Intricately patterned . . . precise and compelling . . . maintains
a relentless hold on the reader's interest . . . a fable about
versions of truth and moral responsibility. It also belongs to a
very British tradition: the mapping of non-Europe as a nightmare world in which the European psyche confronts its own
dark madness'
Aamer Hussein, *Independent*

'All the characters are memorably described. No less vivid is the
author's depiction of the landscape, whose treacherous rivers
and menacing tracts of wilderness provide a suitably unstable
backdrop to this tale of shifting loyalties. Here and elsewhere
in his fiction, Edric writes compellingly about relationships
between men'
Christina Koning, *The Times*

'A very gripping story . . . the reader is drawn in inexorably to
discover what horror lies at the heart of it . . . an apocalyptic
fable for today'
John Spurling, *TLS*

Also by Robert Edric

WINTER GARDEN
A NEW ICE AGE
A LUNAR ECLIPSE
IN THE DAYS OF THE AMERICAN MUSEUM
THE BROKEN LANDS
HALLOWED GROUND
THE EARTH MADE OF GLASS
ELYSIUM
IN DESOLATE HEAVEN
THE SWORD CABINET

THE BOOK OF
THE HEATHEN

Robert Edric

BLACK SWAN

THE BOOK OF THE HEATHEN
A BLACK SWAN BOOK : 0 552 99925 3

Originally published in Great Britain by Anchor,
a division of Transworld Publishers

PRINTING HISTORY
Anchor edition published 2000
Black Swan edition published 2001

1 3 5 7 9 10 8 6 4 2

Set in 11/13pt Melior by
Kestrel Data, Exeter, Devon.

Black Swan Books are published by Transworld Publishers,
61–63 Uxbridge Road, London W5 5SA,
a division of The Random House Group Ltd,
in Australia by Random House Australia (Pty) Ltd,
20 Alfred Street, Milsons Point, Sydney, NSW 2061, Australia,
in New Zealand by Random House New Zealand Ltd,
18 Poland Road, Glenfield, Auckland 10, New Zealand
and in South Africa by Random House (Pty) Ltd,
Edulini, 5a Jubilee Road, Parktown 2193, South Africa.

Printed and bound in Great Britain by
Clays Ltd, St Ives plc.

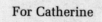
For Catherine

Imagine how we might now be forced to reconsider our understanding of the situation were the so-called heathen of the Bula Matari (Congo Free State) to contain among his multitudes men capable of keeping accounts of these terrible events, of this shameful history told only once – imagine his own books and what they might tell us – imagine then how we might be forced to live with our disgraceful part in all of this.

Roger Casement
Diary, 20 July 1893

... thou knowest the people,
that they are set upon mischief.
For they said unto me
'Make us gods, which shall
go before us ...'

Exodus, 32, 22–23

Marked in the personal Bible of
N.E.S. Frere (1864–1897)
The Pitt-Rivers Museum, Oxford

The Ukassa Falls Concessionary Station

The Congo Free State
May, 1897

PART ONE

1

Across the river the Custom House gun was fired, and at the instant it sounded I raised my pen from the chart on which I was working so that my momentary distraction might not become a waver, an irregularity on the contour where none otherwise existed, a tree in the treeless desert, or, worse still, a blot, the map-maker's clumsy footprint.

It was two in the afternoon, and the gun was normally fired only at the start and close of each day's trading; for it to be fired then suggested an unexpected arrival or some alarm.

I rose from my desk and removed the weights from my chart, allowing it to roll stiffly inwards until all its new country was lost. I knew that no arrival of any consequence had been anticipated that day, and that none of the usual business of such arrivals – none of the excited gatherings, the shuffling of the smaller vessels, the congregation of the traders and middle-men – had preceded the gun.

I waited as the shot faded in its smothered echoes, and even before these were gone my mind turned from the possibility of a vessel to the near-certain conviction that what the gun heralded was the return of Frere.

I remained where I stood, unable to act upon that conviction. He had been gone from us for fifty-one days – and perhaps I alone knew that much – and fifty-one days was a lifetime in that place.

Securing my chart in a strong-box, I went outside.

The river beyond the compound was broad and high, and the far shore was so crowded with vessels and stalls and men moving among them that it was impossible to determine what might be happening there.

Fletcher and Cornelius emerged together from one of our warehouses, and they too stood and looked across the water. I heard Fletcher say something and then laugh. Cornelius came to me, and I knew without asking that he shared my concern regarding Frere. He pointed to where a drift of pale smoke hung above the trees. We searched the river in both directions, but saw nothing.

'Perhaps Hammad,' he said, but with no real conviction.

Fletcher walked closer to the water's edge. He raised the binoculars from his chest and focused them on the distant shore, slowly scanning whatever he saw there. We watched him for several minutes, waiting for him to tell us what he'd seen.

Cornelius wiped an already saturated cloth over his wet face.

'We'll know soon enough,' he said.

I had been about to suggest finding someone to take us across to the Belgians, and perhaps Cornelius suspected this, for he repeated, 'Soon enough,' and then left me, his words a check to my impulse.

Soon after, a second, lesser shot sounded across the water, but this was of no consequence, a pistol or a rifle in the hands of a man who fired it with no more

18

thought for the consequences than a child throwing a stone.

I stood in the full heat of the sun for several minutes longer before returning to the relative cool of my room and the smaller, more calculated dramas of my map.

It was a joke they played in those mongrel towns of Yaba, Kabinda and Boma. Each newly arrived European was met and told there was a certain place to be seen and a decision to be made prior to his journey inland. It was a joke less frequently played by the French and Portuguese, and not at all by the Belgians since the Lado debacle – something better suited, everyone was agreed, to the schooled and face-saving determination of the English. And the joke was this: someone would await these excited newcomers, greet them effusively and then take them to the nearest overgrown graveyard, whereupon they would be asked to pick out a grave-site for themselves and then be asked whether they wished to be buried facing the sea upon which they would never sail home again, or inland, where they were certain to die.

Some saw the joke for what it was and despised the men who played it, the men who moved not ten miles in any direction year in year out. Others grew angry and marched cursing away from the bone-yards. And others still, those men so unexpectedly and painfully conscious of everything they had left behind them – men whose entire lives and their every possession, their names and futures included, still hung in the balance – took the joke at its true worth and pointed to the particular plots they might prefer. Some even went so far as to conquer the joke and the men who played it and put down a deposit on their chosen sites.

I learned all this from Fletcher. He and Abbot were

taken together to the graveyard at Boma. Upon realizing their purpose there, Abbot, already weak and emaciated from his illness at sea, vomited a fine spray of yellow bile over his feet. Fletcher, having been aware all along of what was happening, took out his pistol, pushed it into the cheek of the Zanzibari who had taken them, forced him to his knees and told him to wipe Abbot's boots clean with his sleeve. The man laughed and begged not to be shot. He prostrated himself, and Abbot retched again, this time over the man's head and shoulders. Fletcher watched for a moment, looked slowly around them, and then pointed his pistol to the side of the man and fired into the dirt. Scavenging dogs froze briefly at their digging, waited, and then resumed. The Zanzibari screamed and clasped his hands over the back of his head.

I heard all this on Fletcher's return to the Station. He had been gone two months on rubber business, and had planned his visit to Boma so that he might collect Abbot, our new senior clerk, and travel back with him on the mission steamer. Upon their return, Abbot, still suffering, demanded to be shown to his quarters and to be left alone there. I asked Fletcher what he thought of the man, but all he would say was, 'Untrustworthy,' – the shaky plinth upon which Abbot for ever afterwards stood. Then Fletcher told me how much he had paid for his own burial plot at Sinda almost twenty years earlier, and how he had demanded a certificate of sale to prove his ownership of this unthinkable future.

James Charles Russel Frasier. My name. A staff and guide of a name. The Leicestershire Russels, the Northamptonshire Frasiers. A history and a geography of a name. Two baronets, three members of parliament, one secretary of state; two lord justices; one bishop, still serving, and military men beyond number garlanded with praise and burnished by success. A cradle to grave of a name.

I have seen none of these people for three years, and neither sent nor received any communication for ten months.

Educated at Rugby, Trinity and Sandhurst, I served with the Seventh Fusiliers in India and Kandahar, and afterwards with Brackenbury in Egypt. I believe the phrase is 'Served with Honour and Distinction'. I was wounded twice at Tel-el-kebir and still bear both marks – one on my shoulder, the other across my thigh.

And now I have lost all that. I am not a man given to exaggeration or melodrama, but, equally, I am a man no longer in possession of that history and geography, that staff, guide, light and sustaining warmth. The great enterprise upon which I and the others here were once embarked has collapsed and left us barely recognizable as the men we once were.

As a girl, my mother was a companion of the young Queen, and my father walked the corridors of state as though he were passing along the clean, dry stalls of his stables. My great-uncle – whom I will not name – swept his palm across a map and thousands of men moved one way and then another. As a small boy I imagined him just as capable of controlling the ebb and flow of the tides. A man possessed of faith in himself is possessed of everything, that great-uncle once told me. By extension, I can only assume that a man who once had that faith and who has it no longer is possessed of nothing.

When I was four years old and about to be dispatched to the first of my schools, my General uncle visited me and presented me with a short sword. He told me something of the man he had killed and from whom he had taken it. He spoke of this man – an Afghan tribesman, I remember – with great respect, affection almost. At the time I was a frightened child with a frightened child's grasp of the spreading world and I understood little of what he was telling me.

When I first came here, the whole world was devoted to the unstoppable profit of our enterprise. Profit at a cost we none of us then truly understood; or a cost we carelessly ascribed elsewhere. On the occasion of my being introduced to Fletcher by Cornelius we were interrupted by the arrival of three Kallisa River savages who had escaped from the diamond beds there and who had brought stolen gems to sell to us. Cornelius examined these. It was a poor crop. But the savages remained excited about the size of the stone still in the stomach of the third man, which he was having difficulty passing. Cornelius squeezed and prodded the man's stomach, saying that if what he could feel was a diamond, then judging by its size it was a valuable one. Fletcher pushed the three men out of the room, accusing them of wasting our time. If the diamond could not be produced then it was of no value. He told the men to come back when it was in their hands. Two of the men returned the following day with the gem. Fletcher quizzed them on the whereabouts of the man who had carried the stone, and they became evasive, saying he was in the forest tending to his wounds.

'It could have been worse,' Fletcher said. 'They could have brought us his corpse.'

Cornelius concurred with this, and he washed the stone with brandy before handling it.

For the rest of the day I remained distracted, unable, despite sitting at my desk for several hours longer, to concentrate on the minutiae of my charts. I sought

22

no-one out and was visited by no-one. The work of the compound went on around me.

Late in the afternoon, I went to find Abbot. At his insistence, our meetings now took place daily. He falsely imagined the two of us to be allies because of the complementary nature of our work here. In addition to being the appointed map-maker, I am also employed as a 'technical overseer' to the Company's various concessionary enterprises. Upon long ago enquiring what this entailed, I was reassured that my work would become obvious to me upon my arrival. I was told this by a senior Company official who laughed softly at everything I asked him and then laughed again at his own indulgent and dismissive answers. This secondary role, I soon discovered, was merely to inhabit the spaces left by those already here. Accordingly, I had some relation with all the senior officers, but Abbot was the only one among these keen to establish our shared functions and responsibilities in any formal or official – for which, understand officious – manner.

He was a man much given to facts and figures, a man who did not believe he had fully mastered or understood the nature of a situation unless he had reduced it to his meticulously kept columns and pages. Needless to say, his understanding of a great deal was, of necessity, incomplete and superficial. He had come to the Company straight from the Merchant Taylor's School, had worked in the Tilbury office for two years as an excise collector, and had then, I imagine, pleaded to be sent here.

Upon meeting Abbot, I had guessed his age to be twenty-two or -three and was surprised when he angrily declared himself to be nine years older.

He was not in his office, where I expected to find

him, surrounded by the ledgers and files with which he clothed himself, and I was told by Bone that he had been seen earlier at the quarry. 'Sticking his nose in,' was what Bone said. I debated abandoning my search for the man, but had I not sought him out he would in all likelihood have come looking for me later and then filled the evening with the talk he considered to be conversation.

The quarry stood almost a mile from the Station and its river anchorage. It was the first of the Company's endeavours in the region, inherited from its previous owners in a distant and increasingly profitless transfer of shares. Its original purpose had been to provide ballast for a proposed railway east along the line of the Lulindi towards Lake Albert; and following that the stone and foundations for a new town. Like a great deal else, neither of these projects progressed much beyond the impressive-looking maps upon which they were first planned. The railway started its journey, the town was staked out, the forest felled and foundations laid, but there everything ended. Now the quarry sent its stone elsewhere. Some thin veins of iron and gold had been struck and a smelter built. Labour was unending and cheap. Twenty years ago, a bed of cloudy emeralds had also been discovered, and this was enough for the operation to be expanded in limitless expectation.

I exhausted myself on the climb to the ridge overlooking the workings. I saw Abbot ahead of me, gesticulating to a group of men sitting around him. As I approached he lowered his voice, and one by one the men rose and walked away from him. Some wore cloths around their loins, but most were naked, though with the appearance of being clothed by virtue of the clay which coated them.

Abbot saw me approaching and immediately stopped

24

shouting. He took out his watch and studied it, perhaps hoping to suggest to me that he had been betrayed by it into missing our rendezvous.

He was standing alone by the time I reached him.

I waited for him to speak.

'They work for an hour and rest for an hour,' he said. 'They have no idea.'

I looked down the steep slope beneath us and saw the line of men follow a narrow path to the floor of the hole. Several hundred others worked elsewhere, most visible only by their motions, unseen when they stopped moving against the shovelled earth.

'Take their names,' I suggested.

'I did.'

'They will have lied to you.'

'I know. But I took down their lies all the same.' He tapped the ledger he held beneath his arm.

'Is it progressing?'

'It always progresses.' It was a common enquiry and answer, as all-encompassing and as meaningless as the collision of two clouds. He began to point out to me where rock had recently been excavated, to where a band of one per cent ore was being followed. Within the greater scheme of things – and we were forever being made aware of this greater scheme of things, the excuse of the receding future – it was decided that when the work in the quarry was completed the excavated hole would be filled with diverted river water and afterwards be employed as a reliable source of power to drive the turbines of either a larger smelter or whatever industry arose within the proposed town. I knew from a cursory study of the geology of the place that none of this was going to happen. Abbot alone professed faith in these impossibilities.

'You needn't have come,' he said, as though I were

his subordinate and he my beneficent superior. He looked away to the far side of the quarry. 'Will you survey the new work for your charts?'

'Of course.' It was clear to me that he wanted to ask me about Frere.

'You heard the gun,' I said, unwilling to indulge him beyond the few facts of the matter. It was by then common knowledge that Frere sat in the Belgian gaol.

'Can we be certain it's him?' he said.

'I think so.'

Abbot had been the source of a great deal of amusement to Frere, and though seldom openly hostile towards each other, there was a degree of antagonism between the two men, nurtured and shaped mostly by Abbot, which, prior to Frere's disappearance, had grown increasingly uncontainable. Upon Frere's disappearance, and then again upon the tales of his actions reaching us, Abbot had become brave and had openly condemned him. Now, with Frere's return, he was again less certain of himself and his accusations. He understood my own attachment to Frere, but never doubted that this was misplaced, and that he, Abbot, might provide a more suitable companion and confidant. 'Suitable' was the word he used.

'What will happen to him?' he said.

'I don't know.'

'He surely won't be allowed to stay here.'

'I don't know.'

He paused. 'What will *you* do?'

Like Cornelius, he harboured some notion of Frere's contagion; unlike Cornelius, he did not understand the true nature of that contamination.

'Someone ought to keep a full record of events,' he said, looking away from me as he spoke, almost as though the suggestion had not been his, merely something he was repeating. And meaning that he had already started to keep that record.

I looked pointedly at the satchel at his feet.

'It's the proper thing to do,' he insisted.

'I know.'

My insincere concession exasperated him further. 'He killed a child, for God's sake,' he said.

'We don't know that.' I kept my voice low and even.

'Everyone says so. And worse.'

'Is that what you've already written?'

He picked up the satchel and held it to his chest.

'Even *you* can't close your eyes to what's happened. Why do you insist on defending him?'

'He may not require defending,' I said, knowing this was untrue, but not in the way he had meant it.

'I have to go,' he said. He was a man of hourly appointments, again at his own contrivance. Hourly appointments in a place where others counted month to month on their fingers.

'Of course,' I said, relieved to see him go.

I waited until he was out of sight before following the same curving path back down the hillside.

It rained heavily through the night. I set out my containers and watched the water pour in. I checked that my charts and books were safe from this assault, and then waited to ascertain where new inroads had been made. Old leaks dried up and new ones appeared. It was Cornelius's task, as our Senior Quartermaster, to ensure that our dwellings and the Company offices remained habitable, but where these downpours were concerned there had long existed a policy of partial defeat and compromise.

Earlier, I spent the afternoon with Cornelius and his warehousemen. We played cards, and they drank the

27

liquor they either distilled themselves or bought from the Manyema traders who delivered it in pails, the variable potency of which could never be truly ascertained until long after it had been consumed.

The warehouse in which we sat and waited out the rain was better protected than most, containing as it did the more profitable of the Company's dry goods, our own provisions included. Periodically, Cornelius and I rose from the game and made a brief tour of inspection, pausing to listen for the noise of the water where it could not be seen. Small birds flew back and forth in the high roof above us. Water ran in sheets over the unglazed openings along the lower walls and gathered in puddles on the floor.

Outside, men came and went through the downpour as though it were not happening.

Upon our arrival here together, I had helped Frere set out his rain gauges and had accompanied him on his rounds to record their findings. On one such outing, after a particularly heavy downpour, we came to each of the delicate instruments to find them smashed and useless. I expected him to be distraught at the discovery, but he merely remarked on his own stupidity at not having better protected the glass phials and funnels. It occurred to me then that some agent other than the rain had caused the damage, that the instruments had perhaps been regarded as unwelcome totems or fetishes and had been accordingly destroyed.

Less than a month later, Frere called on me to help him set out his new gauges. These were made of tin and wood and were considerably larger than the original instruments. He showed me the plans he had drawn up in designing and constructing the boxes. Each was as precisely drawn and measured as the vital parts of an engine might be drawn, and as accurately sketched as any of the countless thousands of beetles or butterflies he had drawn since.

It was clear to me that Cornelius had taken me away from the card-players to discuss Frere. I knew that of all the others, he alone came closest to sharing my concern for the man. He and Frere had shared a great many interests, and both had formed an attachment to the place beyond that demanded by the terms of their employment. Regardless of his own doubts, I knew that Cornelius alone might be my only ally in attempting to achieve something on Frere's behalf, even if neither he nor I yet understood what that might be, and how little, in reality, it might amount to.

'About Frere . . .' he said, prompting me.

'Whatever happens, the facts of the matter will need to be separated from all the wild tales and speculation,' I told him, forcing conviction into my voice.

'And you believe that is possible, you truly believe that the two can be separated, one from the other, like so much chaff from grain?'

'Perhaps not, but it will be our responsibility to try.'

He remained unconvinced.

Upon first being introduced to Cornelius van Klees, he looked to me – perhaps because of his age and his meticulously kept beard and moustache – like someone who might once have been painted by van Eyck or Holbein, a courtier perhaps, a wealthy merchant or ship-owner. Despite the length of time he had lived there, his face bore none of the more usual signs of the place. He was a quietly efficient and courteous man, who treated his workers well, who knew when to indulge them, and how afterwards to recoup that indulgence.

'Ought we not to expedite matters by sending him directly to the coast?' he said.

'And let them deal with him there?'

'It might be the correct thing to do.' The more agitated he became, so the more pronounced his accent became, along with the formality of his language. He must have known that the Company directors would not countenance the removal of Frere from the Station.

It occurred to me then what he was having such difficulty in saying to me.

'You think *I* should question him, draw up a report?'

He stopped pacing. 'You are his closest friend here.'

Neither of us spoke for a moment. Everything that needed to be said had been said.

'I'll go and see him, of course,' I said. 'And, hopefully, return with him.' We had our own gaol, for the exclusive use of Company employees, and our own gaoler in Sergeant Bone.

'You think that wise?' he said.

'It will at least remove him from the scrutiny and condemnation of others.'

The gaol across the river, built originally by Hammad to house his slaves, was little more than an underground warren in which more men died than lived, and in which dead men had remained manacled to the walls for days after they had died.

'Which of the tales do you believe?' I asked him.

He shook his head. 'I merely wonder at their details, at the way they are so consistently and insistently repeated.' There was a warning in his words and I heeded it. 'We live too close to the new era,' he said, slapping his palm against the tin wall and causing it to shake.

The remark, and the violence of his gesture, surprised me.

'What new era?'

'This, all this, Africa. Once it was all a game, a board upon which to play, but all that has gone.'

I regretted this sudden turn in his pleading. I told him I didn't understand him, but in truth I understood half of what he was telling me.

'I mean that once we did all this unnoticed, unwatched, forgotten.'

'And now the eyes of the world are on us?'

'The greedy eyes of the world. Everything we do is examined, sifted and sorted for its countless other meanings and significances.'

He had lived in the country for forty years, arriving as a nineteen-year-old. It was said that he had returned home to Belgium only once in all that time, three years after his first sight of the place. It was rumoured that when Cornelius finally went or died, then the Belgians would close their fist on the last of our concessions here.

We were distracted from our thoughts by calls from the card-players to return to them.

The men had finished their first pail of drink, and another sat at their centre. They dipped their cups into this – some scooped out the liquor with their hands – and with their increasing drunkenness, so their gambling became ever more theatrical and reckless.

We sat with them but declined their entreaties to rejoin the game. A few notes and coins lay on the ground beside the empty pail, but the substance of the gambling now lay more in the noisy expectation and soon-forgotten promises which littered the place, and which were added to with the turn of each torn and dirty card.

2

A further three days passed before I crossed the river to visit Frere. The water at the Station was too high and the boatmen who plied the crossing awaited their customers a mile upriver, negotiating the rapids and exposed bars while being carried downriver as fast as they were able to pole and row across the flow. Crossing in this way, one invariably arrived on the far shore soaked from head to foot, and steaming in the heat. One of the first lessons I was taught by Cornelius was to learn to judge the river and then to walk as far upstream as I deemed necessary. There would always be someone waiting, he told me, and invariably there was.

I left my room before dawn, wanting to be beyond our outer perimeter before the first light of the day fell in on us. I told no-one of my intended visit, knowing only that by then everyone expected it of me. Little further news of Frere had reached us during those three days.

I followed a trail through the tall grass. The smoke of early scattered fires hung low around me, in places so perfectly level and unmoving that it might have been so many ponds.

I studied the river as I went, reassuring myself that I understood the vague calculations I was making. In truth, whether the water was high or low, fast or barely moving, I frequently walked to the same low promontory where the same old boatman was waiting.

I passed several others asleep in their vessels. Some had their wives and children alongside them, all sleeping in the river mud and against the banks, all appearing more animal than human in that half-light.

I arrived at the promontory and saw the man and boat beneath me. The man was awake and waiting, facing the river. Beside him squatted a child whom I recognized as the deformed and stunted boy who frequently inhabited the compound, and who was employed by some of us to undertake those menial tasks upon which we would not waste our own time. He excavated and then later emptied our cess pools; he scraped our specimen hides; he cleaned dirty rubber and tended its choking fires; he sang and danced for us; he gathered up our spent cartridges and sold them as charms.

The boatman and the boy were often together, but I was not aware of any family connection between them, and it was only as I saw them there that morning, outlined against the sheen of the river, that I realized I knew neither of their names.

At my approach, the man identified me and then stood aside from the path to his boat. The boy went immediately to the vessel and pushed it into the water. Seeing the orchestrated simplicity of their actions, it was not difficult to believe that they had been waiting for me.

I offered my greeting to the man. He was formal in his response, nodding but saying nothing. And then he raised the short stick he held and pointed to one side of me. The deformed boy, who was mostly devoid of language, made a blowing sound and rubbed his arms vigorously, as though warming his muscles for the task ahead. We all called him a boy, though I suspect his size and shape belied his true age and he was much older – perhaps eighteen or nineteen, say – than any of us imagined or wanted to imagine. I was distracted by this sudden noise, but then drawn back to the boatman by the jabbing motion he made with his stick.

I looked to where he pointed. Another man sat further along the bank, again distinguishable only in outline in the half-light, and by the glow of the cigarette he smoked. As I looked, he rose and came towards us. He called out to me by name. Bone. I felt myself tense at the voice. It was clear that he too had been waiting for me, and I cursed my predictability. The boatman, having served his warning, pushed his stick into the mud at his feet and picked up his long oar instead.

'What kept you? Been here two hours,' Bone said. 'Fletcher said you'd wait for a quiet day and make an early start. Five, he reckoned. Five. Been here since four. Just me, him and the idiot.' He clapped his hands. I imagined the boatman had watched him come and had then stood and watched him in silence until my own arrival.

'Shall we go?' he said.

'Is it any business of yours?' I said to him.

'What?' He seemed genuinely surprised by my rebuke. But I knew even as I spoke that, of all people, he, Bone, would have some small official, *judicial* part to play in the proceedings, and that his involvement could not now be avoided. I conceded all this, and what it might mean for Frere, as he continued towards

34

me, his expression changing from one of amusement to surprise and then to anger as he came.

'What business is it of mine?' he said. 'What business is it of mine?' It was clear to me that this prodding remark masked his own uncertain grasp of the situation.

'My apologies,' I said. 'Of course I need your advice on the matter.' It was my intention to have Frere transferred from the Belgian gaol to our own, and it occurred to me only then that Bone alone – however unwitting of it he might have been – possessed the paper authority to effect such a move.

'I would have reported back to you later,' I said to him. He now stood directly in front of me. 'I merely wanted to make this first visit to ascertain what condition Frere might be in.'

'What difference will that make?'

'I don't know. I simply wanted to find out before any *official* proceedings were started.' Merely and simply: soft gloves of words.

'What proceedings? What are you talking about?'

'I'd hoped you could tell me. I assumed you would be the man responsible.'

'Me?' He reassessed the situation as quickly as he was able to, and it amused me to see his anger turn back to surprise, and then, as the thing became clearer to him, to something approaching pride.

'You,' I said, driving home this sudden idea of responsibility.

It was by then much lighter, but still dark along the line of the river. A larger vessel passed us silently at the centre of the channel, distinguishable only by the lights it carried and by the dull clanking of its bell. The old boatman turned to watch its progress. I imagined him to be following it so that he might better assess our own course, but even as the vessel drew level with us, and the noise of its engine and the smell of its soot reached us, he turned away from it and back to where Bone and I stood.

'What did Fletcher say?' I said to him.

'Nothing. Said you'd go and see the murderer and get him brought back to us.'

'Did he think I'd succeed?'

He nodded reluctantly.

'Even though everyone else wants him to rot – to die, preferably – where he is?'

He nodded again.

'And so they dismiss completely your own involvement in the proceedings. Did none of them ask *your* advice on the proper course of action now to be undertaken?'

He considered this provocation. With Bone, you were either his friend or his enemy; the middle-ground, to his mind, was forever filled with people facing one way or the other.

'Presumably because they understand where the responsibility and, ultimately, censure will fall.' I made a point of appearing disinterested as I spoke, but at the same time I pointed my finger directly at him.

'Me?' he said.

'Perhaps. Perhaps not. Perhaps the whole situation is already so far beyond any of us that we would all be well advised to stay away.'

He must by then have been aware that I was manipulating him into the position which best served my own interests, but, equally, he could not entirely dismiss from his mind the fact that he might have had some significant role of his own to play: Frere was still a Company employee, and Bone was still the arbiter of justice on behalf of the Company – a role in which

36

some small but unassailable power might yet be wielded.

He turned away from me to consider all this without allowing me to read his face.

Without waiting for him, I went to the boat and climbed into it. The boatman followed me.

'Are you coming?' I called to Bone.

He came immediately.

The boy pushed us away from the shallows, wading until the water reached his chest. Bone and I sat together at the centre of the boat. The boy climbed aboard and shook the water from his limbs. The boatman made the first of his slow, assured pushes with his pole. The water rose within inches of the craft's low sides, and already it seeped into the bottom around our feet. Tin cans lay scattered the length of the floor.

We moved further out and I felt the tug of the current to which we abandoned ourselves. The steamer which had passed us earlier was by then out of sight, its more certain passage marked now only by the fading rattle of its bell. I shielded my eyes to await the sun rising out of the growing brightness, but was foiled by the canopy of the trees, and by the river which turned us one way and then another on our passage across it.

The story of Frere having killed a child came to us first from a feather-trader who had heard the tale from one of his gatherers at the confluence of the Lomami and Pitiri rivers. There was a small Station there, little more than a guard hut, manned only during the trading season. Frere, apparently, had arrived at the Station and gone into the forest beyond. The country was mapped along its main watercourses, but the ranges beyond these remained uncharted. It was assumed that the hills rose and fell west and east until they reached

37

Boendie Post in the west or Port Francqui on the Kasai to the south, and it was upon hearing these names that I recalled Frere long ago expressing an interest in the place, in the fact that it remained unknown and unappealing, and, more significantly still, that it was reputed to be the home of cannibals even fiercer than the Matari.

The feather-trader said his collector had been present when the girl had attempted to rob Frere of one of his journals, and Frere had grabbed her arm and then swung her so violently against a nearby tree that he had broken her neck, killing her instantly. Apparently, Frere was either suffering from a sickness or had just then been woken from a delirious sleep, perhaps by the child herself lifting the journal from his lap. The girl's father had witnessed the whole incident. In fact, it was said that it was he who had encouraged the girl to become a thief, the pair of them having come across the sleeping Englishman so far from where any Englishman had been before. And so the delicate crystals of the story grew.

Frere had held the lifeless girl by her wrist, and had offered the small corpse to the man confronting him. The girl's father, seeing that she was dead, had started shouting and had drawn several other men out of the trees around him. All of these others had been armed, all intent, according to this slender branch of the story, on avenging the dead girl. Frere had then laid the body down and had attempted to reason with the approaching men. One of the new arrivals seized the journal the girl had been attempting to steal; others picked through the remainder of Frere's belongings scattered around the tree against which he had been resting. Attempting to avoid being robbed a second time, Frere, still confused and alarmed, had then struck out at one of these men, whereupon the others had retaliated and had clubbed him until he could no longer stand. A further blow had knocked him unconscious, and when he came round he found himself being half-carried, half-dragged in the direction of the Lomami, where he was eventually brought to the guard hut and the recently arrived feather-trader.

The rest of the story remains as speculative as the country beyond. Nothing of how he came to be in the hands of Hammad, who brought him back to us, nothing of his journey from there to here; nothing of what deals were struck with the dead girl's father or of the ransom paid for such a valuable hostage. Only unconnected details. Frere was unable to stand for three days, unable to flex his fingers for a week after that.

By the time of his return, he had either been stripped of all his belongings, including his boots and most of his clothes, or everything had been returned to him, including his precious journals, and everything he owned was now in safe-keeping alongside him in the Belgian gaol. Yet another story said everything had been lost – including the lives of three porters – when a boat had misjudged the Boloko rapids and had overturned there; or when yet another porter had abandoned Hammad in the night, taking Frere's possessions with him in lieu of unpaid wages.

All the places mentioned existed, though few had visited them – and certainly no-one from the Station – and although some of the men involved were known to us, the chief participants – the dead girl's father and the other witnesses – remained stubbornly beyond our reach and questioning.

*   *   *

I searched ahead of us for any sign that we had been observed. There would always be someone watching a vessel cross the river, but hopefully on this occasion no-one who would guess our business in coming. Lights shone in some of the larger buildings. A line of men ferried timber from a boat moored downriver. The sun was by then well risen behind us and already pouring its light into the darkness.

I was pleased that our arrival had not attracted anyone to the water's edge, but then, as the boatman poled in through the channels of braided sand and mud, and as the boy crouched ready to leap overboard and pull us to the shore, Bone raised his rifle and without warning fired three times into the air.

I asked him what he was doing.

But he simply grinned at me, and then nodded once over my shoulder to the water's edge.

A solitary man stood there, his arm raised to us, and in my momentary confusion, the noise of Bone's shots still rising above us, I imagined that the man on the shore was none other than Frere himself, that arrangements had been made without my knowledge, and that this was the reason for Bone coming with me. I was so convinced of this that I almost called out Frere's name to the waiting man.

And then he lowered his arm and came closer to us, and I saw that it was not Frere, but a man of a different build entirely, shorter, thinner, slighter than Frere, that it was in fact a man called Proctor, a Belgian sergeant who fulfilled in this Station the role played by Bone in our own.

My disappointment was evident to Bone, who said, 'See, you aren't so clever,' and then jumped from the boat and waded ashore ahead of me, stirring up clouds of silt in his wake.

The two men greeted each other.

The boatman pushed his oar ahead of us and the keel scraped us to a standstill. Both the old man and the crouching boy waited for me to rise and climb out before leaving the canoe themselves and pulling it free of the water.

I went to where Bone and Proctor stood together. Proctor held a bottle, which he offered to Bone, and from which Bone drank in long swallows. My boots were filled with water and I raised my feet in an unsuccessful attempt to let this run free.

Proctor was in command of the gaol where Frere was being held, and whatever else happened that morning, I would need his support to ensure decent treatment for Frere. I approached the two men and held out my hand to Proctor. He made a point of ignoring the gesture. Bone watched me over the neck of the bottle. I had encountered Proctor before and there existed some animosity between us. Two months earlier he had insisted on having one of our porters flogged for petty theft. The man had afterwards died of his wounds and I had made a formal complaint to the Belgians concerning this. Nothing had come of my approach, but I later heard that the dead man's family had been compensated in some small way, and that Proctor had been either reprimanded or made to contribute towards this payment.

'Been waiting three days,' he said to me. 'Your Mister Frere is not in a good way, not a good way at all. Fact, he might already be dead for all I know. Saw him last – ' he paused and rubbed his chin for effect – 'must have been this time yesterday. Crying like a baby, he was. He can't believe you'd leave him up there to rot like this. Especially you, his so-called friend.' He added a cold emphasis to the word. The man's face and

41

forearms were covered with the waxy fingerprint scars of some old affliction, keeping his skin pale and glossy, and giving it the appearance of being easily broken. Cornelius said it was the scarring pattern of syphilis.

'He has yet to be charged with any crime,' I said, regretting the remark immediately.

'But he stands accused of more than a fair few,' Proctor said. 'You wouldn't believe the tales we're hearing. How long was he gone? And nobody going after him. Surprising what a man can get up to in that length of time, him lost, the sun on his head, and with that taste in his mouth.'

'I'm sure everything will be noted,' I said.

'They keep on coming in every day, his accusers, adding a little bit here, a little bit there, to the stories.'

It was clear to me that he knew as little as we did, and that if he did know more, then he was not prepared to divulge it to me.

'Am I to be allowed to visit him?' I asked him.

His grin fell for an instant, and I knew in that unguarded moment that I would not be prevented from seeing Frere, that the senior officers at the Station had already briefed Proctor on the course of the events ahead.

Bone nudged Proctor.

'Bone here has asked me nicely,' Proctor said.

'Then I am grateful to you both,' I said, entering this charade of petty responsibilities and untested authority.

'He's grateful to us both,' Proctor said, mimicking my voice.

Unwilling to indulge them any longer, I walked past the two men in the direction of the gaol. They ran to join me, one on either side.

The gaol stood some distance from the main buildings of the Station, upriver, upwind, the largest part of it now derelict, its walls crumbled, its log beams rotten and collapsed. At the gateway stood the unlit garrison house in which Proctor was billeted with his command. I had seldom seen these other men, and was aware only that – again like our own garrison – they were the remnants of a once much larger force.

The Belgians had long since secured their territories by treaty, and their military presence now was devoted largely to internal and commercial affairs. The last of the French concessionary stations had been abandoned twelve years ago, most others long before that.

Proctor paused at the open door and shouted inside. Two men appeared, both in a state of undress and angry at being woken. Proctor told them who I was and why I was there.

One of the soldiers went inside and reappeared with a rusted key the length of his hand. He gave this to Proctor, who told the two men to get dressed and follow us to the gaol.

We approached the building across an overgrown parade ground, a lantern hanging at its door and a fainter light showing from within.

'I was wondering . . .' I said.

'Wondering what?' Proctor said quickly, anxious for the first of my bribes.

'If I might be permitted to see Frere alone.'

'Impossible.'

I took the folded notes from my pocket, unwrapped one and gave it to him.

'It's Bone arranged all this, not me,' Proctor said, hoping to double the sum.

'But Bone and I work for the same employer,' I said,

affecting surprise. 'Neither of us would countenance a bribe for fear of the consequences.' I turned to Bone. 'Am I right, Sergeant?'

Bone, caught between fear and greed, could only nod.

'However, should you personally wish to share your own good fortune with a fellow officer . . .'

Proctor scowled at me and went to unlock the outer door. He gave me the key. 'Poor Bone,' he said to me softly as we parted.

I went inside. The room was bare, with the exception of a solitary table and chair. The inner light came from a lamp on the table. Along one wall were the three doors of the cells beyond. The same key opened each of these doors.

I paused for a moment, preparing myself for what I might be about to see, for what I might learn. I heard the voices of the men outside, Proctor explaining to Bone that he would have to wait for his share of the bribe.

I went to the first door and stood with my ear to it. Silence. I opened it. The darkness inside was complete and I could see nothing. I returned to the table for the lamp. The cell was empty.

As I tried the second door I heard a sound from within, and imagining this to be Frere, I composed myself before opening the door fully and holding up the light.

But it was not Frere. Instead, a native knelt in the far corner, both hands clasped over his face, a man as black as the darkness which enveloped him. I spoke to him, but he made no response other than to turn away from me and press himself harder into the corner. Only as I closed the door behind me did it occur to me that the terrified prisoner might have been awaiting a

44

beating, or worse, and that he imagined me to be the instrument of that punishment.

I stood for some time at the final door. After several minutes I knocked on it and called in to identify myself. There was no reply. I pressed my ear to the wood and called again. Behind me, at the far side of the room, Proctor appeared in the open doorway and watched me.

'He's in there,' he said.

I knocked and called again, turning the key as I did so. This third door opened as stiffly as the others, and I regretted that it did not swing open freely, affording me the opportunity to step back with the light so that it did not shine into the cell so abruptly or so harshly, and that Frere might see me and recognize me instead of being blinded and seeing only the shape of a man looking in at him. I held the lantern to one side, causing its light to shine only against one wall, before drawing it into the doorway and spreading its glow over the whole of the small space.

Frere sat against the opposite wall, a hand over his eyes.

'It's me, Frasier,' I said. I waited, but he made no attempt to answer me.

His other hand was held in an iron ring set into the wall.

I repeated my name.

'I know who you are,' he said. He spoke hoarsely and slowly, his free hand still over his eyes.

'I've come to see if—'

'Don't,' he said.

'Don't what?'

'Don't try to help me. Don't even come inside.' The words were a great effort for him and he began to

45

cough, unable to catch his breath. Saliva ran onto his chin.

'But this is barbaric,' I said. 'Unnecessary.' I could not be certain, but I imagined he smiled at this, his mouth covered by his sleeve. He shuffled his legs until they were spread ahead of him. The low ring would have made it impossible for him to rise above a crouch.

'You need help,' I said.

He sat gasping, breathing in long draughts.

'At least let me try and bring you across to us.'

He made no effort to speak again.

'Do you have water? Are you being fed sufficiently?'

He nodded once to each question.

I was distracted then by a shout from Proctor, who told me that my time with Frere was at an end. I regretted my small bribe.

I knelt so that my face was level with Frere's and put the lantern between us so that we might see each other more clearly. His free hand was still over his eyes, but I knew that it was not held so tightly over them so as to exclude all sight of me.

'I *will* help you,' I said. If I had expected some small gesture of acknowledgement from him, some sign that the friendship and understanding between us was still intact – however worn or slender a thread it might now have become – then I was disappointed. For rather than lower his hand and look at me and speak to me, relieved that at last someone had come to him, he remained silent, and not only did he refuse to speak, but he then lowered his head until his chin rested on his chest and he looked through his fingers to the ground. I felt each of these small, deliberate getures like a blow.

I remained where I was, examining him for any obvious sign of injury or suffering. The wrist of his chained hand was rubbed sore and bleeding, and he was gaunter than I had ever before seen him, and dirtier, his hair lank and matted; but other than this I could detect nothing that might require treatment.

'I have to go,' I said to him. I rose, took up the lamp and backed out of the small space. In the darkness I saw him straighten, draw up his knees and raise his head. Shocked by his response to me, and having anticipated so different an encounter, I realized as I withdrew that it had been beyond me even to touch him.

3

I was kept occupied over the next few days. Abbot complained to me that he was falling behind in his work because I was neglecting my own. He referred to my visit to see Frere as an 'unnecessary diversion'. He wanted to know if my day-books reflected my absences and lack of progress.

I worked late into the night. I visited the quarry and the quartermasters' stores when there were few people present. I surveyed and recorded, and to save even more time I trusted the judgements and estimations of others, filling pages with the reckonings of both Fletcher and Cornelius. Neither man shared my urgency, though they too were constantly urged on by Abbot.

'Tell him what he wants to hear,' Fletcher told me.

'Just as *he* tells our masters what *they* want to hear,' Cornelius added. It genuinely saddened him to see how run-down our enterprise had become, how dependent it now was on almost rubber alone. He had helped control it during the years of its supremacy, and now he sometimes seemed to me like a man picking through the waste of its ruins like a dispirited child prodding a stick through weeds. We had all heard his tales of what had once happened at the place, of how extensive its influence had been, of the value and diversity of the goods which had passed through it.

Even Fletcher sat and listened when Cornelius spoke, and I sensed that he too – though he would never have confessed as much – regretted how little was now actually undertaken at the Station. Recently, there had been talk of the Belgians making yet another bid to end our concessionary status and to buy up our sheds and wharves to expand their own considerably more profitable enterprise. But they would neither confirm nor deny this when we approached them directly; there was a great deal to be gained by them in maintaining this uncertainty.

'Does anyone ever see Abbot's reports?' Cornelius asked.

Fletcher and I exchanged a glance and shook our heads.

'He sends them monthly,' I said. 'Sealed canisters.'

'Where?'

'First to Leopoldville, then onwards to London, I suppose.'

'Reports about what?'

'About our work here. Profit and loss. What we achieve and what we fail to achieve. Viability. Prospects for the future. Who knows?'

'Reports on each and every one of us,' Fletcher added.

I told him I didn't fully understand him.

'I've known what Abbot was doing ever since he arrived,' Cornelius said. 'I've seen a succession of Abbots. Men who come here only to be disappointed – for whatever reason; take your pick – but men who will never admit their disappointments, men who go on building things up, surrounding themselves with adventure and achievement where nothing can be either verified or questioned at such a distance.'

'You think he makes the Station a more viable prospect than it is?' I asked him.

'Look around you,' Cornelius said.

'We still trade at a good profit,' I insisted.

I knew by the silence which followed that neither man was willing to be drawn into revealing their own uncertain hopes for the future of the place.

'For all we know,' Cornelius said, 'the decision to sell or abandon might already have been taken and the letter despatched. How would we know? For six months we would all go on doing what we do like clockwork toys slowly winding down and walking round and round in ever decreasing circles banging ever more weakly on our small tin drums.'

Fletcher laughed at this. 'Don't look so concerned,' he told me. 'He's been saying the same thing for the past twenty years.' Fletcher had been at the Station only twelve years.

'Perhaps,' Cornelius said.

'But we all have contracts,' I said.

'Even Abbot,' Fletcher said. 'Even Abbot.'

A moment later we were distracted by the ringing of the bell used to signal the approach of a vessel to our wharves.

'Is anything expected?' Cornelius asked Fletcher.

Fletcher shrugged.

We rose together and went outside. It was late afternoon and the bulk of the day's business was over. The four vessels moored at our jetties were empty. Steam and smoke rose from the single boat preparing to leave. The crews of the others lay asleep around their decks and in the shade of their awnings.

The man ringing the bell ran towards us. Few others paid him any attention. He was a man proud of his position as our human alarm and sat in silence for days on end scanning the empty river. He grabbed Fletcher's arm and indicated where half a dozen small boats negotiated the upriver current on their way across to us. Fletcher studied these through his glasses.

'Ivory,' he said.

Cornelius snorted his disappointment at this. 'Anything else?'

Fletcher continued looking. 'Hard to say.'

The boats approached closer. Even without binoculars I could see that their loads did not amount to much.

'I have work to do,' Cornelius said, and left us. Several years earlier he had submitted a report to the Company recommending they abandon the ivory trade, and to concentrate instead on the gathering of valuable timbers – teak, bomba, mahogany and ironwood – for export to Europe, and for larger scale trade in staples such as caoutchouc, palm oil, groundnuts and gum, but the profit still to be made on tusk and horn was too high to be ignored. It was not out of any thought for the slaughter of the animals which caused Cornelius to make his appeal, but the knowledge that most of the ivory was stolen from other collectors, and that small but vicious wars were still being fought to acquire it. He was convinced that any man bringing more than a dozen pieces to trade brought them with blood on his hands, and for this reason he had relinquished this part of his work to Fletcher. I was once with Cornelius at the Belgian Station when he pointed to a twenty-foot length of boxwood trunk and told me there was enough there to make a thousand clarinets.

'Perhaps you want to go with him and keep your own

51

hands clean,' Fletcher said to me, his glasses still fixed on the approaching boats.

I indicated to him that I would remain, if only to stay beyond the reach of Abbot.

Then he said, 'Amon,' and wiped his eyes.

'You might have guessed he'd be involved in some form or other.'

'But only as Hammad's whipping boy. We owe Hammad too many favours.'

'Will his involvement push the price up?'

He considered this, but said nothing.

By then the boats were within hailing distance and Fletcher shouted to Amon. The man – whom none of us trusted – drew back his white hood and returned the greeting.

'If he's come with the ivory, then the chances are it's a good load. It's valuable and he's come to keep his eye on it as Hammad's agent. It's the first we've had for a month.'

He waded into the water and grabbed the prow of the leading boat. Amon leaped from it and the two men embraced. I could imagine the look on Fletcher's face as the Syrian grasped him. The remaining boats were secured.

Amon saw me and came to me. Our greetings were less effusive. I had hitherto had little to do with him and he remained mistrustful of me. He bowed and offered me a salute. I shook his hand. I was incidental to the proceedings; my presence had no bearing on the price he would be paid. He returned to Fletcher, shouting for the men on the boats to uncover the ivory.

'Bring it ashore,' Fletcher told him.

'But you may not wish to buy it. We may be forced to go back across the river with it.' Amon bowed his head as he spoke. He then called for one of the loads to be carried ashore. They were long, white tusks, most taller than the men who carried them.

'He's cleaned them up,' Fletcher whispered to me. He went to inspect the tusks.

'Nothing buried and dug up here,' Amon said. 'All freshly gathered. Look closely and you may even see some blood.' This was meant as a joke, but only he laughed.

'And the rest?' Fletcher said.

Amon called for a single tusk from each of the other loads to be carried ashore.

Fletcher tapped them with his cane. He ran his hands along their curved lengths. He sniffed deeply at their sawn ends, or at the yellowing roots where they had been pulled whole from the slaughtered animals.

I had been present a year ago, along with Frere, when Fletcher had been called upon to kill a rogue elephant that had trampled the crops of several nearby villages. Our excursion had lasted only an hour, at the end of which Fletcher downed the animal with a shot to each of its front knees, and then by a succession of shells into its eyes as it knelt trumpeting and lashing its bloody trunk at the men who tried to approach it. The price for this had been the better of the creature's two ten-foot tusks, both of which were extracted before it was dead. Even when the flesh and muscle of the sockets had been hacked away and the ivory extracted, the creature did not die, and sat turning its sightless head from side to side for a further hour as the blood continued to pour from its wounds. Fletcher left immediately his work was done, but I remained behind with Frere while he attempted to sever one of the creature's feet, and as he cut off its tail and then removed foot-square pieces of its hide. I wondered aloud if there was anything we might do to put the animal out of its lingering misery, but Frere laughed at the idea.

Down at the jetty, more of the ivory was brought ashore. I was surprised at how quickly Fletcher concluded his bargaining with Amon. I saw what a game was played in their transactions and how secretly reluctant they were to conclude their business. Fletcher shouted for drink to be taken to Amon's boatmen. Amon himself did not drink.

Scales were set up and each of the tusks weighed.

Abbot appeared and watched all this from a distance. He would be angry that he had not been called sooner to record the transaction. He called for Fletcher to go to him, but Fletcher pretended not to hear him, though most of the others turned and looked. Each tusk was weighed and the necessary calculations made. Realizing that he was being deliberately ignored, Abbot turned and walked away.

'He'll write it all down,' I said to Fletcher, still not fully convinced that Abbot was the spy he and Cornelius accused him of being.

'Your name will be in there, too,' Fletcher said. 'Did you not hear him calling you? Perhaps *you* were the one who didn't answer him.'

A word about Bone. Almost thirty years ago, Bone, then a corporal, served in Hobart Town. At that time, a cousin of mine – my mother's brother's son – twenty-three years my senior, attempted to make his name under the auspices of the Aboriginal Protection League by studying the last of the pure-bred native people then living there. He was directed to the garrison, where he encountered Bone. The man's name was Fairfax, my mother's maiden name, and having spent five months in Hobart, he contracted some fever or other and died there. All his work was subsequently lost – whether never completed, whether stolen from him by the aboriginals or lost at some point along its journey home remains uncertain. No-one in the family tried particularly hard to ascertain the truth of the matter. There was some disgrace attached to the venture, but I never knew what that was. I knew vaguely of all this as a boy, but was more forcibly reconnected with the facts by Bone himself, who began to tell me the story one night not knowing that I was a distant relation of the man. I do not recollect ever meeting the scientist, except possibly as a very small child, knowing only that his line of the family had encountered some trouble following the suicide of his father and that he had gone to Australia to live beyond this shadow.

Bone, it transpired, afterwards succumbed to the same fever, but survived it. He told me about the illness, comparing his greater suffering to that of my cousin, and looked upon his survival as an achievement of his own making. A large number of the Hobart garrison had also died and been buried in unmarked graves. As a direct result of this, Bone had risen from corporal to sergeant. This, too, he regarded as being the reward of effort and ability.

Less than a year afterwards Bone was allegedly the protagonist of an incident in which two old native women had been killed. Bone's story was that he had been attacked by a tribe of killers and that the old women were merely the unlucky victims of his fight to defend himself. The two small fingers of his left hand had been severed in the attack, the rest of his hand saved by a Government surgeon. After that, Bone was transferred, first to Sydney for five years, and then God knows where.

He was here at the Station before me, and six months passed before we discovered this connection.

Now, in these present circumstances, his behaviour towards me was becoming ever more unbearable – one moment gloating and condemning me for what had happened, the next speaking to me as though we were equals, as though *we* were related by blood, men who might share confidences, men who did not stand in daily contemplation of each other from the opposite sides of the abyss.

4

I was surprised on my second visit to Frere to discover that he was no longer chained to the wall, and that a table, two chairs and a lantern had been taken into his cell.

Proctor unlocked the door for me and then withdrew before I opened it. He again gave me the key, and I made a remark about being entrusted with it, about helping Frere to escape, but he simply looked hard at me and then at the surrounding trees.

It was midday, and the ante-chamber to the cells was already airless in the heat. I saw the lines on the dirt floor where the table and chairs had been dragged across the room, and only then did it occur to me that they might have been taken into Frere's cell for the purposes of questioning him.

I was surprised, too, by the change in the man sitting at the table. It had been a week since my last visit and I had anticipated finding him in an even worse condition than previously. But he had evidently been well treated since then and had recovered further from his time in the forest. During the crossing I had calculated how best to pursue my own questioning, but seeing him as he was, sitting at the table reading a book, I was caught off-guard, uncertain of how to even begin.

'James Charles Russel Frasier,' he said, rising to greet me, speaking before I was fully visible to him in the doorway. I heard the distant echo of our first encounter and was encouraged by it. He held out his left hand to me. The wrist of his other was bandaged and I saw that he held his fingers stiffly. His voice, too, remained little more than a hoarse whisper. The natural light of the ante-chamber flooded into the small space, transforming everything it touched.

'They told me you were coming,' he said. He carefully marked the page of his book and laid it on the table. There were other objects in the room that had not been there previously: several containers, plates, cutlery, other books, a small tin case and a mirror.

'Are you being well treated?' I asked him.

'Only you would think to ask me that particular question,' he said. 'Two days ago our friend Proctor asked me if I would prefer to move to another of the cells.'

'To what end?'

'Who knows. Perhaps it was just by way of being offered something. As you can imagine, there is not a great deal else.'

'How did they know I was coming?'

'The same way everything is known in this place.'

He filled two cups from a jug of tepid water. The door behind me remained open and he kept his face to the light. His skin was a better colour, he had combed back his overgrown hair, and the sores on his cheeks and neck were faintly discoloured, as though someone had dabbed them with iodine. I considered all this as I wondered what next to ask him.

I had left the compound accompanied by Bone, whom I had encountered supervising the stacking of bricks and timber alongside our own dilapidated gaol. I placed no significance on this – supplies and materials were frequently laboriously manhandled from one place to another on the grounds that they might be closer to where they might one day be needed, and that regardless of their eventual use, even this pointless labour was preferable to idleness.

Bone had walked with me to the water's edge, but then came with me only a short distance along the path there. He knew where I was going, and I was prepared to agree to him accompanying me. I sensed something in his manner and in the things he said which suggested he knew something concerning Frere that I did not – something he might perhaps have learned from Proctor – something he was not at liberty to tell me, and I was intrigued by this, knowing that if it had been anything to his advantage then he would have been unable to resist telling me.

But he told me nothing, and he left me where the long grass gave way to the soft clay of the bank. The river was lower than previously and the old boatman waited closer to the quarry.

'Did Proctor say anything to you?' Frere asked me. He feigned indifference, but I caught his concern.

'Regarding what?'

'The powers that be – *their* powers that be – wish me to be returned across the river.'

'Then surely that's good news. I've been trying myself—'

'Good news?'

'For you to be with us, there, among friends, among your countrymen, than to be held here—'

59

'Among the heathens?'

'To be held here where you have no voice. What else do you know?'

'Only that there have been changes in the government on the coast.'

'There are tales of changes every month.'

'But I suspect these are to be believed. I was visited yesterday by the almighty Hammad, who informed—'

'And you believed a single word of what he said? A man motivated solely by greed? A man who, by common consent, has done more to counter the stability and proper government of the place than – than . . .'

He waited for my anger to subside.

'Of course not. I know him for what he is, and he, of course, understands that. You have always underestimated him, James.'

I acceded to this in silence.

Hammad had been there long before the Belgians, slave-trader, unofficial governor and war-lord of a region so vast that his hold over it was beyond all understanding.

'And whatever you think of him, he is a reliable source of information. He has been in Brazzaville recently. He came here only to negotiate the sale of some of his assets.'

And to take delivery of you from the feather-trader, I thought, but said nothing. Hammad had always seemed to me to be a man surprised by his ability to make money, and then afterwards one intoxicated by it. I had heard accounts of his achievements and excesses on the voyage out. He was a man either venerated or despised by all who knew him. His cruelty to his native employees was well known, and yet they had never truly risen in revolt against him, nor even deserted him in the numbers and with the regularity ours now left us. It concerned me to see how much faith Frere still had in what the man said, but I was unclear in my own mind how much this concern was simply the result of hearing that which I did not wish to hear, and how much it was born of my belief in Frere and his own judgements.

'Delegations are meeting even as we speak,' Frere said. 'Balances of power going up and down.' He made scales of his hands as he spoke.

'And what bearing will all that have on you?'

'Quite simple. I may soon – if indeed I am not already – be eligible to stand trial in the country – in the new nation, say – in which I am accused of committing my crime. Imagine that – tried here and not in my own country.'

There was no alarm in his voice, but rather a growing excitement, as though he were rising to another of his challenges. I did not know what to say to him, everything having raced so far ahead of my expectations in coming to see him.

'In short, again according to Hammad, my presence here – here among the benevolent Belgians – has become something of an embarrassment. Steps are being taken to have me removed.'

'Have you brought across to us, you mean?'

'In the first instance, yes.'

Again, I could not help but feel relief at the prospect. It did not then occur to me to ask him why he had not been brought to us directly.

'Where,' he went on, 'I shall presumably become an even greater embarrassment and liability. To be handed over to a native court – and there are lawyers and judges among these men, James – by the Belgians, despised corrupters of this fabulous paradise that they

61

are, is bad enough, but imagine being forced to be handed over by your own countrymen.'

I could think of no answer. A galaxy of flies circled above us. The sound of distant men came faintly into the room.

After several minutes, he said, 'And all of which, never let it be forgotten, will acquire a considerably greater significance in the eyes of the watching world than my crime itself. Hands will need to be washed, copy-books kept clean.'

I had known since the time of the first of the stories that he was the last man among us to deny anything he had done, and that whatever this was, he refused to speak of it now for my sake alone.

'There are too many conflicting tales,' I said.

'I imagine there are.' He put his hand on my arm to impress his meaning upon me. 'I shall tell you, James Charles Russel Frasier, but it would serve neither of us for me to tell you now. I imagine the details of what happened are already being rendered superfluous to the greater purpose they might soon serve.'

'Then tell me one thing,' I said.

He withdrew his hand.

'Did you kill a child?' It was the most I could ask of him.

He breathed deeply and bowed his head.

'A death in which you – however indirectly – were in some way involved, and for which you are now being held solely responsible?'

He raised his head. 'Please, not now.'

Again, I acceded. 'I'm beginning to sound like a lawyer,' I said. I had said the same to him once before, long ago, and he had remarked then that it seemed a profession for which my character was well suited. We had been in the company of the others at the time and they had all agreed with him, listing those of my attributes which suited the profession. As this listing continued I saw that Frere regretted having made the remark, and afterwards he apologized to me. I told him it was of no consequence, but both he and I knew that I had been stung by some of the comments made. It was why my reference to the fact now made him smile and helped release the small tension between us.

'And if you were one, then I would certainly employ you,' he said.

I asked him if he had been allowed outside the cell since my last visit, and he said that he had, that Proctor came regularly to take him into the yard. 'Bone will no doubt insist on parading me around in a similar manner upon my return,' he said. He dipped a cloth in one of the bowls of water and wiped his face and hands.

'When I was here last,' I said, 'you refused to speak to me. I said your name and you behaved as though you were no longer the same man.'

'Nor was I,' he said immediately. I had anticipated some reluctance from him.

'Meaning what?'

'It would be hard for me to explain, even to you.' He wiped the last of the moisture from his face with his fingers. 'Do you recall when we were held up at Port Elys by the failure of the steamer that was meant to take us to the Pool?'

'Three weeks.'

'And how anxious we were to leave the place behind and come onwards into what we still wanted to think of as the Great Unknown, the place where our names were to be made . . . Well, I remember some advice we were both given there by the Governor General.'

63

I remembered the dinner that had been held in our honour, brief diversion that we were.

'He told us to write all our letters, to do all the things we needed to do while we were stuck in the place, and then, upon our departure upriver, to leave our old selves behind. It struck me then as a strange remark to make.'

I vaguely remembered something of the sort being said. But it was a common enough remark to make – old hands impressing new arrivals, experience impressing itself upon expectation – and I had paid it no mind.

'Do you remember how many letters I wrote in those weeks? To my father, mother, sisters, to Caroline, to our employers, even to my old professors and tutors.'

I told him I remembered.

'Well, that's what I was doing. I was leaving myself behind. Not in my essentials, of course; the man who arrived here was the man who left there, you might say, but I felt the need – if that is not too strong a word for it – to establish myself in all those essentials in that place before I left it. Do you understand what I'm saying? I needed there to be a common understanding of that man in Port Elys – of *me* – of the man who had re-created himself in all those letters before I left the place itself and confronted whatever awaited me here. Did you feel no such impulse yourself?'

'I certainly wrote plenty of letters,' I said. We had been warned of the irregularity of the mails. At least with the sea still visible at our backs and seeing the great ships coming and going upon it we might still have had some faith in our letters being delivered.

'It was more than that,' he said, and I saw immediately that I had disappointed him by my imperfect understanding of what he was trying to tell me. We had also been told to dispatch all those letters and then to clear our minds of all thought of the people to whom they were sent, as though the past and its trappings needed to be stripped from us to make us better able to cope with whatever lay ahead.

'Do you think you achieved this?' I asked him.

He considered the question before shaking his head. 'At first I believed so.'

'And afterwards?'

'Afterwards I saw what an impossible task I had set myself.'

'Then why deny your name when I spoke to you last?'

'Because by then the child was dead, and whether you wish to believe it of me or not, I had had a hand in her killing.'

I felt a sudden chill at hearing from his own lips that it was a girl who had been killed.

'And you believe that by your actions in the matter you were changed?'

'How could it be otherwise? A dead child.'

'And so who – what – do you believe you have become if you are no longer the man who left us all those weeks ago?'

'Fifty-one days,' he said. 'Twenty-four since the child died.'

'Do you regret what happened?' I apologized immediately for the question.

'Regret is an indulgence,' he said. 'I will not deny the truth, my part in it all, the facts of the matter.'

'I know that,' I said. It was the wall which separated us.

At that moment the outer door opened and Proctor called in to me. My visit was over.

On our return across the parade ground I gave

Proctor more money and asked to be kept informed by him of the arrangements to return Frere. He considered this without answering me and pushed the notes between the buttons of his jacket.

I next saw the deformed boy two days later. He was asleep on the ground outside my chart-room door. As I approached him, he woke and stood up. He considered me for a moment before beckoning me towards him. The gesture amused me. Though his life was lived mostly in silence, I had always imagined him a shy and reluctant near-mute. I was surprised even more when he spoke to me in broken but understandable English as I reached the door.

'Come in?' he asked me, by which I understood that he wanted to enter the room with me.

I let him inside, and he stood for several minutes examining the cabinets and the maps and plans arranged around the walls. He moved closer to these, running his hands over them. I imagined they might be incomprehensible to him, things of wonder almost.

I stood beside him and started explaining the features of the map he studied.

He stopped me with the word, 'Wrong.'

'Wrong?'

'No mountains.' He placed four fingers and a thumb over the cones of five peaks several hundred miles to the north-east, beyond the limits of the Ituri.

'Yet many men have seen them,' I told him.

'You seen?' he said.

'Not personally. That is not my map.' I wondered at his new bravery.

'Wrong,' he said again.

'Do you know the country?'

'One cliff.' He drew his arms apart to suggest the

66

extent of this. 'Then flat.' He was describing a vast, high plateau. The map was thirty years old.

'Is it grass, forest, desert?'

'Grass.'

I was about to ask him more when he wandered from this chart to another, a map of the original compound as conceived and built by its first owners. He studied it as though he might once have known it in this state. Only a quarter of the original buildings remained in use, and most of the once-cleared land further back from the river had been lost, first to the grass and then the trees.

I studied him more closely. His spine was twisted, forcing him to lean both forward from the waist, and then in on himself, and his head was turned at an angle opposing this, as though he were making a constant effort not to have to face the ground.

I offered him a seat, but even this posed problems for him, forcing him to turn sideways and then lean backwards to face me. I positioned my own chair so he might look directly at me with the least effort. There was no malformation of his arms or legs, though the curve of his spine forced these to stick out at their own ungainly angles. I saw how much more comfortable it must have been for him to lie on the ground or in the bottom of the boat than to either stand or sit in a chair. Because of his bowed and twisted head, I had seldom before seen his full face, but looking at it then, I saw that it too was perfectly formed. He avoided my eyes, raising his hand to his mouth when he spoke.

'Frere,' he said, instantly drawing me to him.

While the rest of us had previously had little to do with the boy, Frere had allowed him to accompany him on his local expeditions, his crooked back laden with satchels and cases.

'Where are you from?' I asked him.

'Bassam.' I guessed from the way he said it that he would never return there. It was Frere who told me how few children survived their first few years in that place, and how those who were even suspected of some infantile sickness or weakness were either killed or left to die by their parents. The deformed boy would not have lasted an hour under such circumstances. His survival had intrigued Frere, and he had quizzed him on it. But the boy had kept his secrets.

I imagined now that he wanted to know what was happening to Frere, and I started to tell him, but he silenced me by covering his ears.

'I know,' he said.

'Do you know where he went, what happened to him?'

He looked up at me, his eyes moving rapidly from side to side, as though he were about to make some revelation, but then their motion slowed and ceased and he shook his head. He was not being entirely truthful with me. I also sensed that he had come to me for some purpose other than to reveal his attachment to Frere.

'Are your parents living?' I asked him.

He shrugged.

'I once thought the boatman was your grandfather.'

He shook his head.

'Where do you live?' It was a ridiculous question in a place where men lived and slept where they stood and fell. Another shrug.

And after that, perhaps because he was unwilling to tolerate my questioning any further, or perhaps because his brief visit had achieved its uncertain purpose, he rose awkwardly from his seat and left me.

*   *   *

Hammad's home stood three miles from the Belgian Station, along a well-kept road, and was surrounded by a high wall, beyond which lay orange and pomegranate orchards, and fields of millet, rice and sugar cane. It was built – as all his homes were reputed to be built – in the Moorish fashion, with a courtyard, colonnades, minarets and high-domed roofs. This particular residence also possessed an ice plant, a series of inter-connected yard pools with water running between them, and was planted along its walls with date palms transported half-grown from the Nile. Whenever one of these trees toppled or succumbed to some disease, then another was quickly sent for to replace it. The trees were a symbol, not so much of Hammad's wealth, but of his power, of his attention to detail, and of his ability to satisfy his every whim. His wealth was estimated in literally countless millions regardless of currency.

He inherited his position and his business from his father following his education in London, Paris and Berlin. He had travelled to India and to the United States; he enjoyed proclaiming that his commercial empire spanned the world. Only here did it serve him to be considered a brutal and, occasionally, an uncivilized man. We on this side of the river had all long since understood that, were Frere ever to be located in the wilderness, then he would eventually find his way to Hammad, and then from Hammad back to us. No price would be put on his return – though its cost made plain – and once again we would find ourselves in irredeemable debt to the man.

I had been only once to visit him on the far side, summoned six months after my arrival. Frere and I had been called together. It was impossible not to be impressed by what we saw there, what we were shown, what we were told and what we were invited to inspect and to sample. Hammad's wives and servants gathered round us and expressed an interest in everything we said. We had taken gifts with us – including a pair of Wheelock hunting pistols – and saw immediately how inadequate these were. Hammad, however, made a great deal of them, thanking us profusely and then going out into a courtyard to practise shooting with them. We were given gifts in return and invited to what amounted to nothing less than a feast. Hammad, I noticed, behaved as though I had never before met him.

In truth, it served his purpose to have us – the English – there, just as it had once suited the Belgians to have the surrounding country in thrall to Hammad's power and reputation. It was an uneasy existence at best, but one from which none of us could now easily withdraw.

He asked Frere and me on that occasion if there was anything we needed from him, and I told him there was nothing and disappointed him. Frere, however, listed the great number of animals, birds and plants he hoped to collect. He also told Hammad that he wished to meet men of the surrounding tribes who would be prepared to tell him of their ways of life and customs; he wanted to learn about their religious ceremonies, about how they farmed, hunted, built and traded.

Amon was also present at this encounter, seated behind Hammad, and I saw that he made notes concerning everything that was discussed. I also noticed that whatever Hammad did, his agent mirrored in some way. This was not so obvious or as simple as mere repetition, but achieved by some reinforcing action so as to suggest to any audience that there must be no misunderstanding of his master's wishes, and that the two of them, master and agent, were, in the manner of these transactions, indivisible.

The centre-piece of the feast that evening had been a whole roast ostrich, plucked, cooked and then with its feathers ingeniously replaced so as to make the bird look almost alive again. Hammad, I saw, belying his size and weight, ate very little, and I learned afterwards from Amon that his master preferred always to eat alone. As a young man, apparently, one of his rivals in the trade had attempted to poison him, and it had been a lesson hard learned, I saw how much this lesser man fed upon the greater, how his own power was that of a moon orbiting its sun.

At the corner of his mouth, Amon bore a small scar, a snick across both lips, barely visible other than as a crescent of paler flesh. I had been told by Cornelius that Hammad himself had done this to his newly appointed agent upon overhearing his gossiping about his business. I could imagine in its every clinical detail how the punishment had been carried out, how reasonable Hammad would have made himself appear, and how deserving of this reminder Amon would have declared himself.

On my every meeting with Amon since, I had found my eyes drawn to the scar, and occasionally I had seen him feel it with the tip of his tongue.

The feast had been over two years ago, and I had since encountered Hammad, and then only briefly, on fewer than half a dozen occasions.

Ever since Frere's return, and learning that Hammad was in some way involved, I had expected to be summoned again by the man, even if only to be made aware of the true nature of our debt to him. Instead of being called for, however, word reached us by a messenger that Hammad intended crossing the river to visit us, and he came scarcely before the news of his coming had grown cold.

He possessed a fleet of steamers, and he came on the largest of these, accompanied by two others. A space was cleared at our wharves and the work of the day was suspended during the visit.

Hammad went first to Cornelius and embraced him. Then he went to Fletcher. He called for something to be brought from the steamer. It was a rifle, not a gift, merely something Hammad had recently acquired, and he gave it to Fletcher to test its action, and to ask Fletcher if he would align the weapon's sights before he left.

Abbot and the junior quartermasters were ignored.

I was approached first by Amon, rather than by Hammad himself, and told by the agent that Hammad wished to see me privately later in the day.

Hammad was accompanied by forty or fifty men and half that number of women. Most carried trade goods and proceeded to unload these and to barter with the traders here. Some of the women, I imagined, were Hammad's wives, but others I recognized for the whores they were, and they too began to ply their trade, accompanying men away from the river and into the sheds and trees beyond.

'It's a great honour to have Hammad come to us and not merely to be summoned by him,' I said to Amon. If the man detected the coldness in my voice, then he did not respond to it.

'A great honour indeed. And one you would do well not to forget for the sake of the child-murderer.' He smiled as he spoke. Thus was I told everything I needed to know concerning the purpose of the visit, and of my own part within it.

Amon was then called for and he returned to walk beside his master.

I was then propositioned by several of the women. They grabbed my hand and pressed it to their exposed breasts and arms. I shouted at them, but to little effect. They continued to pester me as I walked among the boats to see what had been brought. The women painted their eyes with kohl, and anointed themselves with oil. Once, they had been kept out of the compound, and then punished when they were caught selling themselves there, but now there were so many of them, and they came so frequently, that we tolerated them, only now and again making an example of one of the women if she was caught stealing.

I was forced to wash myself, scour my hands before returning to my maps and awaiting the return of Hammad.

He came finally mid-way through the afternoon. And with him came Amon.

Our greetings were as elaborate and as insincere as those earlier.

Hammad motioned for Amon to remain apart from us, to stay as far from us as was possible in the room. Accordingly, Amon remained in the doorway. He took a small book from his pocket and pretended to read from it, pretended not to overhear every word that passed between Hammad and myself. I wondered how Hammad was served by having this recorder present at all his transactions. Perhaps Amon persuaded him it was necessary; or perhaps it was a way of safeguarding his own precarious position.

'I am so pleased you are able to divert yourself from your work to talk to me,' Hammad said.

'The pleasure is always mine,' I said, our strategies opened.

'Particularly under such circumstances, eh?'

I affected not to understand him, but he dismissed this with a slight wave of his hand. Frere was right: I did underestimate the man.

He hesitated at my clumsiness, but said nothing. He went to my desk and considered the partially drawn map there.

'Do you know the country?' I asked him.

In answer, he smoothed his palms over the paper and breathed deeply, almost as though he were possessing the place, or some fond memory of it. 'In Cairo, I have a collection of maps and charts numbering almost two thousand. You would not imagine so many had ever been made. It seems a mania. I employ my own map-makers. They show me where I have been and where I am going. I daresay you draw yours to serve an entirely different purpose.'

There was a great deal of empty space on the map before him, and he ran his hand into this whiteness, left it there for a moment and then raised it to his face and studied it, as though an imprint of something might remain. Then he held out his palm, fingers splayed, to me and asked me what I saw there. At first I didn't understand him, had misunderstood the rules of the game we were still playing.

'I see the rivers and paths of your hand,' I told him.

He considered this for a moment and then burst into laughter. He repeated what I had said to Amon, who did not laugh, exactly, but who produced an open-mouthed grin from which Hammad's own laughter might at that moment have been coming.

This ceased as abruptly as it had begun.

'I believe we understand each other, you and I, Captain Frasier.'

I no longer used the title. I had told him this at our first meeting, but he had insisted then that it was something hard-earned, something to be proud of, and so I had unwillingly acquiesced to his use of it. He himself carried a great many honorary titles, awarded

74

to him, presumably – or so it suited me to believe – by people who confused fear with respect.

On that first visit to his home, Frere and I had been shown the specially constructed cabinet, inlaid with gold and mother-of-pearl, in which all the various medals and insignia attached to these titles were kept. Four locks secured the cabinet and its massive feet were bolted to the floor. I gained then some notion of the vanity which fed the man's appetites.

'Are we talking about Nicholas Frere?' I asked him, keen to bring this circumvention to an end.

'We are indeed.'

'Do you know the circumstances of his disappearance and discovery?'

'And a great deal else besides.' He continued to look around me as he spoke.

'Then was it you who found him?'

In the doorway, Amon flinched at the harshness of my words and all they implied.

'Indeed, and as you already well know, it was not. I did, however, have the opportunity to speak with the father of the dead girl.' This was his counter-blow. 'And it was he who told me everything that had happened.'

'And are you going to relate the story to me, here, now?'

He smiled at this. 'Ah.'

'Then tell me what you wish to tell me, ask whatever it is you are going to ask of me.'

'Ask of you? Ask what of you? I merely wished to see you to tell you that, whatever the outcome of this unhappy affair, whatever the fate of that disgraced and unhappy man – the murderer Frere – that I am prepared to present my testimony to whatever court wishes to try him in the matter.'

'But whatever you said would only be hearsay, the words of another, not your own.'

'Ah, of course.' He locked his fingers, pretended to consider what he was about to say next. 'Perhaps I am not making myself clear. What I meant to say was that I would be happy not only to appear before any such court, but that I would also be happy to ensure that the girl's father appeared, that I will guarantee this, and that I shall do whatever I can for the grieving, disconsolate man from this time until that. The loss of a daughter, and under such circumstances as those – can you or I ever truly understand how that poor and wretched man must feel?' The tone of his voice changed as he spoke. There was now no attempt to suggest concern, and he spoke solely to make his own unspoken demands clear to me.

'Is it possible to see this man?' I said.

'The feather-collector? I am afraid not. But rest assured, he is well cared for. He says he wants to die, that his daughter was his only remaining child, her mother long since dead or left behind or whatever.'

I knew now that he was embellishing, but knew also that a lie repeated was no more or less of a lie for that.

'You believe that we will be overtaken by events elsewhere?' I said. 'That Nicholas Frere will not be sent home to face trial, that he will be tried here?'

'How perceptive,' he said. 'However, I shall travel to London, if necessary. And gladly.'

'And your witness?'

'Ah. The man would be persuaded.'

'With you as his protector, how could he refuse?'

'You see, we do understand each other.'

'But better if this place were granted some degree of independence from foreign government and Frere were tried here.'

' "Some degree of independence." How generous. And do not forget, Captain Frasier, it is largely at *my* insistence that Mr Frere is being returned to you. Who do you imagine had those barbaric chains taken from him?'

The same man who built the prison in the first place and then had the chains fitted to the walls. But I resisted saying this.

He turned to Amon, who immediately held his small book closer to his face. 'Amon, I fear we have offended Captain Frasier.'

Amon pretended not to have been aware of what had happened, but, as with Hammad's own pretence, he made no real effort to convince me.

'Perhaps I have been over-generous, conceded too much. Perhaps the distraught father might yet break into Frere's cell with a sword and chop off his head and then vanish into one of those empty white spaces never to be seen again. Perhaps even a lion or some other such beast might attack Frere and savage him until he is dead.'

Amon's eyes widened at both suggestions.

'What do you want me to do?' I said to Hammad.

'Do, Captain Frasier? What do you imagine yourself capable of doing?'

'I might discover that the tales of whatever Frere is supposed to have done are just that – tales.'

'Ah, so he has denied everything? He is an innocent man.'

'He is an honest man.'

'Whose life is worth more than the small ignorant savage whose life he took? Is that what you believe, is that what you truly believe?'

I could not answer him honestly.

He saw this and said nothing to provoke me further. He motioned for Amon to open the door, a signal that our conversation was over.

5

I first met Frere in the Company headquarters in Knightsbridge, where, unknown to each other, we had both been called to our interviews on the same day.

I had been in London for a week, staying with one of my father's business partners. I had dealt with some business for my father, largely concerning the shares he held in the various London companies connected with his own, and everywhere I went I was treated as he would have been treated. His partner attempted to dissuade me from accepting the Company position, but when I told him I knew he had been briefed by my father on the matter, he gave up trying.

On several occasions when my daily round took me close to Knightsbridge I had walked back and forth in front of the Company headquarters and studied the building. It was part of an impressive terrace, with a crest in gold and black above its double entrance, and reached via a high flight of steps, on either side of which stood polished marble pillars. It was an imposing entrance into that life, one that inspired confidence and every investment a man might be willing to make.

On the day of my interview I arrived over an hour

early. I cannot explain why I did this, nor why I attempted to explain to the porter who showed me in that I had only just then arrived in London and did not wish to waste my time elsewhere. He took out a book from beneath his desk, opened it to the present date, and slowly searched for my name with his finger.

'Twelve-thirty,' he said.

It was then barely eleven.

'Are all those others being interviewed for the same position?' I asked him. I was dismayed by the long list of names amid which my own sat.

'Not my business,' the man said.

'May I wait?' I indicated the glazed door against which the November rain was just then starting to beat.

He considered my request as though I had posed him a conundrum, pinching his nose and pursing his lips. I understood then the full extent of his domain.

'Follow me,' he said eventually.

He led me to a first-floor room up a wide, portrait-lined staircase, and, as intended, I felt the eyes of all those other men looking down at me as I ascended. We came to a door marked 'Library', and he showed me inside, closing the door behind me before I could ask him if I would be called for or be expected to present myself elsewhere at the appointed time.

I had thought there might be others waiting there, but I was alone. The room was lined from ceiling to floor with book-filled shelves. A fire burned in the broad fireplace, around which were placed several leather armchairs. I went to one of these and sat down. Above the mantel was a giant map of Africa, and beside it two portraits, life-size, of warrior kings. A lion skin was pinned to the wall between the high windows, and I went to inspect this and to look down at the street below. It was raining more heavily by then and the water ran in sheets over the small panes. Directly opposite, a building had recently been demolished and a blaze of timbers burned at the centre of the site, filling the street with its sodden smoke.

I returned to the hearth, sat for several minutes, then rose and looked along the shelves. I quickly realized that most of those volumes I had understood to be books were, more accurately, bound reports and journals. The whole of one of the shorter walls was taken up with volumes of Company minutes dating from its foundation seventy years earlier. I took down the most recent of these and returned to my seat to examine it. I doubt there was a country in the world which was not in some way represented in its pages. Reports on mining, agriculture, quarrying, logging, farming and fishing from Chile to Australia, from the Baltic to Cape Horn. I remember how encouraged I was to see so many badly drawn maps accompanying these reports. I searched the volume for that part of the world for which I was hopefully bound, but found nothing.

It was as I was about to return the volume that the door opened and someone else was shown in by the porter.

This man stood for a moment, accustoming his eyes to the dimmer light of the room. At first he did not see me. He, too, went to the lion skin. He pulled a chair to the wall, stood on it and examined the animal's head more closely. I heard him talking to himself, remarking on what a poor job had been made of preparing the skin. I rose then, making as much noise as possible to announce my presence to him. I expected him to climb down from the chair and come to me, but instead he searched for me, saw me against the glow of the fire, and asked me if I had ever seen a less fearsome-looking lion.

I went to him, the volume still in my hand.

'Are you a committee member?' he asked me.

'I'm here for interview,' I said.

'Ukassa Falls, the concessionary Station?' He leaped down and came towards me with his hand out. 'Nicholas Edwin Stephen Frere,' he said. 'When I was five, my dying father confided to me that I had been an unwanted child, that I was unlikely to inherit anything from him, and that I was called Stephen against my mother's wishes after the saint who was stoned to death.'

'It seems a lot to take on at such an age,' I said.

'Death-bed confidence. And you?'

I told him my name as we shook hands. He repeated it, grasping my hand more firmly. He closed his eyes for an instant, opened them, and said, '*Some Technical Difficulties Concerning the Azimuth Mapping of Near-Polar Latitudes.*'

It was the title of a paper I had published two years earlier; four pages long with a further seven pages of calculations and two sides of references. Sixty copies of the off-print still sat in my bureau; twelve copies of the journal in which it appeared sat in my bookcase. I had submitted three further articles on the strength of this acceptance, and all three had been returned. It was hard for me to believe that anyone else had read the article, then or since.

'Were you long at the Pole?' he said.

'At the Pole?'

'Mapping.'

I had been no further north than Edinburgh and told him this.

'I imagined as much,' he said, and burst into laughter. He pulled the chair back to where it had stood and pointed me back to the fire.

'I'm surprised you remembered it,' I said.

'I have a curse of a memory. Practically everything I read or see or do, I remember.'

We sat in seats on either side of the fire. He seemed perfectly at home there, as though he were a regular visitor.

'Was this what you expected to find?' he asked me. 'All this, this room, this building, all this ostentation, all this marble, brass and mahogany?'

I told him I hadn't known what to expect.

'And which position are you here for?'

'Map-maker.'

'Good.'

'Good?'

'I personally am offering my worthless self up for the post of – ' he pulled a folded sheet from his jacket – 'Officer in charge of Acquisitions and Chief Cataloguer. Two posts.'

'What will they involve?'

'Who knows? Means and needs, I suppose. Much like your own position.'

'Are you hopeful?' I asked him.

'Hopeful that when my money bond is paid it will be sufficient.'

I knew that this was how these positions were often acquired. My father had written letters of rec- ommendation; I had brought sealed envelopes to his business partner.

I wished I had known then that Frere had published fourteen articles and papers, six in the same journal as my own, and that he had written and published two books, the first at his own expense, concerning the classification of microscopic fauna. But I knew nothing of any of this until we were quartered together on the *Alpha* three months later. Another man might have made more of my solitary article merely as an introduction to his own, but not Frere, and when, a fortnight out of Tilbury, I confronted him with his own body of work – I had gone in search, following the trail of footnotes from one piece to another – he said he was no longer so keen on devising his system of classification and cataloguing of dead specimens, and that what interested him now were the practices and customs of living people.

'What will they expect of you?' I asked him.

We were both conscious of the fact that elsewhere in the building a committee of men was already conducting its interviews.

'Whatever they expect, I shall give it to them – give it to them in spades – and I shall continue working on my own behalf,' he said.

I showed him the poor quality of the maps in the volume I still held, and he looked at these for several minutes before speaking.

'They serve the Company's purpose,' he said, and I heard his note of warning clearly enough.

'I shall bear that in mind,' I said.

He slapped the volume shut. 'Just remember that *we* are the men they need,' he said.

'Why us?'

'Why us? Look at us.' And if he was disappointed by my lack of enthusiasm on that occasion, then he did not show it.

'*Frère*,' I said, as though by this simple expedient I might understand something vital of him. 'From the French for "brother"?'

'From the English word "friar" – monk or fish salesman via a, shall we say, socially aware family who might or might not, at one time or another, have visited France, or possibly met someone else who had been there and saved themselves the trouble.'

'You could change it back,' I suggested.

He shook his head. 'It suits me. Besides, I long since redressed the balance of my disappointment by losing the accent.'

At that moment, when our laughter was at its loudest, the door opened again, and this time two old men came into the room. They were two of the fattest men I had ever seen, and one wore a top hat and carried a cane, which made him look even more ridiculous. Frere stopped laughing immediately.

'Which of you is Frasier?' the man in the top hat called to us.

I rose from my seat, uncertain if I was being asked to follow them to my interview. I had lost all track of time since the arrival of Frere.

But instead both men came towards me, smiling and with their hands extended.

I remember stepping forward to greet them, and as I did so I braced myself against the first of them telling me how well he knew my father.

'Congratulations,' Frere said softly beside me, and he too rose to greet the men.

6

I was approached by Cornelius, who asked me to accompany him to the Jesuit mission at Kirasi.

'Not a great deal to see there these days,' he said, 'but once the place served some good. It used to be part of our duties here to supply it and to arrange passage for the people coming and going, but since we abandoned them they avoid us.'

I knew that many years ago there had been some philanthropic connection between the mission and the Company, that our services had been offered and that we had extended our hospitality to the people moving between the mission and the river on their way to Stanleyville. I had hoped Cornelius might tell me more about this, but he answered my queries only reluctantly, and ventured few opinions of his own other than to let me know that he regretted this severance, and regretted even more what had happened to the place ever since. There had once been a hospital for incurables, meaning lepers, at Kirasi, but the inmates had either died, left or been sent elsewhere in recent years.

We still maintained the small tin chapel alongside the garrison for the use of visiting missionaries and other workers on their overnight stops going up-river.

I knew that Cornelius had been more involved than most with the mission, and that, of us all, he alone – and against Company wishes – ensured the chapel remained in a state of good repair, and that he went there every Sunday morning to worship. Upon my arrival with Frere he had taken us to the place and invited us to accompany him at the next service. We had imagined he meant that everyone at the Station would attend, that the chapel would be filled with worshippers, but at our first attendance both Frere and I saw what a private ritual we had intruded upon and we afterwards stayed away.

Cornelius made no secret of these solitary practices, and he could often be heard offering prayers and singing hymns at the top of his voice as though he were sitting at the centre of a large congregation.

The journey to Kirasi was an easy one. The path was broad and much-used; it lay across open terrain for the most part, and then through a sparse forest for its final few miles. The land surrounding the mission buildings was cultivated, and people paused in their labours to watch us pass. Cornelius pointed out to me the small crucifixes nailed to each of the trees which bordered our path.

I had tried again along our journey to quiz him on his involvement with the place, his reason for visiting it now, and for asking me to accompany him, but as on the previous evening, he had been reluctant to tell me any more than I might have learned from a dozen others. I had leavened our conversation by saying that at the very least I might ask the missionaries to pray for Frere.

'Do what you please,' he had said harshly. 'But *I* wouldn't ask it of them.'

As we approached the main building, a delegation gathered on the road and came towards us. Seeing this, Cornelius stopped, wiped the dirt and sweat from his face and buttoned up his jacket. I copied him. He shielded his eyes to examine the people approaching us.

'We'll disappoint them,' he said coldly. 'They'll think we're new converts.'

It seemed a strange remark to make. He walked several paces ahead of me towards them.

They were led by a small man in a black jacket and trousers with a white collar. At first I imagined him to be a native, but as he came closer I saw that his face was heavily tanned. Recognizing Cornelius, this man stopped, held up a hand to halt the others behind him and then took off his cap. His short hair, cut close to his scalp, was vividly white in the sun.

I looked beyond him and saw that immediately behind him stood two nuns, both native women.

The priest came forward alone to greet Cornelius. It was a cold greeting, a handshake and not an embrace, and neither man prolonged it. They spoke briefly, but kept their voices low and I could hear nothing of what they said. I waited where I stood until Cornelius turned and beckoned me to them.

'Father Klein,' he said.

I shook the priest's hand and felt it thin and fragile in my own. He made no effort to reciprocate my grasp, merely letting his hand rest in mine for an instant before withdrawing it. When he stood with his arms by his side the cuffs of his sleeves fell to his fingertips, giving him the appearance of a child in a man's jacket. It was difficult to guess his age, but I imagined he and Cornelius to be contemporaries.

As though in answer to my thoughts, Cornelius said, 'Father Klein and I are both from Ypres.'

'But neither of us will return there,' Klein added quickly. 'Cornelius because he is too long away from the place to ever call it home again, and I because this is where my calling lies.'

It seemed an unnecessarily cruel remark to make. He motioned for the two women standing in attendance behind him to come forwards. By then a considerable crowd had gathered around us and I sensed that everything the priest now did he did with an awareness of these other watching eyes.

The two nuns came to stand alongside him, moving in a fluid, practised motion, as though it was something upon which they had been instructed. I bowed slightly to each of the women and Klein laughed.

'You think they are nuns?' he said.

Neither woman spoke.

'How could they be nuns? They came to us here from Gran' Bassam, from that illustrious palace of pleasure.'

'And so are damned for all eternity and will burn in hell,' Cornelius said. I heard the provocation in his voice and remained silent.

'I am afraid so,' Klein said.

I looked more closely at the two women. Their outfits, I saw, were crudely constructed of poor, heavy cloth. The hoods shielded the upper part of their faces, through which only the whites of their eyes showed. They both looked at me, transferring their gaze at the same instant to Cornelius, who said, 'Perpetua and Felicity,' and went forward to embrace them. I saw the look of disgust on Klein's face as he did this.

Then Klein turned to me and took my arm, leading me away from Cornelius and the women.

'So you are James Charles Russel Frasier,' he said. 'There was a woman here once who was a great friend of your mother.'

The remark caught me off-guard. 'Oh?'

'Yes. Lady Edith Pemberton. She came twelve years ago. Her husband was stationed briefly at Stanleyville. She was with us for four nights. Twelve servants dancing attendance on her, four porters for her wardrobe and another to carry her cosmetics.'

I had some vague recollection of the woman, whom my mother had met through her charity work. To the best of my memory she had made a name for herself by sketching the poor and the destitute of the East End of London and then selling these sketches to her wealthy acquaintances to support her African work. She herself lived in great style and comfort in several houses. I remembered, too, that she once employed a household of black servants for a season, and then replaced them all as unsatisfactory. There was a small, poorly executed painting of a native child in our Leicestershire drawing room. Perhaps this was one of hers.

'You know her, of course,' Klein said.

I told him I did.

We walked towards the mission. The people around us returned to their work in the fields.

Cornelius waited until we were well ahead of him before following us in the company of the 'nuns'. Their voices came to us as we walked, and Klein strained for some idea of what was being discussed.

'Why do they dress as nuns if they are not nuns?' I asked him.

'That was my idea. I hoped it might instil them with some, shall we say, loftier notion of life and all that might be achieved were virtue to be applied.'

I nodded in agreement with this, wondering if some more precise meaning had not been lost in his glib translation.

As we walked, I saw for the first time that he carried a slender cane, no more than a switch, which fell from his hidden hand to the ground, where it trailed behind him and left a thin line in the dust.

'It was the saddest day of my life when your great lords and masters saw fit to withdraw their support from us,' he said. 'So much that might have been achieved here had we not been so brusquely abandoned. We continue to do what we can, of course, but without that vital support I'm afraid a great deal has been lost.' Then he said, 'Did van Klees tell you that I am to accompany you back to Ukassa in the hope of securing some assistance from your competitors on the far shore? Our mother mission in Yaliembe was informed that their trading enterprise was expanding and that, in return for any assistance we might proffer, we might in some small way be remunerated for our help.'

I did not know how to reply; I was not even certain of what I was being told, or why. I felt I had been used by Cornelius.

'Are you returning with us alone?' I said.

'Myself, and those of my congregation who wish to accompany me.'

'Have you been offered anything definite?'

'Definite?' He said it as though he did not understand the word, but instead of asking me to explain myself he quickened his pace and walked ahead of me.

Over the next hour we were given a tour of the mission, its chapel, its dormitory, its school, its small hospital. Everyone there worked in fear of Klein, bowing to him and clasping their hands in prayer when he approached them. Some of them even raised their knotted hands to their lips and kissed them as they answered him.

There was a great poverty about the place, spiritual as well as material, and this was reflected in everything that went on there. The children in the school were all younger than five or six, and the lessons were of the simplest sort. The man who taught them carried a switch similar to Klein's, and he conducted them with it in their shouted answers. In a lesson clearly prepared for our visit, they answered him on the members of the Holy Family and told him what Heaven and Hell were. When one child, a small girl, faltered, he flicked the side of her head with his switch.

In the hospital most of the simple beds lay empty, and those few that were occupied contained men and women who received no treatment, it seemed, other than to have their faces wiped by those who attended them.

Following this tour, Cornelius told Klein that he wished to be alone with me, and the priest immediately withdrew.

'Why didn't you tell me we were here to collect him?' I said.

He dismissed my remark with a shrug. 'Our chapel was consecrated by him; he believes he owns it.'

'And do you believe you – you personally – exercise some control over him because—'

'Because I understand him, and he knows me,' he said. 'I didn't ask you to come with me to receive your blessing in the venture. He knows as much as you or I do regarding Frere, and with or without our permission or assistance, he would have come to tell everyone what he knows. He owes us no favours. He had a comfortable life here until the Company withdrew its money and its so-called good name.'

And I heard in this cold pleading that the man had some hold over Cornelius, too.

'You've known each other a long time,' I said, probing, holding his gaze.

'And, naturally, you suspect something between us that connects us in some other way.'

His words convinced me of it.

We walked together back to the main entrance and followed the shaded walls of the buildings until we were a good distance from anyone working there.

'My daughter is buried here,' he said.

'I never—'

'What? You never knew, never imagined, never believed? What?'

Whatever I said would have insulted him.

'What was her name?'

'She was called Magdalene. It was not my choice. Klein called her that. It was the stick with which he beat me. The child was only seven when she died of haematuric fever. I saw her seven times, came once a year. The year she died was the year our connection with the place was severed.'

'Is her grave close by?' I looked around us at the cultivated land.

'Somewhere. It was never marked. There is a cemetery here, of sorts, but the child, being what she was, was not allowed – he—' Cornelius stopped speaking, his mouth dry.

'Was your wife . . . ?'

'She was never that.' Meaning she had been a native woman.

'Was that why Klein refused the child a Christian burial?'

He nodded. 'I knew the child was coming, of course, but the first time I saw her she was almost a year old. That was when I learned her name.'

'Did her mother live with her here?'

92

'Klein sent her away in disgrace. And kept the girl here for the same reason.'

'Is that why you still come here, despite everything?'

'Despite *him*, you mean. I come because I still feel a sense of unfulfilled responsibility towards them both. If she had not been banished then I would have brought her closer to the Station and provided for her. I loved her. I know how difficult a notion that is for some men to understand, let alone give credence to, but it was how I felt. And if the girl had lived I would have done everything a father does for his daughter.'

'And Klein denied you the opportunity to do either.'

'All the while proclaiming that he did what was best in the eyes of God.'

'How do you feel about him coming to the Station?'

'I wish he weren't, of course I do. But having withdrawn our support from him, we no longer possess the authority to deny him.'

I saw then that this was why Cornelius had maintained the fabric of the chapel and why he kept his vigil there.

'Did you ever discover what happened to your – to the girl's mother?'

He shook his head. 'I made every effort, but she was banished. She disappeared. I don't know what there was for her to do, where she might go. The coast, perhaps.'

'What was her name?' I said.

'I called her Evangeline. I imagine it was the least of everything she had to lose.'

We continued walking until we reached the first of the trees. Cornelius peered into them, as though it was here that his lost daughter was buried. It seemed to me that I had learned more about the man during our past hour together than in all the time I had known him, and I wished I had understood all this sooner. There had been tears in his eyes at the thought of his lost daughter.

'Will Klein return here?' I asked him.

'Only when he realizes that this alone is where his power resides, that no-one apart from these few indoctrinated wretches will do his bidding.'

'You have some affection for his "nuns".'

'They nursed my daughter and then washed and buried her corpse.'

He left me then to wander among the trees. He was making no real attempt to search for the overgrown grave, wanting merely to convince himself of its presence. We were watched from the fields, and I stood guard between him and these others, though no-one attempted to approach us.

Later, I saw Perpetua and Felicity come searching for us. They waved and called to us like excited girls.

It was a great joke among my sisters, when searching for their presents for me upon my appointment, that I would be kept awake at night by the constant and infernal beating of drums in the surrounding forests. Just as I would risk grappling with crocodiles or hippopotami each time I went near the water, lions, snakes and elephants in the jungle. Just as I would doubtless be tempted by the charms (I can still hear their laughter, ever louder with each repetition of the word) of the native women. I indulged them in these fantasies. I knew in my own mind what to expect upon my arrival, and I knew what others might imagine to be awaiting me. They made me their hero, their intrepid explorer, their only brother, and their anxieties and concerns for me were contained and concealed in these appeals to my behaviour and safety.

Their biggest joke was the drums, perhaps because these were the easiest to imagine and believe in, and perhaps because of all their wild imaginings, they represented the least threat to me. I played up to this joke to such an extent that, on the eve of my departure, and following the presentation of everything else I was given, following the speeches of my mother and father and some uncles brought to the house especially for the occasion, I was presented with no fewer than twenty small cases of earplugs of various types and manufacture. I was told to experiment with these and then to write and let my sisters know which brand and type were the most effective at keeping out the drums and allowing me to sleep. A week beforehand, I had woken in the darkness to the sound of all three girls – women, I should say – beating gently and in rhythm upon saucepans with wooden spoons outside my bedroom door.

By that stage, and at my insistence, Frere had visited our home several times, and I saw even then that there was the beginning of an attachment, a fondness, between himself and Caroline, my middle sister – but one already tempered by what lay ahead of him and the time he would be apart from her.

His latest passion then was photography, and each time he visited us he brought with him one or other of the cameras he owned, posing every member of my family and the household staff for their portraits, singly and in groups, indoors and outdoors with the house and grounds as his backdrop. Needless to say, my sisters were the ones most impressed by him and by all this – though they already possessed countless portraits of themselves – and his photographs of them outnumbered all others.

I confronted him one evening when the two of us

were alone in London, in the rooms he had rented in Greenwich while making his own preparations to depart, and asked him of his feelings towards Caroline. He told me that had she and he met under different circumstances, then he would have insisted on seeing more of her and perhaps of preparing in some way for their future together. I saw immediately what a disservice I had done the pair of them.

He came to the house at my every invitation, and invariably he brought small presents for all three of my sisters, and for my parents too – nothing of any great value financially, because he did not possess such things, but personal gifts which no other man could produce. For my father he brought a whalebone inkwell which he himself had carved, and for Caroline he once brought an amber necklace which he had strung himself from small pieces he had collected on the Suffolk coast. My father owned a dozen inkwells, mostly of silver, and Caroline had a room strewn with jewellery, but I knew that each of them treasured these gifts above all others.

In the way that we all mould ourselves in the shapes of others, I saw then in Frere those attributes – of openness and generosity, of flair and kindness – that I knew I should myself enjoy possessing, and which might be appreciated in me by others, just as my sisters admired them in him.

He and I were frequently compared, inevitably to my detriment. He was worldly, whereas I, for all my military service, had lived a cloistered life; he was open to all new experiences, whereas I insisted on being forewarned of everything; he was a man moving back and forth on contradictory currents, whereas I was a man set rigidly in full sail in one and only one direction. I knew that these remarks were not intended to hurt me, and that my persecution was never anything but playful – Frere himself always arguing in my defence – but at the time I heard in them more truths than I wished to acknowledge. At the slightest indication that I had been stung by their comments, my sisters flocked to me like birds and covered my face with enthusiastic kisses.

A week before our departure, Frere and Caroline spent a day together, left alone by the others, who knew instinctively that something of this playfulness was at an end and that he and I were already beginning to detach ourselves from the comforts and the certainties of the lives we then lived.

It was decided that no-one should accompany me to Tilbury to see me off. My father suggested this and I agreed with him immediately. In truth, however, I regretted not having someone standing at the quayside and waving to me as I was taken slowly away from them, but it was beyond me to put this to him.

He was right: in fact, I left the house at four the following morning, when there was no-one but me and my mother to mark my going. I remember looking up at the windows of my sisters' bedrooms, hoping that they had learned of this early departure, and that I might see them there, ghostly figures in their nightgowns waving gently down at me while tears passed silently over their faces. I even had a tin of the earplugs in my coat pocket which I would have taken out and held up to them to cheer them up and cause them to laugh.

At Tilbury, Frere told me that he had spent long hours during the past week composing a letter to Caroline, expressing his feelings for her, confirming her feelings for him, and then suggesting how these might now be adapted and constrained during their time apart. I suspected he was telling me much more, that he had asked her to forget him and not to allow him to remain a shadow on her life. It was her twenty-second birthday two days after our departure, and he had included a gift with the letter. When I asked him what this was he refused to tell me.

Waiting until we were out of sight of land, he presented me with photographic miniatures of my parents and sisters, the five people I held dearest to me, and though I already possessed others, packed away amid my softest clothes, these five were the most recent, and, framed together in a single piece, they were where, for ever afterwards during my absence from home, those five people lived most fiercely for me.

PART TWO

7

Frere was returned to us two days later. We heard nothing in advance of this, and it was not until the boat bringing him was almost at our shore that we understood what was happening. I heard of it from the deformed boy, who banged on my door and then stood pointing when I answered.

Frere was accompanied by Proctor and three of his men. His hands were tied and a rope was looped loosely around his ankles. Proctor and his men all wore their dress uniforms and carried rifles. Their polished buttons and the gold braid of their caps and epaulettes shone in the sun as they came. I had never seen the man dressed like this before, and the formality of the occasion made me cautious.

The boat was moored and the five men waited on the jetty while we on this side formed ourselves into a group and went down to meet them. As we approached, Proctor called to his men and they stood to attention. They were not well drilled, but again the gesture and all it implied made me uneasy. I stood with Cornelius, who told me to wait and to remain silent.

Proctor came forward and took out a piece of paper.

He announced who he was and what he was there to undertake. He required several signatures and various guarantees before he was prepared to hand Frere over. All of these were duly given. He insisted on handing over directly to Bone. Bone, however, had not so far appeared. Fletcher sent someone to find him. He asked Proctor to hand Frere over to him, but Proctor refused, and we waited an hour until Bone was eventually found and brought to us, and then even longer as his own men were gathered together. There was only one other Englishman with Bone, a private called Clayton, the rest of his squad being natives, most carrying only clubs. I saw the look of contempt on Proctor's face as he inspected his counterparts.

'Why are we tolerating this charade?' I whispered to Cornelius.

'Because that's what it is. And because it serves someone else's purpose. Look at them – when did you ever see Proctor or his pretend soldiers dress like that before? Somebody, somewhere, wants all this done properly.'

'They're washing their hands of him,' I said. I looked to where Frere stood, his head down, his hands held together in front of him. He looked much as I had seen him on my last visit. I wanted to attract his attention, to signal to him that he was finally safe, but he kept his eyes resolutely on the ground, determined not to see me, not to have to respond to what was happening around him.

'Perhaps,' Cornelius said. 'Or perhaps it's more a question of them wanting us to properly understand our own responsibilities in the matter.'

I asked him what he meant, and he answered me by nodding in the direction of the far shore. A line of men stood there, none of whom I could identify at that distance and through the watery haze between us, but whose identity I might easily guess at.

There was a further delay while Bone went through the painstaking task of signing his own name on the various documents.

'Why don't they cross, too?' I said, meaning the distant figures, perhaps Amon, perhaps even Hammad, among them.

'Because this way we understand them more clearly.'

'Then why not at least warn us that they were sending him to us?'

Cornelius turned his back on the proceedings. 'Has it not occurred to you over the previous months that we hear less and less, are told less and less, of anything connected to us? Do you not see that even a year ago we heard of signatures on documents five thousand miles away which affected our trade, that we were informed of trading opportunities, of tariff and custom charges, that we were even informed of goods which never came, of men who never came. What *didn't* we hear of in those days?'

'And now?'

'And now this.'

'And you believe there is a purpose to it all, Frere included?'

'Possibly. I was merely remarking on the fact that once we were the kings of our own little kingdom, and that now . . .'

I wished he and not Bone were conducting the arrangements on behalf of Frere. Bone's men were no longer standing beside Frere, but were squatting on the ground.

'Are you satisfied?' Fletcher said to Proctor, as the man made a point of reading all the signatures that had just been signed. But Proctor played to his advantage and refused to be hurried. He slowly divided those pages which were to be returned to the Belgians from those which were to be left with us. He then shouted to Bone and said that he'd been told to take Frere all the way to our gaol and to see him securely held there before leaving. Fletcher said this was unnecessary, but Proctor insisted. He signalled to the men on the jetty and they came forward.

Frere was prodded in his back by one of the men with his rifle and he cried out at the unexpected pain of this. Proctor saw what had happened and looked round at the rest of us to see who might attempt to intervene. None of us did, and this disappointed Proctor, who called for his men to stop goading Frere.

For the first time, Frere raised his head and looked around him.

A considerable crowd had gathered by then. Men I had never before seen began to shout out, to condemn Frere for what he had done. Someone threw a clod of earth at him which burst into dust on his chest. Someone else cheered the shot. A group of women pushed through the crowd and spat at Frere. Proctor told them to get back, but made no real effort to restrain them until they had finished their protest.

Fletcher came to Cornelius and showed him the documents that had been signed. Cornelius read them.

'We accept full responsibility for him,' he said. 'And we hold him here until further action is necessary.'

'Next page,' Fletcher said, his eyes on the procession passing us close by.

'A delegation to be sent to assess the facts of the matter and to establish the most suitable manner in which to proceed with whatever action is deemed necessary.'

'They don't want him sent home,' Fletcher said. 'They want him tried and hanged here.'

'Hanged?' I said.

Fletcher and Cornelius shared a glance.

'Our gift to their new republic, or whatever,' Cornelius said.

'And don't look so surprised,' Fletcher said. 'You could have guessed all this from the very beginning.'

It was then, just as the slow procession passed in front of the chart room, that Frere stumbled and fell forward, grabbing out at the man in front of him and pulling him to the ground as he fell. From where I stood, it was difficult to see any more precisely what had happened. There was further cheering from the crowd as Fletcher pushed through them. Then I heard a call from Bone, and watched disbelievingly as two of his native guards ran forward, pulled Proctor's man to his feet, and started clubbing Frere where he lay on the ground. The cheering from the crowd grew even louder. The beating continued, with both Bone and Proctor looking on, and with neither man making any effort to stop it. It was ended finally by Fletcher firing his rifle into the air and pushing through the circle that had formed around the three men. Cornelius and I followed in his wake.

I had not noticed him previously, but as I approached close to where Frere lay on the ground, I saw Abbot standing in the open doorway of my office. I had locked the door behind me on coming out. He saw me approaching him, but made no effort to disguise the fact that he had been in among my maps without my permission. Instead he stared in fascination at the man on the ground and at the two men still hitting him. It was only as Fletcher fired again, and as the crowd finally fell silent and parted, that Abbot looked up and acknowledged my presence.

Frere lay on the ground without moving. There was blood on his cheek and forehead. Fletcher knelt and spoke to him, eventually helping him to his feet. Only then did Bone begin to admonish his men, but in a manner which made his own feelings clear to us and the watching crowd. The two natives retrieved their clubs and stood together with them cupped in their palms as though they were rifles. Bone then apologized to Frere, who wiped at his bloody mouth with his bound hands.

'Just get him to the gaol,' Fletcher said to Bone. 'You have a duty to him.'

'But not to you,' Bone said, angry at being spoken to like this in front of all these others.

'Perhaps,' Fletcher said, helping Frere as he resumed his hobbled walk. 'But you do seem to have signed your name to an awful lot of papers recently. Not me, not any of the rest of us – *you*. And what do you imagine that means, Bone? What do you imagine you've committed yourself to in your eagerness to sign?'

This had not occurred to Bone, and he looked at Fletcher without answering.

'At least now they've got someone to blame,' Fletcher said.

'Blame for what?'

'For whatever happens to your prisoner – *yours*, that is, not ours – before they can try him.'

Bone became alarmed at what he was being told. There was some truth in what Fletcher said, but he made more of it than it warranted. Bone looked down to where Frere had been on the ground, at the marks and stains in the dust there. Then he turned on the closest of the gathered men and women and told them to go. Few paid him any attention, but most wandered away of their own accord.

Cornelius left me and returned to his work.

I went to where Abbot stood and asked him what he wanted of me.

'With you?' he said. 'Nothing. Why?'

'You were in my room.'

'I was in a room owned by the Company, filled with Company maps. I wanted to ascertain how far behind you were in your work.' He carried several ledgers and folded his arms across these as he spoke. 'He makes quite a spectacle of himself, wouldn't you say,' he said, indicating Frere and the men around him. 'A great pity that neither you nor Cornelius could not have arranged to have him returned a little more discreetly.'

'We had nothing to do with it,' I said. 'It was beyond our control.'

He smiled at this. 'Of course.' He turned away from me. 'Forgive me, I have a great deal to do.'

I stood in my doorway, waiting until I saw Proctor and his men march back to their boat. Once out on the water, all four men fired their rifles into the air and were answered by shots from the distant shore.

8

I had hoped to visit Frere the following day, but circumstances worked against me. On that morning a vessel arrived at the centre of the river flying a yellow flag. The waterways on either side of it emptied immediately, and I could not understand why the small steamer had dropped anchor there rather than continuing downriver. An hour later, a second vessel arrived, also showing a fever flag. These two joined themselves stern to prow and continued on their way together.

The rest of the day was filled with speculation. It was Cornelius's opinion that they had come from the mission at Mohta, but we were at a loss as to what contagion they might have carried. There had been men working on the decks of both vessels while they waited.

Several hours passed before anyone crossed the river, almost as though something of the boats' sickness might remain diluted in the water. There was some complaint from our consignment traders that the vessels they were expecting had been kept away by the flags. Later, we received word that a cargo of palm oil and block attar had been diverted to Biembo at word of the flags.

The incident left us unsettled; these things seldom

occurred in isolation. An order was given to all the independent traders due to leave over the following days to conclude their work more quickly and to leave before nightfall. When they complained at being hurried like this, Fletcher told them either to leave or to take back on board all their recently unloaded supplies. Few persisted in their complaints.

'If it is an outbreak of something at Mohta,' Cornelius said, 'then the boats will be back and forth.'

Seven hundred women and children lived at the mission. Cross-river traffic ceased for two days afterwards. Abbot complained that everyone was over-reacting, and that our business had been delayed and disrupted enough over the previous months without this.

Cornelius waited for him to leave us before saying to me, 'I read Proctor's papers last night. The Company was informed within an hour of Frere's return. They'll know already down in Boma.'

Boma remained our administrative centre in preference to Stanleyville, where the Belgian presence was too great. Sea-breeze Boma we called it, where life was easy, and departure forever on the minds of the men who worked there.

'Someone will be sent to examine the facts of the matter. Frere might even be returned with whoever is sent.'

'Is there no chance that we might be left to sort it out for ourselves?' I asked him.

'Those days are over,' he said. 'It seems we can no longer be trusted. Besides, there are other considerations.'

I regretted having asked. He told me nothing I had not considered a hundred times over through the previous night.

He went on: 'All I'm saying is that it is in all our interests – especially Frere's – to be aware that these things are about to happen to us, for us to be ready for them to happen, and then for us to act accordingly.'

'Which, you believe, involves us keeping our distance from the man.'

'Whatever.'

'Are we going to sacrifice him so readily?'

He shook his head at this remark. 'I am as powerless as you,' he said.

I asked if anyone had been to see Frere since his return.

'Bone is under orders to keep everyone away for the first few days.'

'Why?'

'Perhaps to give Frere time to prepare himself.'

'And to imagine that we here, his friends, have all abandoned him.'

'I doubt he will believe that.'

'Has Bone set a guard on him?'

'Bone himself, honest, decent, conscientious little man that he is.'

'Hardly our greatest conversationalist.'

'And perhaps that is the last thing Frere needs of us for the time being.'

'And after this embargo?'

'Then presumably whoever wishes to see him will be free to do so.' I heard the note of caution sounded in the remark.

It was as we discussed the other matters of the day – primarily the anticipated arrival of our monthly consignment of rubber and indigo – that Fletcher arrived with news of an accident at the quarry, a landslide beneath which four workers had been buried, believed killed. I took out our ledger of employees from my desk and asked him if he knew the men's names.

'Who among us knows *any* of their names? Abbot's up there now, flapping around like the headless chicken that he is.'

'Will it hold up the digging?' Cornelius said.

'Apparently not. The fall was on an old face.'

It was unlikely that the diggers' bodies would be retrieved unless they were either visible or easily accessible. In the past, men had been killed in the quarry and abandoned beneath the rock and earth which had crushed them. Their families were afterwards sought and compensated depending on how loyal the workers were deemed to have been – another division of Abbot's authority – and how long they had worked for the Company.

At the news of a single death, ten families would immediately petition Abbot, and then sit for days on the quarry floor until they were either driven out or they abandoned their useless appeals. We were regularly sent directives on how every type of payment and compensation was to be calculated.

I went with Fletcher and Cornelius to the quarry, where we were joined by Abbot. It was clear where the wall had collapsed: a slope of bright red earth and soft rock, fifty feet high, near-liquid in appearance and spreading outwards over the quarry floor. There was some effort still being made to search the surface of this by men probing with long canes, but little hope remained for the buried diggers.

It was Abbot's opinion that only three, not four, men had been lost, and that this ought to be remembered when the wailing women arrived. He made no attempt to supervise the search for the men, leaving this to those who had been working alongside them when the fall occurred, and those who knew how much easier it was to search than to continue working elsewhere. Abbot calculated that the work of twenty men would be lost for half a day. Fletcher asked him if that included the three dead men, and Abbot said it did.

I went with Cornelius to the quarry floor, to the outermost edge of the debris.

'They cut it too sharp,' he said. He indicated the high, sheer faces all around us.

'That's because there's less and less to recover,' I told him, knowing that within a year the place would be abandoned. We watched the naked men on the slope above us. There was little apparent order to their searching, but even they must have by then understood that they were digging for corpses.

A man higher up the slope began suddenly to scream. He scrabbled in the earth at his feet, and a moment later he pulled free the lower part of a man's leg and foot. Others scrambled up the slope to help him. Letting go of the corpse, the rescuer then cupped his hands to his mouth and let out a cry which reverberated around the enclosed space.

'Now Abbot will have to go to the bother of a burial,' Cornelius said. He started forward up the slope and I followed him.

By the time we arrived at the top, the body had been fully retrieved. It looked flattened, tan from head to foot, both arms and both legs either dislocated or broken, or both. The man's eyes were cleared of the red clay and it was scooped from his mouth. At our approach, the diggers stood aside and fell silent, acknowledging our greater responsibility in the matter. Both Cornelius and I were covered from head to foot in the same red mess. Cornelius told two of the men to drag the body to the quarry floor, and we waited where we stood while this was done.

9

It was raining as I approached the gaol, and water poured from its corrugated roof in a succession of spouts. Bone's own quarters stood to one side of the building, and a third, equally dilapidated structure housed his small garrison. All this was at some distance from the compound, reached by a path through the scrub. In the dry season, when the vegetation died back, the foundations of other, lost buildings could be seen rising to knee height. There was some speculation as to what these had once been used for, and it was generally agreed that, like so many of the buildings across the river, they had been holding quarters for slaves, gathered here awaiting shipment to the coast, or east cross-country, wherever the demand was greatest, and I seldom failed to feel some faint, sour echo of the place and its ghosts each time I passed through it.

Arriving at the gaol, I encountered Bone and Clayton on the building's narrow veranda. Looking at them through the streaming water was like looking at men sitting behind a waterfall. I was by then soaked, and steam rose from my shoulders and chest. They were playing cards and made a show of stopping their game to watch me approach. Bone called out for me to identify myself, saying that he couldn't make me out through the water. Both of them laughed at this. I passed through the water and stood beside them, squeezing the wet from my arms and waiting as it drained into a pool at my feet.

'Rain,' Bone said. 'Only an idiot would be out in it.'

The wet season was by then well established and parts of the compound flooded daily. The river was high, and most of the traders had left our jetties and wharves for the calmer, more reliable pools downriver until the water fell. Everything that might spoil among our dry goods was taken inside under the supervision of Cornelius and the rest was left to sit out the daily downpours.

Bone put down his cards and stood up. Clayton insisted that they continue playing, but Bone took this to mean that the man had a winning hand and told him to go. Clayton protested, and so Bone put his foot against the packing case on which their cards and coins were spread and kicked it over, sending most of the cards and money out into the rain.

'I said go,' he said again; I knew that this small show had been for my benefit alone. Clayton went, cursing loudly as he stepped out into the rain, and we watched him run to the shelter of the garrison.

'I've come to see Frere,' I said.

'You do surprise me.'

'I have every right.'

'Never said you didn't.'

'Can I go in?'

'Not like that.' He indicated the water still flowing from my clothes.

'Is he well?' I asked him.

'How well does he need to be? Don't worry, he'll still be here when they come to get him.'

'Has anyone else been to see him?'

'The Old Man.' He meant Cornelius.

'Recently?'

'The day he came back.'

This surprised me, and he saw this. 'Thought you had him all to yourself, did you, your own little lost cause?'

'Not at all.'

'Yes, you did. You going to save him, are you? The Old Man came, stayed ten minutes and then went. Probably just here to tell him to keep his mouth shut and take what he's got coming to him.'

I refused to rise to the remark.

'Perhaps you're right,' I said.

'And perhaps I'm not. But, either way, it won't make any difference to him, will it?'

Unwilling to delay any longer, I left him.

'Door's open,' he called after me.

The outer room was filled with old furniture, possibly gathered up long ago from those other abandoned buildings, and most of these pieces had been eaten by termites, leaving mounds of dust beneath them. The heat in the room was unbearable beneath its tin roof.

The door to Frere's cell was open. Someone had lined chairs along the wall, and upon several of these stood mounds of books.

Frere sat at a desk beneath a barred window. He was writing as I entered; other books lay open all around him.

'Am I interrupting you?' I said, expecting him to look up at me and smile at the remark.

Instead, he motioned impatiently for me to enter and

wait. He then finished what he was writing, read it through and blotted the ink, all as calmly and as precisely as though he were a conscientious clerk interrupted at his labours. I half expected him to ask me what he could do for me.

'I heard you,' he said. He indicated the small window, through which Bone remained a third presence. He touched a finger to his lips, and then said loudly, 'I have a plan to kill Bone in his sleep and escape.'

The top of Bone's head appeared at the window. He called in to us that he'd like to see Frere try, and then we heard as he left the veranda and ran splashing through the downpour to his own quarters.

'He's a Philistine,' I said.

'He needs to be. And perhaps if the rest of us were, then all this might at least be tolerable.' He rose and moved stiffly, flinching at a succession of small pains. There was still a bruise across his forehead from the beating he had been given on his return.

'I tried to stop it,' I said.

'Cornelius brought me some sulphur powder and bandages.' He raised his shirt to show me his strapped chest.

'I should have thought to bring you some more,' I said.

He pulled a chair from the side of the room up to his desk.

I had with me a satchel filled with other medicines – mainly vitriol and tartar emetic – and with writing materials, although I saw that he was well provided with these, too.

'For my confession?' he said as I carefully took these out and wiped them dry.

'For whatever you want. Did Bone tell you about the papers he was asked to sign?'

116

'Twenty times. A lifetime of signatures. What else do you imagine he can write?'

'*Is* that what you were writing? Your account of what happened?'

'You make it sound as though it all somehow took place independently of me, as though I were merely watching and not participating.'

'You know what I mean,' I said. I resented his abruptness, these probing remarks.

'Of course I do. I just wish you were able to say it more directly.'

'No, you don't. Every time I ask you something directly, you become evasive, you protect me, push me further and further away from the truth.'

He made no attempt to deny this. He said nothing for several minutes, during which there was a break in the downpour and the drumming above us ceased, followed by the hiss and splatter of running water. My hands still left wet imprints where I rested them. It was common during these breaks in the rain for men to fall silent, listening, knowing only that the rain would return and fall for its allotted span, occasionally timing these periods of relative calm as though they were something hard-won, silent reprieves, islands of dry amid the ocean of the rain.

And it was during these periods of short-lived unreality that I felt most intensely that we there were all players on a small, eagerly observed stage, and that the stillness and silence was only a precursor to the events which were inevitably to follow.

Several minutes passed like this, and then Frere said, 'Tell me honestly, is this what you expected, all this, is it what you truly expected to find? Is your part in it all truly the part you expected to play?'

I knew that he was referring to the whole of our time

there, and not merely to his own recent abandonment of us.

I knew how great and unbearable his own disappointment had become. Not immediately upon our arrival, perhaps, but certainly in the months which followed, as our routines were established and as the never-ending considerations of commerce and money-making usurped all else. In truth, it was not what I had expected, but my expectations had never been so high as his. He had expected a wilderness in which to wander, but instead he found only a place already long since sacrificed to the gods of profit and loss. This is to simplify it too greatly, but it was something commonly understood between us. It was why, during those months following our arrival, we had planned and gone on our own short expeditions – all under the flimsy guise of commercial exploration, and fooling only ourselves into believing that we were going where no others had already gone before us.

Frere was the instigator and planner of these expeditions, and though I was at first keen to accompany him, I became less enthusiastic later. The others complained of our time away. Frere always brought something back to appease them – specimen goods, the knowledge of a new route, new sources of hired labour – but they quickly saw through these subterfuges.

After a year of such expeditions I had pleaded that I was too busy with my maps to accompany him, and he had started going alone, hiring porters to accompany him. These short absences were tolerated only so long as his work at the Station remained unaffected. They were not long journeys, the longest lasting only five or six days. It was why, when he finally decided not to return to us, almost a fortnight elapsed before any of us became suspicious.

'I expected to serve some useful purpose,' I conceded. 'I expected something different, something far removed from anything else I had ever known. I expected to be able to make some genuine and lasting contribution.'

'And this place? Is it what you expected it to be?'

'I certainly don't share *your* disappointments.'

'And therefore life here remains tolerable for you.'

'Was it so intolerable for you? I don't believe you. You were given considerable freedom. It wouldn't have been tolerated, say, of Abbot.' It was a poor comparison to make, and thinking of the man, both Frere and I smiled. 'You know what I mean,' I said.

'I do. And I regret the fact that I cannot contain my disappointments, and that even now I am still forcing you – *you*, of all people – to confront them with me.'

'You force me to do nothing. You're my friend; I admire you. You don't need to endlessly tell me of the things I already know. You don't need to tell me how noble and misplaced my own goals or ideals were – are – compared to your own. You don't need to remind me of all the compromises and allowances I make.' I paused. 'Apart from which, I cannot say that I entirely believe you.'

'Oh?' This turn in our discussion amused and encouraged him.

'When you say your own expectations were so thwarted. You knew far better than I did what to expect. You might have pretended otherwise, you may not have disabused me of my own grand notions on the voyage out, but you knew all the same.'

'And so I am now fooling only myself, making excuses for myself alone?'

I could not deny that this was part of what I felt.

He signalled for me to say nothing more. He inspected the medicines I had brought him. I asked him what else he needed. He asked me if all his journals and notebooks were safe and I told him that they were, and that no-one had yet remarked on the fact that I had retrieved them from his quarters.

'Whoever comes, they'll want to see them,' he said.

'Not all of them.'

'No, not all.'

'I can send the remainder home,' I suggested.

'Afterwards.'

I stopped myself from saying, 'After what?'

'And don't forget,' he said, 'anything you do might be regarded as perverting the course of justice. These things must be considered.' He told me which journals he would like to see and I promised to bring them to him. He asked me about his collections and I assured him they remained intact where he had left them. He was concerned that some of them might be stolen. He told me which cases contained his fetishes. 'Take them out – it doesn't matter which – and spread them around the cases and jars. Put one in each drawer of my desks.'

'Will they keep thieves away?'

'It will keep away the men who believe in them. Tell Cornelius I would be grateful if he would return to see me.'

Above us, the rain resumed its clamour, forcing us to raise our voices.

I was with Fletcher the following day when he was called to the river. A small steamer and a dozen attached canoes, some no more than over-laden rafts, had just then arrived and some argument had arisen. A master at a neighbouring jetty had complained that the new arrival had no right to be there, and that his own unloading was being delayed. We went to the boat and its canoes.

Fletcher recognized it immediately. 'Zoo collectors,' he told me, but whatever the vessel held was hidden from view by tarpaulins.

'Do they have any right being here?' I asked him.

'None whatsoever. They're waiting. Those canoes won't survive twenty miles with the river running this fast. They want to tie up here and wait.'

'What will you do?'

'Get rid of them.'

We walked the length of the jetty and leaped down onto the small steamer. The owner came out to us. He was an Arab. He lied to us about having problems with his engine and needing time to repair it. He spoke in a way which suggested he did not expect to be believed, and Fletcher obliged him in this by saying, 'You're a liar.'

The man pretended to be offended. He offered to pay for the use of the jetty for the few hours he would be forced to remain.

'No,' Fletcher said, already walking away from him. He lifted the canvas on the piled cages to reveal the creatures they held, all brought to life by the sudden light shining in on them. The man pleaded with Fletcher to keep the tarpaulins fastened, but Fletcher ignored him and went from one mound of cages to another, throwing back their covers.

The creatures were mostly small apes, chimps and gibbons, crowded together until they were forced to cling to each other and sit one upon another for want of space. There were some small cats, ocelots and civets, and a variety of antelopes and gazelles. The larger of these were trussed and laid on the floor of their cases. Some of the apes threw themselves screeching and howling at the wooden bars as we looked in at them.

We moved on and the owner followed us, pulling

121

down and securing the covers. He prodded the animals with the cane he carried, provoking even louder outbursts from them. In several cages, the animals were already dead. In one cage of small monkeys, all no bigger than cats, more seemed to be dead than alive, and those that were living looked close to death.

I followed Fletcher to the stern of the vessel, where a solitary large cage was roped to the deck.

'Gorilla, probably,' he said to me. We had seen them before. 'Fetching double what they did a year ago.'

Because the cover of this cage was more securely fastened than the others, Fletcher told the owner to untie it himself. He protested, offering us the money he was willing to pay. Other men stood in the canoes and looked up at us. Most of these lesser vessels rocked precariously each time the men on them moved. The river rolled in close, sudden waves along its bank.

When the Arab again refused to do what Fletcher told him, Fletcher took out his knife and cut the ropes securing the cage. The man became even more agitated and called for him to stop, pushing himself in front of Fletcher.

'Then get on with it,' Fletcher said.

The man set about unfastening the many knots, until the last rope fell limp and he stood back from the cage. Fletcher told him to remove the tarpaulin. There had been no sound from the cage while all this was happening, and it occurred to me – as it must already have occurred to Fletcher – that instead of holding a living creature, the box contained contraband of some sort – arms, perhaps, or unmarked ivory.

Eventually, the owner pulled the tarpaulin clear, and in the cage before us we saw a fully grown giraffe, trussed at its knees and feet and with its neck tied down in a tight, awkward curve to the floor of the cage in order that it might be fitted into it. The creature's mouth was also bound with cloths. Its tongue protruded and its nostrils flared and closed rapidly. It looked out at us with dark eyes the size of cricket balls. I had seen others, but none so large or so close as this one. The animal's tail was fastened to one of its feet. The slats of the cage pressed into its sides, and the bars across the roof bore down behind its shoulders.

'It's a female,' Fletcher said.

I asked him how he knew and he prodded its swollen belly, causing the animal to flare its eyes.

'And it won't even get beyond the Lulindi, let alone to whatever zoo is waiting for it.'

'How can you be so certain?'

'Because it was never meant to lie down or even sit. They sleep standing up. The minute it tries to struggle to its feet – especially one in this condition – its heart will give out and it will die. It won't be able to do it. And even if they do manage to hoist it up in a sling, which is what they'll attempt with something so valuable, then it'll stand for an hour, perhaps even a day, miscarry and then buckle, fall and die. I've seen it happen. It won't even have been fed or watered for the past week.'

He asked the owner of the boat how long the animal had been trussed and caged. The man shrugged and said he had acquired it already bound from a collector at Ankoro. Fletcher asked him where it was going, but the man knew only as far as Port Elys on the coast.

'I'd shoot it in the head here and now,' Fletcher said to me. 'Except then I'd have to pay him for it.'

The animal had fixed its eye on me, though I doubt if it saw much through its fear and suffering.

The Arab overheard Fletcher's remark about shooting the giraffe, and seeing that we had satisfied our curiosity, he hurriedly began pulling the cover back over the cage. He called for help from the watching men below and several leaped aboard to assist him.

'Do you want to see what's in the other boats?' I asked Fletcher.

'Nothing as valuable as this,' he said.

We waited until the giraffe was once again covered and Fletcher told the Arab to go, to untie his mooring ropes and take his chances with the faster water downriver. At first I thought this was a prelude to increasing the man's bribe, but Fletcher made his intentions clear by leaving the vessel and starting to untie the ropes himself.

Minutes later the boat and its attendant canoes were pulled away from us, slowly at first, then ever faster, half turning in the middle current until its steam was raised and its paddle turned fast enough to correct its course. We watched the smaller vessels rise and fall behind it on the swifter water, and heard the muffled cacophony of screams and cries to which this increasing motion gave rise.

10

I next encountered Klein on his knees in the garrison yard. I had gone to the gaol early, hoping to see Frere alone. I had with me the journals he had asked for, and several of my charts – those mapping out the further reaches of our immediate influence – in the hope that I might finally start piecing together his journey away from us. I wanted to start making sense of what had happened to him during his absence, to better understand his reasons for leaving us.

The priest was praying aloud, and I heard his voice as I entered the yard. Bone and his men sat at the garrison door and watched him, deriving a great deal of amusement from what they saw. Occasionally, one or other of the men would say something and they would all burst into laughter. Klein seemed unaffected by this. Perpetua and Felicity knelt on either side of him, and a group of twenty or thirty women who had accompanied him from Kirasi knelt in a group behind him.

I went to Bone before approaching the gaol. Klein had looked up at my arrival, watched me briefly and then resumed his prayers. Bone told one of his men to fetch a chair for me, and then told me to sit beside him.

'How long has he been here?' I asked him.

'Here before dawn. Three hours this racket's been going on. Him and the two black-and-white crows, they been here all that time. The others come and go. It's like he's got them working a rota. Two stand up to leave and two more appear to join in the fun.'

'They been swapping clothes,' the man who fetched my chair said.

'What?'

'Over there,' Bone said. He indicated where a narrow gate led into the surrounding trees. 'The ones who come turn up half naked and the ones who go give them their clothes. Some nice-looking ones among the recent arrivals.'

The men around me nodded vigorously at this. Some sat and stared in silent, hopeful anticipation at what this nakedness still suggested to them.

Bone wiped a hand across his mouth. 'Some real lookers.'

I studied the group of women. Most were young, some barely out of childhood. They were the women Klein held the greatest sway over. Some were as black as our local Manyema, but others were octaroons with fuller limbs and creamier complexions, and several among them looked almost white at that distance. It was these women Bone and his men watched the closest. Occasionally, one or other of those kneeling at the rear of the group turned her head to look at us. There was something suggestive in the way they did this, all the time keeping their hands tightly clasped, as though this alone would betray them to Klein. I watched as two women, both paler than most, rose and quietly walked away from the worshippers.

'See,' Bone said, and he pointed to where two others had come to take their place. These women stood by the narrow entrance inside the yard. Both wore short blouses and cloths tied at their loins. One of them pointed to where we sat and whispered to the other. They came towards the departing women, who took off their skirts and handed them over. There was nothing secretive or furtive about the exchange, and for several moments all four women stood near-naked in view of the watching men.

'How long does he intend keeping this up?' I said, hoping to divert attention away from the women, but no-one answered me.

Bone eventually said, 'Who cares?'

Frere, I thought, but said nothing.

The two new arrivals then walked past us to join the others. They glanced at us as they went, and one of them gave a shy wave.

'It's you she's after,' one of the men said to me. I felt myself blush at the suggestion and the man saw this and laughed. He made some further remark. The girl who had waved paused for a moment and looked at me. She lifted a hand to her chest and brushed something from her blouse. This display was much appreciated. And then her companion tugged at her sleeve and the two of them continued towards Klein. I expected the girl might look back at me before kneeling and beginning her praying, but she did not.

'You should have beckoned her over,' Bone said. 'She'd have come, that one. Been round here a lot the past few days.'

I could tolerate this no longer – not so much the men's behaviour or their remarks, for I would have expected nothing more in the presence of the women, but the fact that they included me among their number, the fact that I was obliged to share in and prolong their pleasure.

Ensuring that my charts were well fastened and

revealed nothing of their contents, I rose and went to the worshippers. I made a point of walking in a wide circle around them until I stood directly in front of Klein. His own clasped hands were pressed into his eyes, his head bowed, but I knew that he had seen me. My shadow lay in a line towards him, and I moved forward several paces until it touched his knees. On either side of him, Perpetua and Felicity kept their heads bowed, but further back, many among the worshippers looked up at me while intoning their words. I stood without speaking for several minutes while this continued.

Klein had attached himself to me for most of the journey from Kirasi, while Cornelius, Perpetua and Felicity had walked ahead of us. On several occasions I had suggested joining them, but Klein had resisted this, saying that he enjoyed talking with me, and bemoaning the fact that it had been several months since he had been able to have such a discussion over a variety of shared interests. He was an impermeable conversationalist, asking my views only as a primer for delivering his own, and expressing these in a manner which made it clear to me that I might now, having listened to him, wish to reconsider my own opinions. He made several derogatory remarks concerning Cornelius and asked me questions about the man I did my best not to answer. He called frequently for one of his attendants to bring him drink. He grew intoxicated as we walked, though swore to me that he was drinking only a tonic for his blood. I quickly tired of him, and wondered if this was another reason why Cornelius had asked me to accompany him to the mission.

I put this to Cornelius later that same night and he said, 'Of course,' and poured me another glass of his brandy. I asked him what he had talked about with Perpetua and Felicity and he became evasive. I knew he had discussed more than his own lost 'wife' and daughter, but we were both exhausted by our day's journey and it was beyond me to pursue the matter.

Upon our arrival at the Station, Klein and his congregation took up residence in the chapel, and he announced that he would hold a service there that same night. None of us took him up on the offer, though he gathered a sizeable flock from our boatmen, loaders and porters, most of whom went, as they often went to these gatherings, more out of a sense of curiosity than commitment. Some went because they had once been at Kirasi, and some went for word of their relatives who had been there. These men and women led such uncertain, fractured lives in our employ, and Klein's service appealed to them as a beacon might appeal to a mariner. Those of us who did not attend could not help but hear the prayers and hymns aimed directly at us through the darkness.

I stood before him now and waited. He made a great play of finishing his prayer, of soliciting its responses and then of concluding it. Eventually, he fell silent, and this silence spread outwards across the yard. I heard the muted applause of Bone and his men.

'A pity they cannot learn to appreciate more what we are attempting here,' Klein said, his hands still clasped, his eyes still firmly closed.

'Is that why you came?'

'You know why we came. We have business across the river.'

'Then why not do all this there?'

'We are still in possession of the chapel, still

129

caretakers of the Lord's house here.' He smiled as he said this, lowered his hands and opened his eyes. I expected him to rise, but he remained on the ground, and I saw what an advantage this gave him over me.

'I doubt he'll thank you for it,' I said, indicating the gaol behind me.

'It is not *his* thanks we seek.'

'Frere holds firm opinions concerning the nature, even the existence of all you hold so dear,' I said, only then realizing that Frere might be overhearing everything that was being said.

'He may have forsaken the Lord, but he will soon enough be remembered by the Lord.'

There was something reassuring in the glibness and the predictability of this answer.

'Remembered?'

'We are all His children. We will all one day be remembered by Him.'

'You seem very certain of that.'

'Certain that Frere will be remembered? Or that he will be remembered sooner than most?' His smile narrowed and he looked up at me, his gaze unflinching in the full glare of the sun, able to see clearly and directly that which I was still reluctant to even glimpse.

'Ah,' he said. 'Your own conviction wavers. You yourself would not deny all that he denies.'

'Is that why you're here – the saved soul of the redeemed sinner? Is everyone beyond your own obedient flock already lost to you?'

Perpetua and Felicity looked up at my words, and I wished there was some way I might signal my apology to them. Behind them, many of the other worshippers were growing restless now that they were no longer unified in their worship. Klein saw this and he turned

130

to look at them, causing them all to fall silent and to bow their heads.

'He'll be in there laughing at you,' I said.

'Oh, I don't doubt it. But our perseverance may yet give him cause to reconsider. Who knows, he may even wish to repent.'

'Like Cornelius repented when you banished the mother of his child?'

He shrugged at this. 'She was what she was. Only *he* refused to see that.' He then clicked his fingers and Perpetua and Felicity came forward to help him to his feet. They brushed the dirt from his clothes, beginning with his shoulders and moving down to his feet. He took no real satisfaction in the attention of the two women, only that I was there to watch them attend so willingly to his silent bidding.

'I am a child to their devotion,' he said to me as the women straightened his jacket and wiped the dust from his legs. He signalled again to them and they stopped this work and withdrew, one to each side of him, a proscribed distance, each handmaiden facing straight ahead, her arms by her side.

'You've trained them well,' I said. I knew that soon two others might be picked from his congregation and the surplices handed over. Perhaps some among the crowd had already played the role and knew better than most how they were being used by the man.

'Have you been in to see him?' I said to Klein.

'I have no desire to see him. He is a murderer. He murdered a child. A murderer. A child killer.' He paused. 'And possibly worse. If you cannot see these things, then it is well that others are looking on your behalf. What brilliant light does that man give off that you are so blinded by it? Oh, but then perhaps you alone are blinded by it because of your connection to him. Perhaps that is nearer the truth.' He went on before I could answer him, his speech of veiled suggestion and condemnation well prepared. 'No, I have not been inside to see him and nor shall I. What is there to discover that I do not already know? Any good I may do, I can do from where I stand.'

I doubt I had felt contempt for any man as I felt it then for that priest.

He turned away from me and held up his hands. He thanked everyone for what they had done. He thanked the Lord for allowing them to be there, and for them to have been guided by His goodness.

'What now?' I asked him.

'Now? Now you and he shall sit together for an hour, and he, in all likelihood, will tell you none of what you came hoping to hear, and to avoid that awkward silence and all it implies concerning your friendship you will fill his head with talk of your tedious life here and of his coming inquisition. You will no doubt share a joke and laughter about my own presence here, just as those others – ' he motioned without turning to where Bone and his men still sat ' – make their own lascivious remarks about my congregation. And then, at the end of your long hour together, having achieved nothing, you will be happy to leave him and he will be even happier to see you go. And no doubt this charade will continue until he confesses everything to you – because, oh yes, that is the role you imagine you have cast yourself in – or until you and he face the truth together and forsake each other for good. There, is that sufficient of an answer for you? What now? What now? Was there ever anything said so useless?'

And with that he turned and left me, snapping his fingers for Perpetua and Felicity to accompany him.

Passing Bone and the others, he called for his congregation to avert their eyes from the soldiers, which most did immediately. He then turned to the garrison and held his Bible towards the men there while the women behind him passed out of the yard and into the trees beyond.

11

I opened one of my tin trunks this morning to find that it had been invaded by white ants and that much of what had been stored inside – books, clothing, a case of pens and pencils – had been reduced to dust. Only the inedible parts of the books' bindings remained untouched, along with a handful of metal buttons, and all that remained of my mapping pencils were the silver clasps which held them together. I could not remember what had been in the case, whether they had been empty journals or full ones, or the novels I had gathered together and brought out with me, most of which had been presents from my mother and sisters.

Each member of my family had presented me with an inscribed keepsake: a toy crocodile and lion from Caroline; a framed sampler of Daniel and *his* lions from Victoria; and a silver hand mirror from Elizabeth. My father had given me a pair of hunting pistols, each of a different bore and calibre, and each with my initials set into their grips. My mother, as I suspected she might, presented me with a Bible, so bound that when it was closed and locked it was sealed tight inside a japanned tin case. Because she had worked earlier in her life for various missionary societies, I imagined this gift was in some way connected to her past, and I saw in it how much of her own thwarted ambition I now embodied.

I sought out all these precious things and took them from their wrappings. I had neither read from the Bible – the place was strewn with other, cheaper, expendable editions – nor fired the pistols other than to show them off to Fletcher. He told me they would be good for shooting small birds. Or fish, he said. Fish? I said, but he was already laughing.

During my first months here I had slept with the toy animals on the cabinet beside my bed, the silver mirror between them. It became my nightly ritual to ensure that all three pieces were in their place. During the daytime I locked them in my desk. I had hoped to send the head of either a crocodile or a lion back to Caroline, but that was when I imagined both were plentiful and might be easily or cheaply had.

My mother gave me the names of a dozen missionaries she had known, and the places they had served along the river. Some of those places no longer existed, and most had changed their names. She told me to try and contact some of the people she had once known and to pass on her regards to them, speaking as though they lived in the next county and I was calling on them for tea. It was only when I realized she was talking of people she had known thirty or thirty-five years ago that I understood the futility of this request. I read out some of the names to Cornelius, but even he shook his head at them.

I took the trunk of dust outside and emptied it. I salvaged the buttons because they had some value, but I kicked away everything else until it was scattered. Several men watched me from a distance and then came over and searched sifting with their fingers through what I had discarded. I told them there was nothing to find, but either they did not understand me or did not believe me. They retrieved the half-eaten pages of unidentifiable novels and gathered these together; they picked up tiny pieces of the gold-painted binding as though it were gold itself. One man even found the metal cap to one of my pens and rose yelling from the other sifters as though he had found a jewel.

On one of our expeditions, Frere and I had gone in search of a lake, supposedly five days to the north-east of us, in Uregga country, and supposedly the home of a monster, a creature the size of twenty elephants, according to the Uregga porters who told us of it. There were many such tales, many such monsters, but we went anyway. The most we could hope for, Frere suggested as we departed, was a variant species of lake hippopotamus, though he was doubtful of even that. It was one of our first expeditions together, and undertaken at a time when he still believed they would be frequent and sanctioned.

We moved into the forest between the Lulindi and Elila. I knew from the maps I possessed of the region that there were other, unnamed watercourses, but I had no idea of the land between them other than that it was forest and that the region further away from the river was populated by the scattered villages of the Uregga.

I asked Frere about these people on the eve of our departure, but he knew little about them, except that they had recently been greatly reduced by war and disease, and that they were a dying people. I asked him if they were likely to be hostile towards us and he said he didn't know. He then reassured me by saying that he doubted if we would encounter anyone prepared to stop us travelling through the region.

According to Fletcher, the Uregga were an impoverished tribe who could not even compete with the scavenging Ayaya living along the river. I sensed that Frere was disappointed at learning all this, that he had expected something more of the expedition than a trek to establish the existence, or otherwise, of the lake itself, let alone the creature it was rumoured to contain.

At his insistence, we left before dawn, crossing the river several miles from the Station.

The shore where we landed was overgrown, and trees lay where they had fallen. There were no staging posts, no markers or other indicators of human presence, and as we disembarked, Frere asked me which path we were to follow. The question caught me by surprise. He had been so certain of our landing point that I assumed he already knew the route of the first part of our journey. But as he waited for my answer, I saw that I had been set a deliberate challenge – that whichever course we followed we would be following it blind – and so I rose to it. I indicated inland along a shallow stream in a steep-sided valley, hoping that this would connect with one of the larger watercourses. Frere applauded my confidence and said he assumed we would simply travel north-east until we encountered someone with local knowledge of the lake. I told him that this had been my understanding, too. I took readings to establish our landing place, and then others to mark the exact line of the water as we left it behind.

The first day's travelling was hard. The terrain was steep, irregular, and more heavily forested than I had expected, and I calculated that in ten hours we crossed barely six miles.

By mid-afternoon a low plateau had appeared ahead

of us. On one of my maps a scarp line was drawn immediately south of the supposed site of the lake, and I imagined this was the raised land before us. I showed this to Frere and we were both encouraged by the prospect.

Here and there we crossed tracks in the trees, though whether they were used only by game or by the inhabitants of the region, we could not tell. Occasionally, Frere told me to wait where I stood while he went into the forest in search of specimens. I called out to him at regular intervals and he answered me. It was difficult to judge both distance and direction because of the distorting effect of the trunks, and because of the canopy overhead. Once he came back with a small, squirrel-looking animal rolled into a ball in his hand, and on another occasion he captured a bird with foot-long crimson tail feathers, which he plucked out before throwing the bird back up into the branches. He killed the squirrel by piercing its spine with a small knife, and carefully arranged the feathers in one of his cardboard tubes.

At one point, approaching the foot of the plateau, and where the trees had at last given way to scattered thorn and scrub, he suddenly held up his hand and signalled for me to remain silent and still. Then he pointed to a low rise ahead of us, conspicuous because of its crown of taller trees, and I shielded my eyes to see what he had seen. We both instinctively lowered ourselves into the high grass.

At first I could see nothing, but then a movement caught my eye, followed by another. There were men ahead of us, and Frere indicated to me that he had seen five. He shed the load from his shoulders. I did likewise, and followed him as he crawled forward into the open. The men on the rise were gathered in a circle and appeared to be working in unison upon whatever was at their centre.

'They've killed something,' Frere whispered to me. He studied the men through the smallest of his telescopes before handing me the glass.

'Do you want to approach them?' I said.

He considered this. 'Wait.'

We sat and watched the men for a further hour, after which they rose together and descended the slope towards us. I searched for signs of a path in the grass, but saw none. I was concerned that they would come upon us and misinterpret why we had concealed ourselves to watch them. I started to move backwards, towards our discarded baggage, but Frere put a hand on my arm to stop me.

The men continued towards us, each carrying a spear or a bow. They were all short, none of them over five foot, but they did not resemble the other pygmies I had seen, and were much darker in colour. It was difficult to follow their movement through the high grass, but at the moment I felt certain we would be discovered, they turned away from us along a track parallel to the trees, as though they were reluctant to enter that darker realm. Frere moved forward to watch them go, and only when the last man had disappeared from view did he rise and beckon me to him.

Retrieving our loads, we went forward to the low rise, and we saw there the stripped bones of whatever game the hunters had killed and butchered. The ground was trodden bare, and with boulders set in a circle. Frere sketched this and made several pages of notes. He gathered up some of the cooling bones and slid them into his pack. Afterwards, he became noticeably more enthusiastic about our expedition.

I took my own measurements and calculated that two

hours would take us to the rim of the plateau. Three hours of daylight remained to us. Frere examined the trees on the rise for any marks on them. He found these and made further drawings.

My calculation had been clumsy: I had been deceived by the apparent height of the plateau, and by the haze which covered the land immediately below it, and it was already dark by the time we arrived at its foot, where we stayed for the night.

After eating, I sat with Frere at a small fire for several hours, and I saw him more excited then – there is no other word – than I had ever seen him at the Station. He insisted on seeing my figures and calculations and then on me translating these into the crudest of maps for him. He told me I might name the small rise after myself, but I declined. I told him I could not be so presumptuous, and that, anyway, the offer was not his to make. He skinned the small squirrel and we cooked and ate what little meat was to be had from it.

The following day we climbed the scarp slope. Our climb lasted until midday, when we were rewarded with a view I believe no other Englishman had ever seen before us. Ahead of us, the plateau stretched away into the distance, and I guessed that we could see for thirty miles, standing as we did at its upper end. It was forested for the most part, and I saw at least three watercourses. An immense flock of egrets passed over the treetops beneath us, and for the first time I started to believe in the existence of the lake, and even that it might have held its monster.

Our travelling that day was considerably easier; the slope was gentle and downhill, and the trees were neither so dense nor so tall. We walked for several hours. At one point I imagined I could smell wood-smoke. Frere confirmed this, and we became more cautious as we went on and spoke only in whispers, adding to our notion of ourselves as true explorers.

We came to a river and I pointed out to him that it was not flowing in the same direction as the others we had so far encountered, that instead of following the lie of the land to the north, it ran in a more easterly direction. So far that day, Frere had gathered nothing but insects and butterflies, all now packed, dead or dying in his jars and cases.

We followed the course of this water, marking the start of our path with a cairn. I took our bearings on the slope behind us, and afterwards measured our progress at more frequent intervals. We passed a fetish, the dried and wizened claw of a small cat pinned to a tree. Frere also found a small arrowhead and several inches of its shaft embedded in the same trunk further down. He gouged this out and told me he considered it his most important find thus far.

At three in the afternoon we followed a bend in the river and ahead of us saw the lake into which it flowed. The sight of this body of water took us by surprise and we stood speechless before it. At best, I had imagined something surrounded and concealed by dense forest, something dark and stagnant, perhaps, plant-choked and dying, but here was an expanse of water as large as any I had seen, clear in the shallows and blue at its centre in the sun, and with the white of gentle waves across its entire surface. Flocks of birds congregated across it in every direction.

We both stood and looked out over the expanse of water without speaking. I could not believe that something so large had not previously been noted and explored. It was possible to see the whole of the surrounding land, but even so, and allowing for the illusion created by the heat, here was a body of water at least ten miles across, and perhaps fifty in circumference.

We discarded our packages and went out into the open land of the shore. Frere was the first to take off his boots and wade out into the water. He pronounced it warm and said that he could see small fish swimming around his legs. I followed him in.

As we stood together, looking out, savouring our discovery, the water to our knees, he said to me, 'We are, of course, being observed.'

I looked quickly around us. 'Where?'

'I imagine to our left.' He continued to look directly out over the water.

'How do you know?'

'When we turned the bend there was the faintest wisp of smoke above the trees. A fire that has now been doused.'

I looked, but if the smoke had existed, it had drifted to nothing by then. All I saw were several trodden clearings at the water's edge.

'Are we in any danger?' I asked him, but he could not say.

I was the first to return to the shore and pull on my boots. And as I did this, I was surprised and alarmed to see him cup his hands to his mouth and shout out, turning left and right as he did so. The echo of his words skimmed back and forth across the water, but there was no answering call.

I added the lake to my chart. It did not matter then to measure its true extent or depth or dimensions exactly, merely to be precise about how it might be again reached. All those other calculations could come later, made by lesser men following in our wake.

I knew, looking out over the bright, clear water that it contained no monster.

That night we retreated to the edge of the trees. We lit a fire, and periodically one of us returned to the open shore to see if any others had been lit there. At first we saw nothing, but as the night darkened, I saw that at least two other fires burned several miles from us to the west. The fact that they had been lit, and that ours was visible to whoever sat around these other blazes, reassured me.

The night, as usual, was filled with its noises. Buffalo came down through the long grass all around us. Hippopotami grunted and splashed unseen away from the shallows. It was the night-amplified noises of these creatures, we decided, that came closest to the roaring of a monster.

'Did you ever believe that there might have been something here?' I asked Frere.

'Not truly. But I was prepared to believe in it in the hope that my expectations would not yet again be driven so far ahead of the truth of the situation.'

'And what if you had seen or heard something – not necessarily the creature itself – to make you think otherwise?'

'Then I would have believed in the monster the same way you believe in God. *That* would have been the nature of my belief or faith in its existence.'

Six months earlier I might have been offended or felt myself challenged by the remark, but not then.

The night remained uneventful. The distant fires burned until dawn. One of us kept watch while the other slept, but the rising sun found us waking together, our packages undisturbed around us.

I spent the morning recording what further calculations I was able to make, and Frere cut branches to fit to his nets and went in search of the underwater life of the lake.

We decided that we would return to the high rim of the plateau before nightfall, and that we would explore east and west along this in the days remaining to us. I wanted to determine why nothing of the lake itself was visible from this vantage point. I imagined that others had climbed the slope before us, and, disappointed by what they saw, or didn't see, had turned back.

I remained convinced that Frere and I were the first Englishmen to set eyes on the lake.

I could not have known it at the time – and if it had occurred to me then, I would have been reluctant to believe it – but that early expedition and the finding of the lake was perhaps my greatest achievement in this place; certainly, nothing I did subsequently created the same sense of wonder or accomplishment in me. For weeks afterwards, the others referred to Frere and myself as their Intrepid Explorers, and I for one was unable to disguise my childish pleasure at the title, however intended.

Several months later, and then by chance, I learned from Fletcher that some among the Uregga people remained notorious for their cannibalism, and that all those months earlier he had tried to dissuade Frere from embarking on the expedition. Frere, he told me, had made him promise not to raise the matter with me prior to our departure. Upon confronting Frere with this, he was dismissive of my concern and accused me of over-reacting. I remembered then the growing excitement with which he had watched the men on the low knoll, and how eager he had been to reach their fire; I remembered, too, his excitement at realizing we were ourselves being watched during our night at the lake. Unable to contain my anger at the way I considered I had been used and deceived by him, I had left him. He apologized to me soon afterwards, saying he genuinely regretted his behaviour. What he regretted most, he said, was that my sense of achievement might now be debased and not enhanced by this new understanding. Neither of us was granted permission to leave the Station for several months afterwards.

12

I was at my desk when the door to my room opened
and Amon entered unannounced. He brought with him
a satchel made of pale leather the consistency of cloth,
and still without speaking to me he came to where I
sat and dropped this bag beside the chart upon which
I was working. I objected to this sudden intrusion, but
he simply took a step back and waited for me to pick up
the satchel. I pushed it to one side and blew on the
drying ink of my chart. Ensuring that no harm had been
done, I covered the detail of the map with a sheet of
blank paper. Seeing this, Amon made it clear to me that
he had no interest in my work, and he yawned to
emphasize the point.

'What is it?' I knew he was not acting for himself.

'Look inside.'

I took out a single slender journal, recognizing it
immediately as one of Frere's. I knew that I would in
some way commit myself if I opened it, and so I left it
where it lay and instead gathered up my pens and
washed their drying nibs.

'Surely you recognize it,' Amon said.

'It's one of Frere's.'

'Are you not intrigued to learn what it contains?'

'Whatever I discover, you will no doubt insist on telling me five times over in case I fail to grasp the smallest point of the exercise.'

He smiled at my anger and raised his palms to me. 'Please, I am merely the messenger.'

I looked again at the journal and saw that most of its pages had been torn out, that its board covers contained only half of what they should.

'How did you come by it?'

'How do you think? Hammad bought it from the feather-gatherer along with your Mr Frere.'

' "Bought"?'

'Whatever.'

'Hammad "bought" Frere from the gatherer?'

'Perhaps it was the only way the man would relinquish his hold on such a prize.' He was now less certain of himself, and to press home my small advantage I looked at the scar on his lips and then allowed his eyes to catch mine as I raised them.

'What does it matter?' he said. 'That,' he indicated the journal, 'is why I am here.'

'Why you were sent.'

'Whatever.'

'You stole it from him.'

'I assure you—'

'Along with the rest of his possessions.'

'Perhaps he had long since abandoned all those so-called possessions. Perhaps he was so overjoyed at being found and rescued from the father of the child he had killed that he forgot all about them. Perhaps he made a gift of all he still possessed to his rescuers. Who knows?' He thrived on the uncertainty and menace of his own making.

'Then if you do not know, I shall assume you stole it,' I said. 'You, or Hammad.'

It concerned him to hear his master's name used so disrespectfully, and I knew he would not repeat what I said. Hammad himself would not have tolerated any of this confusion. *His* message – those missing pages – was clear enough.

'What do you expect me to do?' I said.

'Examine it. See what it contains.'

'It is a man's personal journal, a private thing.'

'It contains your name.'

'I don't doubt it. I don't doubt that it contains all our names, perhaps even the name of someone as lowly as yourself.'

He grinned at this and I saw that my brief advantage was gone. 'No,' he said. 'Only yours.' He retrieved the journal and opened it, flicking his thumb over the torn edges of the missing pages.

'Where are they?' I said.

'My employer considered it judicious to remove them for safe-keeping. As you can see, the first hundred or so have been left intact. He would not want there to be any doubt as to the provenance of the thing.' He handed the journal back to me and I took it.

The remaining pages were filled with Frere's fine and minute handwriting. The first page was dated the day he left us, and a quick examination showed me that two or three pages had been completed for each day he was missing. The pages of the book were wrinkled and stained, as though it had been dropped in water, retrieved and then too quickly dried.

'I assume I will find nothing of any real significance in the pages that remain,' I said.

Amon shrugged. 'Possibly, possibly not.'

'So their purpose is merely to suggest to me the importance of what has been removed.'

'And which my employer now has in safe-keeping.'

'Why?'

'Why what?'

'Why has he taken them? What does he expect from me, us, for their return?'

'He expects nothing. He simply feels that they contain information of such a nature that it would be best if they were kept secure and unseen until someone more qualified to inspect and understand them were to do so.'

I understood then what he was telling me, what true purpose those lost pages served.

'Have *you* seen them?'

He shook his head. 'Only Mr Frere himself, an illiterate man who does not even understand that his own name can be written, and Hammad.'

'Who wishes us all to know that he once again wields a stick over us.'

'What a vivid imagination you possess, Captain Frasier. Why would he want to do that? He is your friend, your ally.'

I was careful after that not to say anything that I didn't want repeated verbatim to Hammad.

'Would he show these missing pages to me privately?' I asked. 'Or if not to me, then to Cornelius?'

It was something Amon had not considered.

'He told me to bring the journal directly to you,' he said. 'To show it to no-one else.'

'But knowing, surely, that I would share it with the others.'

'It is yours to do with as you choose.'

I turned to the last page. A cursory reading of it told me nothing. Frere had sketched a beetle and drawn a map of the confluence of three unnamed rivers. A pattern of small islands marked the confluence, and though I could not place it then, it might have been possible afterwards to locate precisely where Frere had made the drawing, where he had been – in the journal at least – before he had disappeared from sight. The day's entry was incomplete, and so I imagined that the succeeding pages had been torn out with good reason, and that no other clue remained to me.

'The pages removed no doubt explain the circumstances of the crime he is alleged to have committed,' I said.

Amon considered this remark and then slowly repeated my words. 'Do you truly imagine a man might avoid the truth of a matter simply by avoiding using those words which express that truth most directly?' he said.

'Are there any instructions from Hammad?'

'Merely that he wishes you to read the remaining pages and confirm that the journal does indeed belong to the unfortunate Mr Frere.'

'And what if I were to say that the missing pages were all blank, that this was where Frere stopped writing?' I knew this was unlikely.

'I believe you know better,' Amon said. 'But if it is the story you wish to tell, then I am powerless to stop you.' He picked up the fine leather satchel and went back to the door. 'We can all close our eyes when it suits us,' he said, and then left me.

I decided to postpone reading the journal until I was alone.

An hour later, Cornelius came to see me. I slid the book beneath a sheaf of papers as he entered. He had seen Amon departing and wanted to know why he had come. I told him the Syrian had been sent to ensure that Frere was recovering his health. Whether he believed me or not, he left me before my lie to him was exposed.

I had seen less and less of him since the arrival of Klein, and whenever the priest entered a room, Cornelius invariably left. He told me little more about the man, or of their distant involvement, but the animosity between them remained and curdled.

For his part, Klein behaved as though he were one of us – but one of us in possession of information or a secret the others did not possess – entitled to come and go among us where he chose, to indulge himself in our company and conversation, and to share what few small concessions or luxuries remained to us. We tolerated the man, but that was all; we were all growing to despise him.

13

It rained more heavily over the following days than any of us had before known. It came and ended at its usual times, but fell with such ferocity in between that the water rose in minutes to levels which had hitherto taken hours, and each afternoon the compound was turned into a lake, rising to a man's thighs in places, which then drained and dried in the heat of the returning sun, which also seemed in those days to burn more fiercely than usual, as though the two elements were striving to maintain some vital, contested balance.

Work was suspended in the quarry, where run-offs poured with water from the top to the bottom of the faces in vividly red spouts, filling the quarry floor. A new channel was blasted out to the river to allow this to drain away. This was supervised by Abbot, who announced the success of the operation on the day the rain finally subsided and resumed falling in its more accustomed quantities.

Out on the river a new configuration of banks and bars was seen to have formed between us and the far shore, causing some disruption to the traffic there. Floating vegetation caught on these bars and collected there, trapping more with each of the river's dying surges. These new islands would not last – we all understood that; nothing lasted on that river – but it was a busy time of year for the rubber traders on either side, and both Cornelius and Fletcher were convinced that, presented with the obstacles in coming towards us, the traffic would prefer the easier route to the far shore. The two men spent hours out on the bars, examining them and plumbing the channels which braided among them. Whenever possible, Abbot avoided the two men, which had the unfortunate consequence of forcing him more and more into my company.

During the downpours of that week I was able to work on my charts without being called elsewhere. I rose earlier than usual and worked longer hours, often by the light of my lamps. I was determined to keep a part of each day free so that I might visit Frere.

The garrison yard was as badly flooded as the compound, and the quarters of Bone and his men leaked worse than our own dwellings. There were times when the path joining us was so far under water as to be lost to sight completely, forcing those few of us who passed between the two places to make lengthy detours onto higher ground.

Trees were undermined by the scouring rain, mostly along the river, where the crumbling banks were sheared away, and one, an ancient baobab, toppled onto one of Cornelius's warehouses, requiring him and his quartermasters to work through the deluge to cut it to pieces and drag these clear before salvaging the goods inside. It was a common enough sound to hear, these trees falling in the forest, or to hear the drawn-out crash of snapped and over-laden branches dropping from the canopy to the floor below.

I discussed the freak circumstances of this weather with Frere, relieved that it gave us something to talk about other than his own situation, of the events already beyond our reach. I made no mention to him of what I had learned from Amon concerning the lost pages of his journal.

'Measure it for me,' he said on my third visit. 'Measure the rain.' He instructed me on how to set up his gauges and where best to place them. 'Tell me everything that happens with the flooding.'

I did as he told me, keeping notes, embers to fan into the flames of our conversations. Only afterwards did I understand that in his enthusiasm he was as complicit in the deceit of avoidance as I was in the compliance of his wishes. I told him everything I had seen and heard, and in this manner we kept ourselves apart from those other events and their darker consequences for the week of the flood.

He compiled a new journal, which he insisted I should not read until he was gone. I no longer probed him for his own guarded understanding of what was happening to him; for the time being, the water was enough.

On the fourth day there was some damage to one of our wharves when the river rose and swung a heavily laden boat into its supports, crushing several of these and weakening others. The boat's moorings were lost and the vessel was driven towards the bank, slicing away more of the wooden structure as it came. The alarm raised, we gathered to watch. The men on the boat left it at the first opportunity. Some were able to leap onto the decks of other vessels, but these were quickly out of reach. As the collision with the jetty threatened to undermine it even further, some men jumped into the racing shallows and scrambled ashore.

There was nothing any of us watching from further back could do to help them.

The captain of the small vessel stood in his wheelhouse and tried frantically to turn the boat into the main flow of the water, but this proved impossible in its over-laden state. Part of the cargo was stacked on the deck and this was soon lost to the higher waves.

As the boat came closer to the shore, Fletcher instructed some of our men to attempt to push it away from the undamaged jetties into the faster-flowing water. He shouted to the captain that the vessel was lost and for him to save himself. Several ropes were thrown to the man. It would not have been difficult for him to leap from his vessel and wade ashore, but the man refused to leave. Eventually, Fletcher had ten men working the poles and keeping the boat away from the jetties. The rain streamed over them, turning the bank to a quagmire in which they all frequently lost their footing and fell. Their cries when this happened added to the overall sense of urgency and growing alarm. The masters of the other, securely moored vessels stood on their own decks and watched. None made any attempt to help the stricken boat.

Eventually, the floundering vessel was manhandled clear of the damaged jetty and pushed away from us. The man still on board became even more frantic in his calls for our help. Fletcher sent someone to fetch one of his rifles, and he stood on what remained of the jetty looking down at the man.

Soon afterwards, the boat finally lodged among the submerged posts. It was violently rocked in these, but was held steady enough to be safe there until the rain stopped and the water level fell. We heard the loud cracks as its waterline planking was ruptured and saw the billowing water where it rushed in to flood the vessel and destroy what remained of its cargo. Only when this happened, and when pieces of loose planking began to break free and float away, did the captain make any attempt to get ashore. He climbed out onto the canopy which then rose level with the spars of the damaged jetty. His intention, I saw, was to climb from the boat onto one of these and then make his way along the broken posts to solid ground. The attempt seemed easily achievable and there was little concern among us at what the man was about to do. He was protected now from the main assault of the river by his own disintegrating boat, which bore the full force of its flow.

Fletcher went as far as was safe along the unsteady timbers and indicated to the man where to climb next, but the man paid him no attention, and as he passed from one seemingly sound post to another, the second post swayed beneath him and then fell slowly away from the jetty until it lay at an angle, forcing the man to cling to it, and from where he could not reach any other part of the structure. He clung to this post as I had seen small animals cling to the floating branches rushing past us in the floods. Further ropes were thrown to him, but he caught none of these. The post itself was lassoed, but it was beyond even the strength of the ten men to pull it back into its upright position, and with every minute that passed it leaned even further, undermined more quickly by the faster water in which it now lay.

Fletcher cursed the man for having waited so long before leaving his boat. Cornelius inspected the damage done to the jetty and said that in all likelihood it was beyond repair. Abbot disputed this, but was ignored.

The closest we could get to the man clinging to the pole was twenty feet, the water between us more earth than liquid. I imagined the only course of action remaining to us was to leave the stranded man where he was until the rain stopped and the river slowed and fell. But I knew even as I considered this that the rain would continue falling for a further three hours, and that another six hours might pass before the surge was gone from the river, by which time it would be night, and even at that short distance the man would be lost to our sight. It was inconceivable to me that he might remain clinging to the pole until morning.

All these considerations were then cleared from my mind as Cornelius came to me, and said, 'The boat.'

I looked to where the stricken boat, still stuck among the poles and spars of the jetty, continued to break up. It was less firmly lodged than before, lightened by the loss of its cargo, and it rose higher in the water and was starting to swing free of its underwater restraints. Fletcher called for the men with the ropes to secure it, but they were as unsuccessful as before in their efforts.

I considered it unlikely that the man clinging to the pole was aware of what was now happening. Had he been upriver of the vessel, then this would not have mattered – the boat would have drifted free, broken up and been dragged away from him. But he clung to his pole downriver of where this was happening, and it was clear to everyone standing away from him that when the vessel finally rose free of its restraining poles, then it would swing directly onto him, at worst crush him where he was, and at best dislodge him and his perch and carry them both downriver amid the disintegrating wreckage.

I asked Fletcher what he thought might now happen, but it was the question of a man wanting only to confirm and share his own fears, and he did not answer me.

Finally, the boat rose free, spun until it was side-on

to the clinging man and was then rammed into him, crushing him against the pole, and striking him such a blow that he had no time to understand what was happening to him and no time to do anything to avoid the collision. He screamed, but it was a short, truncated scream, and he instantly lost his grip on the pole and was lost between it and the boat in the dark, foaming water. The pole stood firm for several seconds, but then it too gave way with the weight of the boat against it, and once this obstacle was overcome the boat was free to drift out onto the river and away from us.

I heard Cornelius say, 'Thank God for that,' and for the words to be repeated by others around him.

I looked back to where the man had disappeared. It was impossible that he would have avoided serious injury in the collision of the boat with the post: at best his arms, legs or ribs would have been crushed, at worst his spine or skull broken and his agony ended. It was difficult to see exactly where he had been because the pole was no longer visible, but we searched as best we could through the rain for any sign of him. We saw nothing – not even his snagged body on another of the poles – and soon afterwards, the day's drama over, we all withdrew to our offices or rooms.

Later that evening, as I told Frere about what had happened, and as the rain finally slackened and fell on the roof above us with less and less clamour, he asked me why I referred to the events of the afternoon as a tragedy.

'Because a man lost his life when he might have saved it,' I said.

He shook his head at this definition. 'No, a man lost his life because he chose not to save himself and because he made a judgement concerning the value of his life against that put upon it by others – that put upon it in relation to the value of his boat and the goods he carried. That is no tragedy.'

I did not understand the distinction he was making, but I was still too overwhelmed by the events of the day and the brutal death I had witnessed to continue the argument. I would have told him he was dealing with events merely as abstractions devoid of human understanding or feelings, that he would have felt differently had he too stood helplessly by as the man was crushed. But to what end? He might have conceded these points to some small degree to appease me, but he would not have believed me.

Word reached us via the Belgians that a delegation was being sent to us to enquire into what had happened regarding Frere, and that the findings of this enquiry would determine what action was subsequently to be taken against the man.

The document Abbot read out to us was four pages long, and scarcely a single sentence of it strayed from this official camouflage. It was signed by six men, each, apparently, with some part in the 'affair'. None of us recognized a single name other than that of our own Company Secretary. The titles of the others confused us.

We were assured that Frere would be provided with every 'civil comfort' relating to his situation, yet warned that he should be offered no more liberty than was absolutely necessary. We were his gaolers, little more – guardians of his health and his sanity.

Our own testimonies would be sought, however peripheral, however indirectly they related to the events at hand, to those fifty-one days, the true focus of the enquiry.

That all this information had been addressed to and

delivered to Abbot caused us further concern. He told us he was instructed to read it aloud to us, that we were all to attend this announcement, and that the document was afterwards to be kept safe by him and him alone. We all suspected him of a greater part in the proceedings than he admitted.

To the best of my knowledge, he had not so far visited Frere in his cell, and nor had Frere made any attempt to communicate with him. There was pride in his voice as he read out this news of the delegation, something which had thus far remained only an unwelcome rumour, the possibility of which had receded with each passing day.

Cornelius asked Abbot to explain to us who the unknown signatories were, and Abbot went through the pretence of knowing. He spoke of new governmental bodies and the powers and institutions of new protectorates; he added to this tangle of meaninglessness by quoting new rules and regulations to us. He said that deals had been struck elsewhere between the Company and others, between the Company and the concession-granting, tax-imposing Belgians, and between those men and the men of emerging native governments, who might or might not become their partners in the future.

Our minds wandered into the background of these dramas, and we learned nothing solid, nothing of any use to us, other than that Abbot considered himself to be at our centre in the matter, and that anything concerning Frere must now be undertaken through him. He wore this small responsibility like a crown and became even more unbearable than usual in its possession.

He told me that he was liaising directly with Bone concerning Frere's treatment, and in improving the conditions in the flooded garrison, suggesting to me that my own involvement must cease. I told him that there was nothing in the document to prevent me from continuing to visit Frere. This angered him, and though he was forced to concede the point, he made it clear to me that everything I now did and said in the matter might be legitimately observed and noted.

Fletcher asked him how large the delegation was likely to be, and we knew again by Abbot's answer that he was guessing.

The Inquisition would come and shine its light on us in our darkness. Abbot would help direct the light this way and that, and the blaze of understanding would be so great that we would all be dazzled and then blinded by it. Nothing would remain unseen. We had all lived too long in the half-light of speculation and hearsay, of lying and evasion, to have any true idea of how brightly that light of enquiry, and, possibly, of redemption, might now shine in on us. We all understood this, and we all made our own unspoken assessments. The hand behind any one of those six signatures might sweep us all away, might take Frere from us and never again present him to view.

We were reminded by Cornelius that the document had come to us via the far shore.

'Meaning what?' Abbot said angrily.

'Meaning nothing,' Cornelius said, looking round at the rest of us to confirm what we all understood – that whatever *we* knew was already known by others.

'It has no bearing, no bearing whatsoever,' Abbot insisted. 'No-one else has any involvement in the matter.'

Fletcher asked if he might look again at the papers, but Abbot refused him and sealed them in his case.

He left us shortly afterwards.

A bottle of brandy was produced and the rest of us sat together considering the wider implications of the message we had so abruptly received.

Cornelius wondered aloud why we had been fore-warned of what was about to happen, and when I asked him what he meant, he told me instead to imagine how much pleasure Abbot would have in reading the document through the bars of Frere's cell door. I still did not fully understand what he was saying, until Fletcher, sitting beside him, made his hand into a gun and pressed it into his temple. I told him he was being ridiculous, but he refused to argue with me.

Cornelius diverted us by calculating how long it would take the delegation to reach us if it had departed, as we were told, from Leopoldville, eighteen days previously. He calculated that ten days remained before it would be with us. Fletcher put this closer to twenty. He said there would be 'new' men involved, men unaccustomed to travelling in the wet season, and that, besides, there were too many diversions along the way.

I left them and returned to my quarters.

I thought of approaching Abbot alone and asking him if he knew anything more than was contained in the document, but even as I considered this I knew that I would achieve nothing. He knew no more or less than the rest of us, the only difference being that his own ignorance had been sanctioned, had been elevated into an official role within the proceedings, and ours had not.

I sat for an hour in my open doorway, watching all the stars of heaven in the night sky and listening to the calls of unseen creatures all around me.

14

'You didn't see fit to tell me about my inquisitors?' were Frere's first words to me when I saw him two days later.

'Abbot warned us off,' I said. 'Besides, I knew he'd do a good enough job of telling you himself.'

'He did.' He examined his teeth in a mirror as he spoke, seemingly unconcerned about the events now officially set in motion around him, and circling ever faster towards him.

He had been brought back to us with an infection in his mouth and gums, and this had recently become inflamed, causing him some pain. He pointed out to me which of his teeth were loose, and I saw too the white filigree pock of the disease on the inside of his cheeks and starting on his tongue. Because it caused him pain to speak, he spoke with the left-hand side of his mouth closed. The slight discoloration of his cheeks remained, but this might still have been the fading bruise of his beating.

'I suppose he read it to you word for word,' I said.

'Word for word. Through the bars. I trust you didn't think you could protect me in some way by not telling me, that you believed you might hold them off, that I might be better served by not knowing what was happening?' There was no anger in his voice at this air-clearing, only a clenched sense of disappointment.

'Fletcher reckons they're eighteen days away yet.'

'I would have said nearer twelve.' He spoke as though he were advancing to meet them. 'However long they take to get here, nothing will change the facts of the matter, they will still arrive, I will still be waiting for them, you will still be stood to one side wringing your hands and watching.' He signalled his apology to me for this last remark. He was as uncertain as the rest of us about what was happening, but whereas we were still able to play our ignorance to advantage, he was not.

He had been reading through a pile of his papers upon my arrival.

'Are you preparing yourself?' I said.

'Am I undertaking my own defence, do you mean? I might be a fool, but I am not *that* particular breed of fool.' Everything he said was designed to hold me apart from him: where I offered light he added shadow; where I conjured up chance, he saw only risk. It was something he wanted me to understand. He had said it before.

'Is that how you see it – an inquisition?' I said.

'Friend Abbot was very clear on the point. I imagine the man will want to keep a precise and very complete record of everything said. Why else are they coming?'

'They may merely wish—'

'I mean why are they coming as opposed to me *merely* being sent for? A week trussed up in the hold of a steamer would see me gone for ever.'

'So you imagine they wish to undertake something here as opposed to elsewhere, on the coast?'

'Beyond the eyes of the world. Surely you can see

how much more expedient that might be for everyone concerned, myself included.'

'Yourself?'

'Think of the shame, the disgrace this will bring on my family.'

And on Caroline? The thought remained unspoken between us.

'A great deal would depend on your confession,' I said.

He put down the mirror and gently wiped the saliva from his lips.

The door to his cell had been open on my arrival. The previous day, following Abbot's visit, Bone had appeared and told Frere that he might also inhabit the outer room during daylight, returning to be locked up only at dusk.

'He even offered to accompany me around the garrison yard on the condition that I was hobbled to prevent me from running. And so long as I agreed to remain within sight of either him or one of his armed cronies.'

I was surprised at the offer. 'Perhaps they don't want to be accused of maltreating you.'

'No – plenty of time for that after the trial. Or perhaps I am expected to make some attempt at escape.' He saw the concern on my face. 'No, I won't run. Besides, I have too much to do here before the delegation arrives. Work I never finished.'

Reluctant to leave him, I finally told him about the incomplete journal Amon had brought to me. I lied to him and said I had received it only that morning. I had read what remained of the journal's pages, but other than discover where Frere was headed, the path he followed, and what he had hoped to see there, I had learned nothing of the emptiness beyond.

Upon hearing this, he immediately reached across the table and held my arm.

'Did you bring it with you?'

I hadn't.

'To what date are the entries intact?' He shook my arm.

I told him and he released me. He closed his eyes and made some calculation.

'On that final page was there a sketch map of the confluence of the Lomami and Pitiri rivers along with one other?'

I told him there was, if that's what they were, and he let out a long breath.

'Did you imagine the journal had been lost?' I asked him.

'I don't know, I couldn't be certain. I was sick with a fever, delirious for a week before and a week afterwards.'

'Afterwards?'

'After the events it chronicles. I believed then that I was closer to death than to life and I did nothing to draw myself back. There was nothing I *could* do. I can't even remember if I went on writing, though I imagine I did. I remember wanting to write, I remember knowing what I wanted to say. And whether I did or not, I chronicled everything before I fell ill in good enough detail. Good enough detail for anyone looking at it to be in no doubt about what I was saying.'

I knew that sometimes he wrote in code – he once told me that this was done to protect some commercial secret or other, though I had never been wholly convinced of this – and I asked him if this was how the missing pages had been written.

'I'm afraid not. I'm afraid I was all too feverishly exultant in what I had witnessed and accomplished to be capable of keeping any part of it secret. I did not so much write, as *shout* onto those missing pages.'

'And will you not tell me what that achievement was? Others already know of it, and soon it might become common knowledge.'

'And sooner yet, it might become damning evidence against me.'

'But you still cling to the idea that if you told me it would somehow work against you.'

'No – that it would work against *us*. Some things I can afford to lose, others I cannot relax my grip upon – my belief in – to even the slightest degree. Please, try to understand what I'm saying, don't force me to have to explain something in which my own understanding is as imperfect as your own, but which I need to possess, to cleave to above all else while this storm gathers around me. Without your friendship, without your faith in the man I was, there would be no wall for me to stand against and face my accusers.'

'So you wish me to remain ignorant of the facts, perhaps even to be deluded into—'

'You are not deluded, James Charles Russel Frasier, but you are wont to see the best in men, and on occasion to turn side-on to the truth.'

I was about to refute this, but he looked hard at me and held up his hand to silence me.

He went on: 'Soon, that opportunity – that privilege of ignorance – will not exist. It is no longer a possibility for me, and soon it will be lost to you and the others. If you can grasp nothing else of what I'm trying to say to you, then at least grasp that.'

On any other occasion I would have complained at this twisting retreat into seeming melodrama, but I saw that it served his purpose, and I saw too that I might later turn it to my own advantage.

'I will believe you,' I said. 'And I accede to what you want – to my uncomfortable ignorance of the facts – if you promise to tell me what happened during the days of those missing pages if and when my knowing serves your purpose, and certainly before these strangers arrive with their own notions of justice and retribution.'

He again held up his hands to silence me.

Neither of us spoke for several minutes afterwards. The rain had not yet started.

Outside, Bone went through the motions of drilling his men, shouting his instructions five times over and then spending twice as long berating them for their inefficiency.

'I spoke to the humpback yesterday,' Frere said.

'Oh? He was here?'

'He sometimes comes and sits outside the window. We talk without seeing each other. He occasionally runs errands for me. He does the same for Bone and the others. He escorts women into the garrison each night and then takes them away again. He offered to do the same for me.'

'Does he know anything that might help you?'

'He knows better than anyone here what is happening across the river. He knows where the best rubber is coming from and why so little of it is coming to us. He knows that the politicians are rolling their dice again. He knows that the heavy rain has come at a bad time and destroyed the growing crops over a wide area to the north. People are on the move and raiding. Fighting is starting up again all along the Mutua and Chapa Rivers.'

'We hear the same rumours week in and week out,' I told him.

'I believe him. He tells me all this in Wenya. He lies only in English.'

'Has he learned anything relating to what Hammad intends to do? Will he present himself to the enquiry?'

'Of course he will. He will be called. He was my rescuer, remember.'

We were silenced by the sound of shooting in the garrison yard. I rose and went to the small window. Bone and his men were shooting at a rusty drum in the far corner of the yard. Each shot on target brought forth a cry from the man who fired. Watching them, it was difficult to see who fired which shot, and the few successes were all loudly contested.

When I turned back to Frere, he was once again studying his papers. I asked him if there was anything he wanted me to bring him on my next visit.

'There's an old journal,' he said. He spoke without looking up, but I saw that he had momentarily stopped writing.

'Which one?'

He paused before answering me. 'The journal containing the account of our visit to Babire.'

I caught my breath at mention of the place.

'Can you bring it to me? Do you have it?'

I nodded to both questions.

'I do understand your feelings,' he said.

I left him after that, before the onset of the rain.

Outside, Bone and his men had grown tired of their target practice and were gathered around the perforated drum sticking their fingers into its holes. Bone called out to me, but I was in no mood for him and I continued walking. I imagined him raising his empty rifle and aiming it at my back.

15

The days which followed were days of uncertainty and
waiting for all of us – days of activity, of preparation,
of stock counted, of ledgers and accounts completed, of
timetables made good. I was exhorted daily by Abbot to
ensure that all my own accounts and my Company
map-making were up to date. He intended presenting
to whoever was sent to us as complete a dossier as
possible of all our various works, and my maps, he
flattered me, would be as clear an indication as any of
what we had all, in our separate endeavours, achieved
there over the previous months.

He showed me the charts he himself had compiled –
charts on which the columns rose and rose in
accordance with this lofty purpose. And in an unguarded moment he even confessed to me that he
hoped to gain promotion for himself as a consequence
of this inspection. I allowed him to indulge himself
in this fantasy, allowed him to go on behaving as
though *he* and not Frere were the true focus of the
enquiry. In a report I had once read undertaken by
the Native Protection Committee – the greatest joke
of the age – I had seen the members of a now defunct
French Station referred to as the 'cheating and

unscrupulous instruments of rapacious, pitiful and never-ending folly', and the description had stayed with me. Cornelius had read it, too. He said our native workers and gatherers regarded us as flabby, weak-eyed devils, and said he hoped our investigators did not deem it necessary to ask *them* what they knew or thought of what had happened. Sanity and desire, he said, quoting, I imagined, from one of his beloved Belgian poets, become breezes and now winds blowing away from us. Abbot, of course, laughed in the face of all this doom-laden rhetoric.

It was only as he left me that Abbot suggested that the person best served by all our efforts over the coming days would be Frere himself, but when I asked him to explain himself he became defensive and said that his observation needed no explanation.

Cornelius gathered together his quartermasters and began a thorough stock-taking of our rubber and other trade goods. I asked him why he bothered, knowing that his records of stock and trading were the most complete of any of us. He told me he was doing it because whoever was sent to visit us and enquire into Frere would also be required to report on how well or how badly things were going here. He looked around us as he spoke. The same had happened before, he said. No opportunity to inspect us and report back would be wasted. And Abbot, for all his other failings, under-stood this perfectly. He even instructed his native staff to find the Company uniforms with which they had been issued upon their appointments, but which few had worn beyond their first week of work.

As I had anticipated, only Fletcher openly refused to undertake Abbot's bidding. He had started repairs to the damaged jetty, but this was slow work in the swollen river and the wharf would remain unusable for a long time after our visit. This distressed Abbot the most. He authorized the hiring of more labour, but Fletcher told him there was no more labour to be had, that too many men had returned to their homes and lost crops.

With the jetty out of operation we were losing trade. Boats could no longer be tied up to await unloading, and anchorage in even the calmer channels was precarious. Some vessels approached us, were warned of the delay, and then signalled their intent to continue downriver. We had no fixed contracts with most of these men, and berate them or plead with them as Abbot might, there was nothing he could do to entice them to us.

Two days following this unhappy conversation with Fletcher, Abbot had even greater problems of his own.

The fallen wall of the quarry had never been cleared from where it lay once the workers' corpses had been retrieved, and following this, as part of an attempt to better drain the swamp of the quarry floor, Abbot had ordered a mound of clay pipes to be carried and re-stacked beneath the slumped mass. These pipes had already been waiting there three years ago upon my arrival. They were sent originally when that early great expansion was still anticipated, ready to drain the surrounding land for workers' sheds.

According to Abbot's own account, there had been thirty thousand of these pipes, each with an inner vitreous glaze, each a yard long, and each designed to fit tightly inside another. He frequently told us how vast an area of land might be drained when the need arose – something he alone still professed to anticipate. The rest of us considered them something of a folly, home to rats and snakes and whatever else stumbled into them.

It took four days to move the pipes, and Abbot inspected each one of them as they were laid in their new resting place. He discarded those that were cracked or broken, surprisingly few considering how long they had been there. It was his intention to lay some of these pipes out on the quarry floor to show our visitors how he intended to better drain it. I had seldom seen him so enthusiastic – one might almost say manic – in his work. A plan all of his own making, dependent on nothing from anyone else but their labour. He even drew his own map of the proposed drainage pattern. And when the floor was drained, he said, then more of the quarry might be opened up for working, and following that the drained land might be used for building.

This was as specific as he was prepared to be, and if any of us saw the obvious flaws in this plan, then we kept our mouths shut. We saw what he was doing and why he was doing it, but none of us, I believe, accepted his argument that our displays and achievements there would have any bearing on what now happened to Frere.

And then, the night after the pipes had been placed ready for their use, there was a further fall in the quarry when the wall adjacent to the recent collapse, weakened by the heavy rain, gave way over an even wider area and fell. The vast majority of the stacked pipes were smashed and buried, and of all those already laid out in lines, over half were covered and the rest shaken out of their neat, promise-filled pattern and scattered.

The fall happened during the night and the first we heard of it was when a party of workers came into the compound at dawn. They went to Abbot's office and waited in silence for him to appear. Cornelius was the first to arrive, but when he asked them why they were there they refused to tell him, saying that Abbot had warned them to speak to no-one else of his plans. Cornelius knocked on Abbot's door.

I went with the two men and the workers back to the quarry, where we surveyed the damage from the far rim of the excavation. Men were already digging for the pipes as they had earlier dug for their companions. Upon realizing the full extent of what had happened, of what had been so suddenly snatched from his grasp, Abbot fell to his knees and started to groan in his despair. He asked me over and over what had possessed him to move the pipes after they had stood for so long and so safely in one place.

Cornelius and I saw how little had been truly lost in the fall, and how much unnecessary labour was now likely to be wasted. We told Abbot that the situation was not as bad as he believed, but in response to this he simply stared at us and asked us if we knew how much each one of the pipes had cost, and how much besides they represented.

Water continued to fall from the quarry rim in narrow spouts, silvered where it caught the sun, and feathered to spray before it hit the floor. Men used these falls to shower themselves after their labours. Abbot refused to go down into the workings and confront the disaster any more closely.

Even from that height it was clear to us that few of the pipes survived intact.

Abbot pressed his face into his hands. 'What will they say?' he said. 'What will they say?' And for the first time since I had known him, I felt a genuine sympathy for the man. My mother had once told me that there was no distinction to be made between cheap dreams and noble dreams in the minds of the men who harboured either.

174

'What will they say? What will they say?'

And my father had told me I would encounter a thousand Abbots, and that any man of worth, any *decent* man, might best be judged by his *decency*, that he would succeed or fail, live or die by it. I had never fully believed either of them, but looking at Abbot contemplating his own crushed dream beneath him, I came much closer to an understanding of what I had been told.

'What will they say? What will they say?'

Cornelius and I left him and returned to the Station.

16

I sought out the journal Frere had asked for.

We had gone to Babire four months after our discovery of the lake, and only weeks before the dry
season was due to end. There was some urgency in
mounting the trip, and Frere undertook all the arrangements concerning our provisions, guides and porters.
All he asked of me, having secured my agreement to
accompany him and help map our journey, was not
to disclose our final destination to our porters. He
confided in me that our guides would take us only as
far as the mouth of the Babire River and that they had
agreed to wait there for us. I asked him why such
secrecy was necessary. Both Fletcher and Cornelius, I
knew, had advised him against making the journey.

Babire, it transpired, lay between two warring tribes,
and word had recently reached us that several battles
– though we all understood that this was too grand a
name for them – had been fought and a great many
small villages destroyed and their inhabitants either
killed or dispossessed of their lands and homes.

Frere said it was his intention to visit these ruined
villages before they were overgrown and lost to
the forest. He wanted to record and collect whatever

176

evidence of the recent warfare that might remain, and to examine the surrounding country in the aftermath of the conflict. We lost too much of our wild rubber in these unsettled regions. He also wanted to try and understand how these small wars were fought, what savagery was involved, and how completely the people and settlements were consumed by them.

He had also begun a collection of the totems and fetishes left behind at the scenes of such savagery and he wished to add to this. He confessed to me that he had been waiting for news of just such a recent battle before pushing for a visit to its site. Normally, word of these affairs did not reach us until months afterwards – some boatman or other complaining of a delay or the absence of promised goods – and equally often these reports were vague in their details, and of events too far distant for us to be able to reach them quickly enough to satisfy Frere's curiosity.

He had already calculated that, following our journey by river, two days' walking would bring us to Babire. He allowed a further two to three days to examine the site and then to explore the surrounding countryside for whatever he might find there.

I asked Cornelius if he had cautioned us against going because he thought the fighting might still be taking place, but he said this was unlikely. They would not have been lengthy encounters anyway, and relatively few men would have been involved. The brief clashes might have been savage by our own standards, but it was unlikely that anyone now remained to threaten Frere or myself. He said he objected because he felt the journey was of no value other than to Frere personally – he had already accused Frere of dilettantism following our visit to the lake – and because, with the onset of the wet season, there was more than enough work to be undertaken at the Station. I could not refute this, and everything he said made me regret having agreed to accompany Frere. I knew that I had again succumbed to his enthusiasm, and that, despite wanting to again experience something of the sense of achievement I had felt upon locating the lake, I had been given no real choice in the matter; the credit of our friendship had again been drawn upon.

On the morning of our departure, Fletcher asked to look at the rifle I was taking, and when I showed him it – a weapon loaned to me for a price from Bone – he took it from me and insisted on exchanging it for one of his own, his treasured Martini-Henry. I objected, but he would not listen, and then stood with me as I practised loading it and turning the bolt.

When Frere learned of this, he laughed and gently accused Fletcher of over-reacting. Over-reacting to what? I asked him. He took me beyond the hearing of our porters and told me that Fletcher was concerned that one of the tribes involved in the fighting at Babire were again reputed to be cannibals. Before I could ask him if this were true, he reminded me of the tales we had been told concerning the people of the lake country and how little we had suffered there, at twice the distance from the Station, how much we had achieved there. Though he did not say it, I was being accused of the same alarmism I had been accused of then. Our conversation on the subject was ended by him saying that a single shot from Fletcher's rifle would send anyone within a five mile radius running screaming back into the forest. It was rare that he resorted to such easy and evasive answers. I asked him if he anticipated there would still be anyone there – cannibal or not – to be scared away, and he finally lost his patience with me and told me that if I no longer wished to accompany him then he would go alone and that he would not hold my decision against me. As before, my choices evaporated around me.

We paddled and walked to Babire as planned, and left our guides and porters at the mouth of the river. Frere offered good wages, but none wanted to accompany us further. Some of the porters he paid off and they left us the instant the money was in their hands. We learned later that, of the six men left with the guides, a further two absconded during the first night of waiting.

Frere and I entered the disputed territory alone. We had no accurate idea of where Babire lay, and we came upon the ruined village unexpectedly, following a stream into the plundered fields and charred remains of the dwellings that had once stood there. At seeing the place so suddenly before us, we withdrew briefly and unburdened ourselves.

I followed Frere in a wide circle around the perimeter of the clearing, searching for the other paths which led to it. We found four of these, evenly spaced, and Frere followed each of them outwards for an hour in every direction, searching for whatever it was he sought.

He found the well-trodden path by which the attackers had come and then afterwards withdrawn. He found the marks on the trees he was looking for. He found a small, white-skulled doll made of clay and grass set into the path to deter pursuit. And all the time he searched, I kept my eyes and ears open for sight or sound of anyone remaining in the trees around us, and everywhere I looked I saw shapes and movement in the dappled light and shade, and in every silence I heard the whispering voices of watching men. As usual, Frere made a joke of my concern.

The forest around Babire was as dense as any I had previously encountered and our voices penetrated only a few feet on either side of us.

Frere insisted on following this main path even further from the village, and it was not until darkness started to fall and we were two hours from our loads, that I was able to persuade him to return with me. He suggested that I should return alone, light a fire, and that he would join me later. I refused to do this, and seeing that I was angry at the suggestion, he returned reluctantly with me to the ruins of Babire, eventually apologizing to me and admitting that it was in the ruins of the village itself that he hoped to make his greatest discoveries.

Having seen the empty space and its scattered wreckage I asked him what he could possibly hope to find there, and it was then, in his shrug of an answer, that I understood, despite his protestations to the contrary, we were again on the trail of cannibals.

'Anthropophagy, James, anthropophagy.' As though this added an immediate cachet and veneer of scientific respectability to what we did; as though the word itself conferred upon us some protection.

I was repulsed by the thought, but even as I considered it, I knew he was unlikely to be successful in his search. By my estimation, any fighting there had taken place over twenty days previously, and there were enough scavengers in the forest to ensure that nothing would remain. I mentioned none of this to him as we made our return to Babire in the darkness.

We retrieved our loads and lit a fire. I gathered wood from the ruined buildings to ensure that the blaze would be fed until dawn. I had expected to be kept awake by the usual noises, but the forest around that lost village was a peculiarly silent place, and following the day's exertions I was the first to succumb to sleep and the last to wake.

I woke alone, to find our fire a mound of glowing ash. The sun was already above the canopy. At first I was alarmed, imagining that Frere had gone back along his path, but then a motion caught my eye and I saw him come out of the trees at the far side of the clearing. He was carrying a club and a piece of animal skin. He saw me watching and raised his trophies to me.

He came to me and showed me what he had collected. He told me how all the surrounding small cultivated plots had been plundered and their crops taken. He had been searching since before dawn. The club he held was weighted with a band of iron at one end. He could not identify the skin, but showed me the holes where it had once been stitched. He poured from his satchel the few other pieces he had found. It was a disappointing lot, but he remained enthusiastic.

He joined me for breakfast and explained that, according to his calculations, three hundred people had once lived there. I did not ask him if he had yet found any sign of the atrocities believed to have taken place in the village. He showed me the pieces of cooking pots he had collected. All had been smashed beyond use.

'And your cannibalism?' I finally asked him, wondering if he was prepared to keep further discoveries from me.

'Nothing. Nothing whatsoever.'

He asked me to make a plan of the ruined village, to plot where its huts had once stood, where the hearths in these had been located, to examine the surrounding forest for track-ways and other cultivated clearings, and to mark on the chart anything I found that he himself

181

had not already come across. He intended making a more thorough search of the surroundings, admitting for the first time that he hoped to find the body or the remains of someone killed or mortally wounded in the fighting, who had crawled away and died alone and unnoticed amid the trees. He did not imagine that he would be successful in this, but he was determined to make the attempt having come so far.

I expressed my reluctance to be separated from him in such an isolated place, but he merely reminded me of Fletcher's rifle and the faith I had earlier placed in the weapon, and remarked that we would achieve twice as much in the time left to us if we worked separately. He showed me the abundant notes he had already made during the night.

I worked through the day making a plan of the village. It was an accurate map and I was pleased with the result. Every few hours, Frere would reappear and show me what he had found. He showed me a small, broken shield, a snakeskin bracelet and a finely woven grass quiver. He complimented me on my map, and I felt encouraged to add to it. I showed him the few unremarkable pieces of pottery and wood-working I had found. One of these pieces, a ball of ebony, excited him as much as his doll. He said it was broken from another club, a weapon designed specifically for crushing skulls. But the highly polished surface of the black wood disappointed him and he asked me if I had wiped it clean before showing it to him. I disappointed him further by saying I hadn't.

We ate together and then he left me again.

I searched through the surrounding perimeter of trees for signs of once-cultivated plots. I could not be certain in my identification of these and I shaded the areas on my map accordingly. I occasionally heard him working further out among the trees. He sang and spoke aloud to himself as he went.

Later in the afternoon, he returned to the clearing. He carried two sacks of further findings, and he tipped one of these out for me to examine. There was nothing that I hadn't already seen elsewhere, and I sensed that he too was disappointed by the haul. I asked if the second sack contained more of the same and he said it did. I asked him to let me see, but this time instead of tipping the contents out, he reached into the sack and brought them out piece by piece.

First among these pieces were several small bones, and it was not until he had arranged these on the ground that I understood I was looking at a small human arm. I asked him to confirm this and he nodded. He told me where he had found the bones, and that a fire had been lit near by. He took another bone from the sack, this one blackened and broken. Yet another still had some flesh and sinew attached to it. It was clear that they were not the bones of an adult, and the vanished inhabitants of Babire had not been pygmies.

'They are the bones of a child,' I said bluntly.

He held the largest of the bones at arm's length, and when I took it from him to examine it more closely I caught the faint but distinctive odour it still possessed. He took the bone back and sniffed deeply at it, as though wanting to commit the smell to memory.

I asked him what he intended doing with the bones, and he said he wanted to keep them. He did his best to mask the excitement in his voice.

He reached carefully back into the sack and took out something else – something which I could not at first identify, and it was only when he held the thing between his finger and thumb and clear of his palm, that I was able to make out a small black hand with its thumb and one of its fingers missing. I looked from this trophy back to Frere's triumphant grin, the look on his face one of wonder, awe almost, the look of a man who might have found a diamond of the same size.

I told him to put it back in the sack, but either he did not hear me or he had become oblivious to my words, for he went on staring at the small black hand, turning it one way and then another as though to get a better impression of what it represented, of its great value to him.

My revulsion at seeing this was equal to that I felt at seeing the thing itself, and I made my feelings known to him, but he was either unconvinced of these or remained oblivious to them, and I left him alone with his prize, painfully conscious of this unexpected and unwelcome distance so suddenly between us.

Later, I suggested that the small, mutilated hand be buried – that he and I performed the ceremony – and he was angry at the suggestion. Casement and Morel had had their whole sacks of hands, he said, and their skulls, and their shrunken heads. What was this one small specimen collected in the name of science compared to all that? It was an empty argument and he knew this better than I did. The hand was already packed away in one of his jars of preserving fluid. He tried to divert me from my argument by telling me that the Mahdi, the killer of Gordon and possessor of the Sudan had delivered up ten sacks of locusts to the British emissary sent to bargain with him, saying they were the souls of the infidel soldiers killed by him, proof, if proof were needed, of their slaughter, and of the Mahdi's power and invincibility. The insects had clattered all around the delegation as they spoke, seemingly unnoticed by the Mahdi and his followers.

I sensed that somewhere in the tale lay Frere's apology to me, or if not his apology, then his concession to my feelings, and an acknowledgement that he regretted as much as I did the fracture between us.

17

I crossed the river in the uncertain hope of being able to see Hammad. Nor was I certain of what I hoped to achieve by the visit, other than to make a plea on Frere's behalf, or to better understand Hammad's own involvement in the affair. He would certainly have known of our coming investigators by then, and perhaps – or so I also tried to convince myself – the situation might now be sufficiently altered for him to divulge something or other to me. Such was the flimsy and desperate nature of my hope. I told no-one in the Station of my intentions.

I crossed with the old man, having the previous evening sent the deformed boy to make arrangements.

It was not an easy crossing and we were forced to manoeuvre among unfamiliar channels and currents before making landfall a mile downriver. I was warned that our return would need to be undertaken before the day's rain came. Neither the man nor the boy said much to me on the crossing. I asked the boy how he found Frere, but he told me nothing I did not already know. He was reluctant to talk in front of the old man and so I did not pursue the matter. They left me where I was landed.

I arrived at the centre of the Belgian Station and stood for a moment watching all that was happening there. There was a lively air of commerce about the place, and their wharves, in stark contrast to our own, were crowded with vessels being loaded and unloaded. I walked among the market stalls and the tables of their own rubber-buyers. I met several officers I knew and they invited me back to their quarters with them. They repeated the tales they had heard about famine and fighting, about the falling-off of the season's rubber.

Those who knew him, asked about Frere. They said they did not believe the stories they had heard, assuring me that he would soon be exonerated and released. I said nothing in return to either fuel their speculations or to bolster my own long-dead hope. Instead, I remarked on how much trade there was, allowing them to instantly divert their talk and to make the usual traders' complaints – too much, too little, prices too low to sell, prices too high to buy. It was a capricious whim of the river that had forced this difference in our fortunes, and they understood this as well as I did. The balance of profit and loss was seldom still.

I told them why I was there, hoping that one or other of them might be able to help me, but at the mention of Hammad they became evasive, apologetic, saying there was nothing they could do. It was Cornelius's opinion that the Belgians had no intention of handing over any powers to a native government, but that it was currently in their best interests to appear to be about to do so, and that the handing over of Frere to a native court for trial was all a part of this greater subterfuge. It was something I would put to Hammad if I saw him, if he had not already long since worked this out for himself, and now looked upon Frere and his trial in the light of his own ambitions. I saw again how we were all – the Belgians as much as ourselves – in thrall to the man, that he remained at the pivot of that balance, whatever other swings of fortune we endured.

Declining all their offers, I made my way to Proctor's garrison.

I found the man alone in his office, sitting with his feet on his desk reading a newspaper.

Upon hearing me enter, he swung his feet to the ground, but then seeing me he made a great play of lifting them back up and of continuing with whatever he read.

'Six weeks old,' he said. '*The London Times.*'

At first I did not believe him. He saw this and showed me the heading. It cannot be imagined or overestimated what a sudden dart of longing seeing that title and its date sent through me. Our own papers, when they came, were invariably six *months* old, and though we treasured them for what they were, their primary purpose was denied to us. Men who had died were rotting in their graves while we thought them still alive; new-born babies were not yet conceived; civilized wars were started and ended before we even knew any hostility existed; the jigsaw of nations was shaken apart and re-assembled by new hands.

'New man in yesterday,' Proctor said. 'Four weeks at sea, two weeks straight here on the river. Gave me this without even knowing what it was worth.'

I considered asking him if he would sell it to me. Or if not the whole paper, then a page of it, and it was with a great effort that I said nothing, doing my best to not even look at the sheets he folded so carelessly to examine.

I told him my intentions.

'No chance,' he said immediately.

'He may see me out of curiosity,' I suggested.

He shook his head at me, as though I were a child incapable of understanding the simplest thing. 'No chance. A mile up that road – ' he motioned in the direction of Hammad's home ' – he's got a dozen of his own men stopping everyone from going any further. Lot of activity up there for the past week and now not a single one of us is allowed to go near the place, not even the Station Manager.'

'What do you think is happening?' Several barely formed ideas ran through my mind.

'Obvious, I would have thought.' He took great pleasure in my ignorance. He put down the paper and again swung his feet from the desk so that we might face each other directly.

'Not to me,' I said.

'He's been on one of his own trading missions. That's what he calls them. Or if not him, then one of them's come back to him.'

'Trading in what?'

'What do you think? What do you think those dozen Arabs are stopping us from seeing?'

'You think he's gathering slaves?'

'Indentured labourers, if you don't mind. All you ever see of his palace is what he shows you. Walk a mile beyond it and you'll see another side of our Mister Hammad entirely. Buildings for men, buildings for women, buildings for all their screaming brats.'

'And none of this trade comes down through here?'

He laughed. 'Course it doesn't. You're talking about a man who might one day soon – one day *very* soon – wash his hands, sign his name to a piece of paper, raise a flag, and become the king of a new country.'

'Do you really think so?' I made my scepticism clear.

'Why not? He'll be perfectly suited to the place. The talks are going on. What did you think, that we'd get to lord it over them for ever? Perhaps if Hammad does take over, then the rest of us can go home and leave them to it. Place'd be a blood-bath within days while everything got settled.'

I considered the likelihood of all this. I knew what growth this mulch of conjecture and rumour supported, that what Proctor said, despite his own lurid emphasis and my own reluctance to believe it, was not so unbelievable.

It was by then midday and the room in which we sat was an overheated vault.

'No, Hammad keeps himself clean here. He'll send most of them east, I imagine, where they still fetch a good price. That'll be the men, mostly; the women and children he can still sell on the more specialized markets. Still a big call for some of those women in Port Elys or Petit Coeur. And some of those girls, ten or eleven they are, bet you or me wouldn't say no to getting our hands on one of them for an hour. Word is that Hammad likes to break some of them in himself. Either him or one of his guards. Get them trained up, worth a bit less in the short run, but more in the long, if you know what I mean.'

I understood him perfectly, and I saw how he was goading me. The brothels at Port Elys and Petit Coeur were filled to overflowing and their trade never slackened.

Before we put an end to it under Company orders, caravans of these women and children were moved along the paths on our side of the river, sometimes being brought into the garrison yard or compound to await some vessel or other. They were a pathetic sight. Most were bound and yoked, and some were shackled.

The mothers and children were kept apart, and despite how they were treated and what they must have suspected lay ahead of them, they were inevitably acquiescent in their behaviour. I learned later that some of the women were drugged before being bound. Worse, I learned that they were told they would only be allowed to remain with their children if they complied with everything they were told to do. They were also warned that they were resting in our Station under sufferance from us and that we would punish them ourselves if there was any disturbance.

I remember visiting one of the landing stages where seventy or eighty of these women were being guarded while they waited for a boat. They all froze as I went close to them, and some closed their eyes to deny my presence completely. Most of them were naked except for cloths fastened between their legs, and this, I imagined, was done more for our sakes than their own. They might have been so many boulders resting there in the night for all the noise they made. Occasionally, one of the women would be untied and taken elsewhere by the men who traded and escorted them. We knew better than to intervene when we saw this happening, or when a woman or a child was beaten for some transgression.

Cornelius in particular had complained to the Company Secretary that our involvement in the trade, whatever the women were called, and even if only by this association, was detrimental to us. The Company had always replied that they were assessing the situation and that wider considerations further complicated our own apparently simplistic understanding of the matter. Cornelius tore up these answers as soon as they were received. I had not known then about his own lost 'wife' and dead daughter, but I understood afterwards what a large part their memory played in his frustration.

'So?' Proctor said loudly, invading my thoughts.

'And everyone here condones this activity,' I said absently.

'What's it got to do with condoning? Never been made illegal here – not the way these men do it. You have to admire them for that. Highly respected men, some of them, and none more so than our friend Hammad.'

'Highly respected by whom, though?' I said.

'There you go again. You still think it matters to make that distinction. Wait until he's king and ask me again.'

'And whatever I think of him, I'm not going to get to see him.'

'You were never going to get to see him. Who do you think sees him by knocking on his door and shouting in that that's what they want? The old Queen herself could come and this bastard would keep her waiting just long enough to let her know how far from home she was.'

Hammad, who was reputed to have once lined up a dozen slaves, one behind the other, and fired through them with a newly bought rifle to see how effective it was, disappointed and angry when only the first three fell, then leaving the others standing for a day and a night while he decided whether or not to repeat the experiment at closer range.

Hammad, who substituted dynamite for gunpowder to teach a team of idle stump-clearers a lesson they were able to remember only for the final agonizing seconds of their lives.

Hammad, who once lost a canoe of twenty bound men over the vicious Ngula Falls, and afterwards telling the story and saying, 'What a pity, it was such a well-built canoe.'

'Then I've come on a fool's errand,' I said eventually, more to myself than to Proctor.

He surprised me then by asking me how Frere was.

I told him, detailing the preparations Bone had made and what new airs and graces he gave himself. Proctor smiled at the predictability of it all. He opened up and refolded the newspaper. He said he would sell it to me, but that he could get a better price for it among the Belgians for the European news it contained. I asked him if there was anything of any great significance I ought to be aware of, but when he pushed the paper towards me, I found myself reluctant to pick it up and search it, only too aware of the pleasures and pains it might simultaneously inflict on me. I declined his offer, and because he understood why I had declined, he took it back immediately and put it in a drawer.

'I could get word to Hammad that you wanted to see him. What is it – that you humbly beseech an audience with him?'

'Then he'll know I've been and he'll know what's happening here.'

'Too clever for me,' Proctor said, though he understood me perfectly. 'Besides which, he'll already know that you're here and that I'm filling you in on everything.'

'Paid informants?'

'Paid favours, it's all the same.'

'Then do you know about the men coming to investigate Frere?'

'The men coming to solve all your problems.'

'Meaning what?'

'Meaning you haven't been able to wash your hands of him without someone else telling you what to do.'

'Is that what you thought would happen?'

He considered this for a moment and then nodded. 'They were at the Black River outflow two days ago.'

That meant they were less than five days away from us.

'Why did no-one tell *us*?'

He spread his hands.

I rose to leave him, conscious of the coming rain. He held out his hand to me, and I could not help but think that I had misjudged the man, equating him with Bone when they were in fact two completely different creatures.

As though reading my thoughts, he said, 'Send my regards to poor old Bone.'

I smiled at this and told him I would. Then he offered me the newspaper for nothing and again I declined.

'I know,' he said. 'It's full of everything elsewhere. Bring tears to your eyes reading about a cold spring morning.' Then he grabbed my arm and said, 'Don't get slack with Frere. You aren't going to be able to hold his hand and walk him through this one.'

I asked him what he meant by the outburst.

'What I said,' he said. 'Man from Stanleyville said they spoke to next to no-one all the time they were there.' He released his grip on me.

I acknowledged this warning and left him.

My return journey was as prolonged as my earlier one, and again neither the man nor the boy made any effort to speak to me. Still angry at having achieved nothing by the crossing, I resented this behaviour, and when the time came to pay I deliberately tossed my coins towards the boy knowing that he would not be able to turn smoothly enough to catch them and that he would then have to search for them in the silt at the bottom of the boat.

18

The next day I went to see Frere to tell him what I had attempted.

'Stay away from Hammad,' he said angrily.

'It seems I have no choice.'

'No-one has any choice around that man.'

'Meaning you give credence to Proctor's story that Hammad may one day play some part in governing the place?'

He laid down his pen. 'Do you still harbour doubts?'

More of his journals were scattered around the room. Others must have taken them to him. I saw, too, that a Bible sat solidly at the centre of his desk. I looked surreptitiously to see if he had any of his precious photographs with him – of his parents, of Caroline, perhaps – but saw nothing.

He saw my surprise at seeing all this.

'Cornelius came. I asked him. And when no-one comes, I ask the boy.'

'I can do all this for you,' I told him.

'I know you can, but—' He stopped abruptly.

'What?'

'I was going to say that you already have your suspicions concerning me, and that soon, if these are confirmed, you may want to – you may *need* to – sever yourself from me completely.'

'Babire,' I said, marking the centre around which we were both circling.

'Do you imagine I went back there when I left you?'

'No, not there. But I imagine you went in search of something similar. I imagine it formed part of your purpose in leaving us.' He said nothing to stop me. 'You asked me for the journal because it was beyond you to offer the clue to any of the others, even Cornelius. In here you can hide it amid all these others, bury it deep. But I was there with you. I know what you were truly searching for. I know what others can only guess at.'

He held up his hand to me.

'And *did* you find what you were searching for on your wanderings?'

'Before I fell ill and into the hands of those men and then Hammad? Yes, I found it.'

'And you detailed all this in the pages Hammad holds?'

'That was the purpose of my journey, of my deserting you. What more do you need to know? Because whatever I tell you, I will only sink further in your estimation.'

'And you went without telling any of us – without telling *me* – so that none of us would be implicated in what happened. You detached yourself completely.'

He nodded once.

I was about to suggest that he had done nothing else but abuse our friendship, when someone shouted outside and I recognized the voice of Klein commanding his singers into position.

'They come most days,' Frere said, resigned to what he must now endure.

The singing began, the same few hymns I had heard when sitting with Bone.

'Is there nothing anyone can do to stop the man?' I said.

'I imagine he believes he serves his purpose. My redemption, salvation – call it what you will – may not be so impossibly out of reach as most imagine.'

'But it is not something you yourself believe in?'

'I need neither to believe in it nor to insist on others believing in it.'

'Which is a polite way of telling me to stop quizzing you on it. Do you know about Klein and Cornelius, about his dead daughter and the child's lost mother?'

'He told me. He wanted to apologize to me for Klein being here and punishing me instead of him. He offered to try and rid me of the man and his sheep, but I told him not to get involved again, that he'd be gone soon enough. Besides which, I imagine Klein has his own good reasons for being here.'

'Meaning?'

'Meaning he'll be trying to work out where he and his new mission best fit into the coming scheme of things.'

'What possible part will he have in anything?'

'The man's a puppet. He may be of great value to someone who needs to take advantage of whatever influence he has, of what he still represents here, of *who* he represents.'

It did not surprise me to see how swiftly we had come from one path onto another, from mine to his, where something unexpected – something I had not even begun to consider – lay around each bend.

I had been with Cornelius on several occasions recently when we had encountered Klein, and when Cornelius had made a point of ignoring the priest completely, to the extent now of refusing even to return his greeting. On each of these occasions, Klein had been accompanied by Perpetua and Felicity, and the women had remained silent, as instructed by him. Klein spoke to me openly about Cornelius, and within Cornelius's hearing. He made remarks which might have provoked another man – Fletcher, say – into attacking him, but which Cornelius, though clearly angered by the remarks, affected to ignore.

I told Klein that he was mistaken if he believed I would act as an intermediary and that my allegiance and sympathies lay wholly with Cornelius. At one point, when he accused me of being as blind as all the others, when he accused me of clinging to a power I no longer possessed, I told him I despised him as I had despised no-one before. I was trembling as I said this. Cornelius told me not to rise to the priest's bait and led me away from him. Klein stood with a smile on his face and watched us go. I saw how distressing this was for Perpetua and Felicity.

When we were beyond his hearing, Cornelius told me that Klein regularly beat the two women, that all three of them considered it part of their religious instruction, and that this was one of the reasons he dressed them in their heavy outfits. I looked back to where the two women stood in the distance, their heads bowed in supplication as Klein berated them.

'So you think Klein will make himself useful to whoever comes to power?' I said to Frere as the hymn-singing rose around us.

'Oh, indispensable, I'd say. The Lord's mouthpiece.'

'Is there nothing to be gained – by you, I mean – in submitting to any efforts he might be persuaded or bribed to make on your behalf?'

He laughed at this – whether at the suggestion itself or at my naïvety in making it, I could not tell.

'Will what Hammad possesses condemn you so completely?' I said.

'Way beyond any notion of salvation or redemption our friend out there might have.'

The singers paused briefly, rested in the emptiness of their own dying echo, and then resumed even more loudly.

'And doubtless it will not be so straightforward,' he said.

'You're saying they'll make an example of you, that your punishment will be an expedience, done for the wrong reasons.'

'They'll flex their new muscle for the first time. After all, I did what I am accused of doing.'

'You did nothing thousands of others haven't done before you, aren't doing still.'

'Stop,' he said. 'You're making yourself sound ridiculous. *I* did it, *me*. *Me*. That's the difference. That's what you – and you alone, I'm afraid, James – have not yet fully grasped.'

Neither of us spoke after that. Close enough to him to embrace him, and yet I could not even bring myself to look in the same direction he looked.

I had gone to him wanting to talk of Caroline – as much, if not more, for my own sake as for his – and of my parents and other sisters and the times we had spent together with them. But I saw now what a false and contrived note this would sound and said nothing. I saw too what reward and punishment such shared fond remembrance might simultaneously be in the minds of two men – something sweet to one man and yet bitter to the other for precisely the same reasons.

The noise from outside grew louder yet, and ever more discordant in its rising volume, and I went to the small window, showed my face there and shouted for them all to shut up. My words had not the slightest effect whatsoever, and few even glanced up from making their racket to acknowledge my presence. But Klein saw me, and knowing that I was with Frere doubtless added to his pleasure at this pious assault upon the man.

After that we did little but wait for the coming men, our days filled with empty whistles and false alarms. 'Empty whistles' was the term we gave to signals from those boats which did not come to us, but whose masters sounded their whistles or horns or rang their bells at every indication of habitation along the shore, we looking at them, they at us, seldom even waving or calling out to each other during these passing encounters – constant reminders, despite our mirror image across the river, of the vast and mostly impenetrable emptiness amid which we otherwise sat.

During that week – an omen almost of what was afterwards to befall us – there occurred a partial eclipse of the sun. Cornelius warned us that it was coming, saying that it would unsettle our employees, that some among them would refuse to work while this crescent of black – this, to their minds, paring of the unimaginable – lasted. This break in the day's operations was of no consequence to us.

Reports arrived of men approaching us from all directions.

We fastened our collars and pulled straight our jackets, so to speak, and waited. And when these false alarms passed we returned to our unobserved lives almost with a sense of having been cheated.

We learned in the middle of the week that Dhanis's expedition to Fashoda had ended with the mutiny of his three thousand Batetela porters. Some accounts said that Dhanis himself, along with all his Belgian officers, had been killed, and that these three thousand disaffected men were armed and rampaging across the north of the state, causing the factories and the stations there to cease operating, and in some cases to be abandoned when they came under attack.

Later the same day, we heard that Dhanis alone had survived and that he had fled and was now back in Stanleyville. It was said the Batetela were approaching the place with the intention of plundering it. With Stanleyville gone our own major line of trade and communication no longer existed. If the news caused us concern, then we could only imagine what terrors it struck into the hearts of Dhanis's countrymen across the river, many of whom had families living in Stanleyville.

The following day I was with Fletcher when he killed and butchered a small black pig he had bought. He killed the animal by stunning it and then slitting its throat to bleed it. Afterwards he cut open its belly to disgorge its innards, but then, as he paused to sharpen his knife, the creature came miraculously back to life, struggled to its feet and ran squealing around the compound with its innards trailing behind it in a single glossy piece. I helped him chase the animal, both of us helpless with laughter. We called for the assistance of some of our nearby workers, but they refused to intervene, and instead watched wide-eyed as the small pig continued running and squealing. Eventually, the animal succumbed and Fletcher carried it twitching back to the table where he was finally able to butcher it.

At Abbot's insistence we raised a crisp new flag up our pole.

Klein and his congregation marked the ceremony

with a service and more singing, and Bone insisted on his men firing a salute.

Thus did we compose and prepare ourselves, and more forcibly than ever before did the wilderness surrounding our swept-out buildings and laundered flag strike me as something more permanent and invincible than anything else I could imagine, something as potent and as indestructible as evil or truth itself, and something waiting only for our departure to reassert itself and to prove once and for all the insignificance of our brief and unremarkable existence within it.

PART THREE

19

'My name,' he said, 'is Granville Beaufoy Montague Nash.'

A finger gently prodded four times into each of our chests. A name before which a weaker man might have taken a step backwards.

His own men were lined up behind him, all Zanzibaris, porters and guides. We had anticipated that he might be accompanied by other Company men, or by men acting under the Company's authority collected at the coast or Stanleyville. These men stood upright, their arms flat by their sides, as though about to be inspected. Those senior among them wore red fezzes and cotton drill suits. Nash himself wore a brilliantly white topee, varnished boots and an alpaca dress jacket with a stiff masher collar. Afterwards, Cornelius said the man reminded him of a tailor's dummy. It was clear to us all that this one pristine outfit had been saved for this occasion, and that, fitting so closely and cleanly to the man inside it, it was there to serve a purpose, to signal intent.

'Beaufoy?' Fletcher said.

And as though on cue, the man said, 'Henry Beaufoy is my uncle. My father's brother. I was named after him long before I was called here.' He relaxed momentarily, tugged by this distant memory, and then he remembered himself and straightened.

Henry Beaufoy had been, or perhaps still was, the Secretary of the African Association. His portrait had looked down on Frere and myself in that overheated library. The man was a Quaker and well known for being governed in all his actions and decisions by the strictures of his religion.

Cornelius was the first to approach the man in greeting.

'And these are my men,' Nash said, his first time in command, stepping aside to present them.

I recognized those of the porters who had been here before. They were not reliable men. They had come with Nash because, in addition to their pay, there was some novelty involved, and some distant possibility of further pay.

Cornelius, guessing what was expected of him, walked along the line and looked each of the men in the eye. Most avoided him, but Henry Beaufoy Montague Nash did not see this.

We had known of the party's arrival since the previous evening, when word of it had come to us from a fisherman who encountered them a mile downriver. Abbot had gone to them, found them exhausted and in disarray, and had then been sent back to us by Nash, who insisted that he would not present himself in that condition. Abbot had asked him where the other members of the delegation were, and Nash, perhaps imagining he was referring to the porters yet to catch up with him, had told Abbot they were coming. It was why, at this appointed hour, we had expected to see other Englishmen standing alongside him.

I alone, I believe, felt some reassurance at seeing him

standing there by himself, the thinnest of threads between everything that had happened and everything that was yet to come.

As he waited with his porters lined up behind him, others came into the compound to join them. These late arrivals wore only loincloths or tattered trousers and carried small loads, which they dropped unceremoniously in a mound beside Nash. He told them to be more careful, but they ignored him, and only when Cornelius shouted at them in the language they better understood did they lay down their packages in neat piles.

'Thank you,' Nash said to Cornelius. It was the first of his concessions.

Cornelius then invited the man to accompany him to his quarters, where he might wash and change his clothes.

I saw that Nash had expected considerably more of his arrival, to be greeted more ceremoniously. Like Abbot, he was a clerk who had wandered further from his desk than he had ever believed possible, and we all saw that.

'Are there others yet to come?' I asked him, meaning more porters – the forty he had with him had brought the loads of half that number.

'No,' he said. 'I am completely alone.' He looked at the men behind him, his gaze stiffening them further.

I went with him to Cornelius's rooms. Throughout our encounter he held a leather case, and when I offered to carry it for him, he thanked me and declined.

Cornelius asked him about the route he had taken and Nash explained at great length how he had chosen his guides at each of his stopping points, and how trustworthy they had proved. It was clear that he had been misled, that his journey had been unnecessarily prolonged and made more costly by these uninformed decisions. Neither Cornelius nor I disabused him of his achievement.

He spoke at great length regarding his stay on the coast, what he had seen there, what changes were under way, and how often his expectations of the places he had visited had been exceeded. He looked around him as he spoke – we were then passing the most dilapidated of our timber warehouses – making his silent, disappointing comparisons.

He complained of an ache in both his knees, and of cuts – one on his shoulder, another on his forearm – which continued to suppurate. Cornelius reassured him that they would be treated.

'They are of little consequence,' Nash said. 'What man comes here without the expectation of suffering?' He laughed at the remark. He seemed bound by and devoted to his own expectation.

I saw myself in him. I had been ready to dislike him, to be offended by him and his purpose there, but I saw that he had arrived just as I had arrived, the only difference being that I had come clothed in uncertainty, and here was a man whose conviction in his work was as certain and as solid and as much a part of him as the legs which carried him and the spine which held him upright.

'Of course,' Cornelius said.

Around us, men were at work unloading a small half-decked steamer, and he asked me about its cargo. I told him what I knew of it, that it had brought only palm nuts – vividly crimson in a mound ahead of us – and a consignment of greenheart and gum. The load was of little value.

'No rubber?' he said.

Cornelius, I saw, continued to make his own silent assessment of the man.

Arriving at Cornelius's quarters, Nash took off his jacket and undershirts and showed us his wounds. In addition to the two of which he had spoken, there were a further dozen, all displaying various degrees of infection. His chest and neck were covered by insect bites. A lesion ran the length of his ribcage, darkening in the places where the bones came closest to the skin. He studied himself in Cornelius's mirror and seemed genuinely shocked at what he saw there.

He continued to discuss his journey with us, false familiarity in his voice; he mentioned places neither Cornelius nor I had ever visited.

Cornelius washed his wounds and applied iodine and oil of thyme to them. Nash did his best not to show the pain this caused him. Cornelius explained to him what had bitten him, and in turn Nash listed the medicines he had brought with him, few of which would serve him well. One of his porters had died during the journey, an old man who could scarcely manage a quarter-load. He had eaten his meal one evening and then died in the night. Two other men had absconded, one with his load.

I stopped listening to him. We had all been wrong-footed.

'And Nicholas Frere?' I said finally, stopping Nash at the height of another small speech outlining what he considered to be his duties among us.

He looked at me for a moment, angry at my interruption.

'Where Nicholas Frere is concerned,' he said, his tone changed, formal, unassailable, as solid as his conviction, 'I shall determine the facts of the matter – facts of which you are all no doubt already aware; I shall make my assessment based upon those facts; and founded upon that assessment I shall make my recommendations for further action.'

'Meaning you'll send him to stand proper trial,' Cornelius said flatly.

'That may be my recommendation, yes. How can I decide when I am not yet appraised of the facts?' His retreat into written orders continued, disappointed that his own part in the proceedings had been so bluntly and swiftly exposed.

'You will be offered every assistance,' Cornelius said.

'I understand that.'

'Beyond our legal or contractual obligations, I meant.'

'Of course.'

'We want this whole thing resolved as much as you do.'

'As the Company's representative in the matter, I shall ask nothing of any of you that you cannot already have considered a hundred times over prior to my arrival. I do understand the nature and the depth of your feeling towards me. Nicholas Frere was your companion and friend. I understand what that means in a place like this.'

By which he meant that we were to keep our distance from him, that we were more likely to hinder than to assist him should we insist on our involvement in the matter. We were men uselessly beating our heads together.

I left them soon afterwards and walked through the tall grass to the edge of the garrison yard. Bone and his men were there, but no-one else. It had been my intention to visit Frere in advance of Nash, to tell him of the man come to question him, but instead I turned away, and little caring where I went, I walked to our useless quarry and sat for an hour at its rim watching the tiny brown figures beneath me.

A month after my arrival I had been taken by Cornelius and Fletcher to witness a trial on the far shore. A Manyema stood accused of theft and murder and was being tried by the Belgians. Cornelius had some small role in the proceedings and would be called to testify to the man's character. Fletcher and myself were invited to attend in the more debatable capacity of 'official observers'.

We crossed the river on the evening prior to the trial. It was my first time out of the Station, and it surprised me to see how much busier and more obviously prosperous this place was compared to our own.

We were put up at the residence of a man called Henrici, Chief Quartermaster – Cornelius's counterpart – and it was not until late in the evening that I discovered that he was also to be the acting judge in the following day's proceedings.

Alone with Cornelius, I asked him by what authority the man played the role, but he dismissed my remark by asking me how else I imagined these things were done. There was no doubt that the accused man was guilty, having confessed to both his crimes.

Henrici had speculated on the punishment he might deliver, but here too there was little doubt. Cornelius told me to say nothing during the trial. The accused man had also been suspected of stealing from us during the time he was in our employ, but nothing had been done to expose or punish him. I saw then how inextricably all these events and their participants were connected.

The criminal showed no remorse and stood before

211

the court wearing only a pair of blue trousers, his feet and hands tied. He frequently shouted out to interrupt the proceedings, and each time this happened he was struck by the guards on either side of him. One of these men was Proctor, though I did not know him at the time.

A junior quartermaster acted in the man's defence, but this amounted to little more than a recital of his record of employment, doubtlessly compiled the previous day, and being little more than a list of the months during which the man had not been accused of any crime. He was an unreliable and unpopular worker, who stood accused of beating a fellow porter in order to steal a small case of wire rods and polished tortoiseshell. The other man had died of his wounds ten days after the attack, and four days after that the thief had been arrested while attempting to sell what he had stolen.

The court proceedings were perfunctory. At one point, Henrici called for Proctor not to beat the prisoner so harshly, saying that the beatings and the man's attempts at evasion were holding everything up. There was a small space in the building reserved for the public, and this consisted mostly of traders keen on an hour's entertainment while they waited for their customers. There were no seats, and these men came and went.

The man's wife and four children had been allowed into the court at the start of the proceedings, but had then been removed following the woman's constant wailing. She had thrown a fetish at her husband, expecting him to catch it and protect himself with it, but instead the man had simply stared at it where it fell at his feet and had then ground it into the dirt. Henrici watched this and then called for the thing to be removed, saying it dishonoured the integrity of the court. He consulted frequently with the men sitting alongside him, but I imagine that little of any legal consequence was discussed by them.

The guilty man's crimes were frequently repeated. Whatever else happened, there was to be no doubt whatsoever that he was deserving of the punishment about to be handed down to him. Cornelius had warned me the previous evening that there was only one possible consequence of a murder charge being proven and that the man would be hanged. This, he said, would take place immediately following the trial. This was not a place for reconsideration or appeals. I asked him if he thought this was fair – I had not known then how inadequate and compromising the man's defence was to prove – and, suppressing his laughter, he told me I might want to raise the point with Henrici over breakfast.

The following morning, taking his duties seriously, Henrici left for the courthouse before I woke.

The trial lasted two hours, half of which consisted of private deliberations.

Cornelius gave his evidence. He smoked one of his cigars, constantly acknowledging the men he recognized in the crowd. He was asked to tell the court what he knew of the accused man, but everything he said only confirmed what the court already knew. He spoke to those of us in our reserved seats as though we were the members of a jury, and it occurred to me only then that this, unofficially, was what we were.

The accused man was condemned to death by hanging for the murder of his fellow porter. One of the other judges rose at this announcement and asked if there were any relatives of the murdered man present. No-one answered him, disappointing him and causing him to sit back down, his own small role in the proceedings over.

'He would have offered them a part in it,' Cornelius said to me, making no attempt to lower his voice. 'In the name of fairness and retribution.'

There was then a further delay as Henrici announced that he and his judges would now consider the crime of theft.

I asked Cornelius if this was simply another example of the protocol of the occasion being seen to be observed.

'Oh no,' he said. 'They'll probably want to flog him unconscious before reviving him to hang him.'

I thought at first that he was making a cruel joke at the condemned man's expense, but a moment later Henrici announced that the man would receive three hundred lashes before he was hanged. He rose from his seat and read from a ledger. Upon finishing, he handed the book to each of the others for their signatures.

Even allowing for the fact that the man had confessed to both crimes and must have known what awaited him, it was evident to most present that the trial was a charade, concerned with a great deal more than the matter of theft or murder.

At this point, Cornelius rose and asked Henrici if the flogging might not be reduced. Henrici shook his head. The ink had already dried on the paper.

I asked Cornelius why he had made the appeal on the man's behalf.

'Because they'll beat him unconscious more than once and we'll all be kept waiting while he's brought round. There will have to be a doctor present and he will have to certify that the man is fit enough to go on being lashed. After which, he will have to certify him sufficiently recovered to be hanged.'

I asked him how many of these trials he had attended, and rather than answer me, he began to one by one slowly extend the fingers of both hands.

I looked past him to Fletcher. We had all expected to be back at the Station by mid-afternoon.

We ate lunch with Henrici. His manner was grave, as befitted his new responsibilities. He said it shocked and surprised him to see how these people continued to behave towards each other, how little value they put on life itself. But his tone was more one of excited disgust than genuine, humanitarian disappointment in his fellow man. He drank glass after glass of wine with his food.

Later, the proceedings resumed and the condemned man was unceremoniously tied to a crude frame erected in the space outside the court. A larger crowd gathered.

Proctor and two of his men carried out the beating, one man counting aloud each time the cane connected with the man's back.

Mercifully, the flogged man screamed only at the first thirty or so lashes, and after that he seemed anaesthetized by his pain. Blood sprayed the ground in a wide circle around him. I even imagined I felt the finest flecks of it on my own forehead twenty yards from where he was whipped.

After sixty lashes, he fell unconscious, and Proctor and his men revived him by pouring water over him. The man groaned – sufficient for the doctor to signal to Proctor to continue – and the flogging resumed. Men and women in the crowd called out continually and I saw that wagers were being made on how much more the beaten man might endure.

He passed out four more times before the first hundred lashes were administered. After this he was revived, allowed to rest for a few minutes, swilled with clean water, and his flayed back pointlessly sprayed with sulphur powder. The doctor moved closer to oversee this, standing with a cloth pressed firmly to his nose and mouth. The man's injuries did not concern him, merely his capacity to endure having more inflicted upon him.

The flogging resumed, and this time the man passed out almost immediately. It was by then three in the afternoon and the sun was at its hottest. A cloud of flies hung over the beaten man. The men with the canes paused and Henrici went to them. After a brief conference, Henrici announced to the crowd that nothing would be served by further reviving the man and that the flogging would continue even though he was unconscious. The men with the canes worked less energetically at this, and the man counting the lashes lowered his voice until he was almost silent. An air of shameful expediency now hung over the proceedings.

In this manner, the punishment was soon over and Henrici finally called a halt to the proceedings.

The man was again doused, and when, after fifteen minutes, he showed signs of responding to the water thrown over his near-skinless back, he was released from his frame and carried to the tree where he was to be hanged. All that was required now, apparently, was that he was able to stand upright, unaided, for a full minute before his punishment was completed.

Henrici stood in front of him, his pocket-watch in his hand, counting. The condemned man stood upright for only a few seconds before swaying and falling. He was helped back to his feet, but fell again soon afterwards. This happened several more times, until Henrici finally called for a chair to be taken to the man. The man sat on it, crying out when his back was pushed against its slats. After conferring with the doctor, Henrici announced that to insist on the man standing and repeatedly falling was beyond him and that this requirement need not now be fulfilled if the other judges were in agreement. They were.

After this, the condemned man was given a drink of water, and a rope was thrown over the branch of the tree above him and its noose placed round his neck. He seemed barely to notice what was happening to him. A minister approached him and read aloud from a Bible. Then, even as the reading continued, the man was helped up onto the chair and held steady at his waist.

The minister turned from the man to the crowd, still reading, and walked slowly away from him. The slack was taken in from above the man and the rope secured to a hook in the trunk of the tree. Henrici and the other judges stood shoulder to shoulder facing the man on his chair.

A signal was given to Proctor and the chair was kicked away. The man dropped, jerked, appeared to kick out two or three times, and then hung limp, dead, his feet inches from the ground.

The crowd fell silent for a few seconds, and then, one by one, began to cheer and applaud. Henrici motioned for the doctor, who in turn called for Proctor to unfasten the rope. Proctor did this and the hanged man fell into a sitting position beside the fallen chair, his legs splayed. The doctor touched a finger to his forehead and the body fell backwards. The crowd pushed forwards for a closer look at the corpse.

I rose and was caught in the movement, having to fight to extricate myself and push a way through to where Cornelius and Fletcher awaited me. They were determined to leave as soon as possible.

The river, I remember, was low and there was great

demand for the small boats now that the proceedings were over. Cornelius insisted on seeking out Henrici and thanking him for his hospitality.

'Thank him for the show, too,' Fletcher told him.

Cornelius left us and I went with Fletcher to find a boat.

As we returned, I looked out over the brown, sluggish water to see our own Station in its entirety. I saw how whitely our distant buildings shone in the fierce sun, saw smoke rising through the trees in unbroken columns into the windless air. I remember then, in that brief moment of calm after all that I had just witnessed and hoped never to see again, asking Fletcher if we ever held our own trials, and him telling me that we didn't, that we no longer possessed the authority. I remember the relief I felt at hearing this, and at leaving the far shore and all that had just happened there behind me, my thoughts then distracted by the flock of birds which rose screaming all around us at our intrusion.

20

Nash spent the next three days preparing his living quarters and unpacking his loads. Cornelius found a recently vacated room for him. Nash went everywhere in the Station, explored the river, our immediate hinterland, visited the quarry, inspected the garrison and our wharves, and throughout all of this he spoke only to our workers, avoiding all mention of Frere, and discouraging all our own approaches to him.

He came to me on the fourth morning without any prior warning. I had only just risen and was washing. It was not yet six, and the cool of the night could still be felt. The smoke of rekindled cooking fires again covered the ground in a low mist.

The deformed boy had spent the night outside my door, and it was upon hearing him being addressed by Nash that I was alerted to the man's presence. I had spent a largely sleepless night, frequently waking in a sweat, as though I were at the start of a small fever. I had seen the boy the previous evening and had asked him what he wanted, but, as at our previous encounter, he had refused to answer me. I felt almost as though he were there to keep guard over me while I slept. It was he who had woken me with a bowl of heated water on the stand beside my bed.

I heard Nash tell him to leave, which he did. A long silence followed before Nash finally knocked and called in to me.

He had recovered well from the rigours of his journey. He was cleanly shaved, and wore a jacket buttoned to the collar.

'I have disturbed you,' he said. 'I can return later.'

I told him to come in while I finished washing. I wore only my trousers and boots. The water in which I doused myself ran over my chest and back. I felt him considering me as I rubbed myself dry.

'I was always told that this was the best part of the day to do business,' he said.

I sensed his urgency to please, to reconcile himself to us following his spurning of our society.

I offered him tea and he accepted.

'I wished to talk to you about Nicholas Frere,' he said.

I was surprised and encouraged by the remark, and then made wary by it.

'You and he seem to have formed a close attachment,' he said. 'You are friends.' He looked around my room as he spoke, his gaze coming to rest on the much-amended map I had pinned to the wall where he sat.

'We were interviewed and employed together,' I said. 'I knew nothing of him before that. But, yes, I would call him my friend.'

'Should this map not be secured in your office?' he said. He leaned closer to the confused scribble of names and markings.

'There is nothing of any commercial interest on it,' I said.

'In your opinion. No matter. Frere.'

'We came out here together,' I said. 'On the *Alpha*.'

'Ah, the *Alpha*. Sold a month ago. Along with the *Corisco*. Crews paid off. The Belgians wanted her. She was of less and less use to the Company. Sold or broken up, she didn't have long left. And her crew were Company men. They'll find work elsewhere.' He spoke as though expecting me to be impressed by his knowledge.

'Work with the Belgians, perhaps,' I said. 'They've closed their fist on everything else.'

'Perhaps. Can we return to Frere? It is my intention to speak to all the Company officers before I interview the man himself. He may have said something to one or other of you that is of some significance in the case.'

Something he may not now repeat to you, you mean, I thought.

'He holds himself wholly responsible for whatever happened,' I said, raising my voice.

'Please. There is no doubt as to the guilt he pleads. I was talking to Abbot, who—'

'Who presumably told you to visit me.'

'I would have come anyway. But, yes, he did tell me you and Frere were close, and that there were other, shall we say, family attachments to be considered.'

'He had no—'

'I visited your quarry yesterday. What a great pity. The place should have ceased operating months ago, years perhaps. I told Abbot as much. It is a waste of his talents, a complete waste.'

'Talents?'

'Abbot is a highly regarded employee. Surely you understand that?'

'He tells us often enough. Or highly regarded because he sends secret reports on everything and everyone here?'

'Secret? They are merely confidential reports. And they are a part of his contractual obligations to us, to the Company. Why do you insist on seeing intrigue and subterfuge where none exists, Mr Frasier?' My title was clearly marked on the Company file he had no doubt already committed to memory.

'And so *will* the quarry finally close?' I asked him.

'Oh, undoubtedly. In fact, I imagine there will be a great many changes in the coming months.'

'And Abbot?'

'Mr Abbot might better serve us were his talents to be deployed elsewhere. Even you must realize that this whole enterprise is not what it once was.' He paused. 'Or even what the Company expected it might become as a concessionary concern.' He spoke as though these disappointments were his own.

'And the rest of us?'

'Why do you ask? You presumably read your contract before you signed it. You seem concerned. Please, there is no need. You are just as valued as Mr Abbot. I promise you, your capabilities and loyalty – ' he glanced again at the map ' – will not be wasted. Perhaps a job on the coast might better suit your own capabilities.'

I understood only too clearly what I was being told, why Frere's name had been mentioned once and never since.

'Is the Company withdrawing completely, has the concession finally been lost?'

'You surely cannot expect me to speculate on matters of such commercial sensitivity, Mr Frasier.' His gaze remained on the map as he spoke, and he smiled broadly before turning back to me.

'And Cornelius and Fletcher?' I said.

'Mr Fletcher has always been something of a

renegade. He would be the first to admit it. His contract expires in seven months. Did you know that?'

I shook my head.

'Then rest assured, he surely did.'

'And Cornelius?'

'Another loyal and long-serving servant. Perhaps he has had enough of this place. Perhaps he would not wish to stay were his present circumstances to change. He is a man somewhat set in his ways.'

'And the best quartermaster the Station has ever known.'

'Perhaps, perhaps not, but is he a man prepared to move with the times? This is the modern age, Mr Frasier; can you honestly say that he lives within it? I imagine he is owed a not inconsiderable pension.'

There was nothing I could say. Everything I had hoped not to be told, I had been told in the space of a few minutes and at my own insistence. He had come to talk about Frere, perhaps to ingratiate himself with me, and instead he had shone that blinding light into the future and showed me everything that lived and did not live there.

I finished dressing.

'Have you seen Nicholas Frere since my arrival?' he said. He had told us on the day of his arrival that we were not to visit the prisoner until he himself had been to see him.

'No, of course not,' I said. It was a half-lie. Following my approach to the garrison four days previously, I had returned to see Frere and to forewarn him of the man he was about to encounter. But upon asking Bone to let me into Frere's cell, Frere called out for me to leave and for Bone to keep the door locked. There was nothing I could call in to him in the presence of Bone, who made a point of standing close to me, better there to savour my discomfort at being treated like this by Frere. I insisted to Frere that I needed to talk to him, but he refused even to answer me.

'Nash told me not to let any of you get even this close,' Bone said. 'None of you.' I knew then – this was his purpose in telling me – that I would have to pay him not to report my visit to Nash.

I looked at Nash now as he considered my answer and wondered if I had given Bone enough.

He said, 'Your sergeant . . .' But speculatively, and left me uncertain of what Bone had or hadn't said, what new pattern all these more recent allegiances were forming.

'Proud and noble warrior,' I said.

'Doubtless employed at a time when these things did not matter. Is he to be trusted?'

'No, but he can be bribed.'

He looked up at the remark. 'I sincerely hope not.'

'It's what you've already heard from Abbot,' I said.

He lowered his head.

'But he will guard Frere well for you,' I said. 'And that's all that matters.'

'I sense some antagonism between the two men.'

'Enough for Bone to take some pride in his role as gaoler.'

'I see. Then perhaps even there I might insist upon some changes.'

I was growing tired of being used as his sounding-board.

'When will you start questioning Frere?' I said.

'As opposed to questioning you, you mean? I intend visiting him later today.'

'Am I permitted to accompany you?'

'Certainly not. My investigation is above all else a confidential one.'

'Then will I be permitted to visit him at other times?'

'I daresay there is little I can do to stop you if your Sergeant Bone is all you say he is.' He paused and smiled. 'And if it will save you money, then, yes, you have my permission to visit the prisoner at times other than when he and I are together.'

I saw, too, how this might later serve his own purpose, but I was powerless to suggest it to him. If a trap had been set for me, then I had helped him to place it, and once in it I could not be seen to struggle to release myself.

'That boy,' he said.

'Boy?'

'The humpback I encountered at your door.'

'He brought my water.'

'He slept there all night. I have encountered him before. Downriver. He was in a boat with an old man. He warned my porters away from the path they were intent on following. Said there had been some fighting and that an ambush might be laid for us. I suspected him of setting one of his own, wretched creature that he is. I made them quiz him on the path he intended us to follow.'

'And did you follow it?'

'I had already decided on it before he appeared. I thought at first, seeing him come towards us, that he was an ape.' He laughed. 'I was within a minute of shooting him, I swear I—'

'But he gave you good advice, it seems.'

'I do not need advice from the likes of him.' He was aware by then, in this further clumsy attempt to ingratiate himself, of having stepped over the divide between us.

'No, of course not.'

He rose at this and carefully set down his cup and

saucer. 'There is nothing you cannot ask me,' he said. 'You, any of you. Anything you wish to know. It is as much a part of my duty here to appraise you of the wider circumstances within which we all find ourselves as it is to determine the facts of the matter relating to Frere.'

I went to the door with him and saw him out, trying to understand what he had hoped to achieve by this encounter, whether the balance of understanding and revelation had swung in his favour or our own.

I watched him as he walked away from me, as though even by this something might be revealed to me. He was a fastidious and a conscientious man; this much had become clear to us. But his methods and intentions were not yet fully revealed, and nor did we fully understand our own lesser roles in the drama he was there to conduct.

He paused at a kuka tree and snapped off several of its lilies, arranging them in his hand as he continued walking.

The boy sat at the centre of the compound, leaning back on his hands so that he might lift his head high enough on his curved spine to look directly at us.

Nash walked to within a few feet of him, looked down at him and then altered his course away from him. The boy watched him go, after which he rose awkwardly from where he sat and half-walked, half-ran towards the river. To me, too, he looked like an ape, running in fright, clumsy and vulnerable, out of the safety of the trees.

The onset of the rain brought everyone inside. I was standing with Cornelius and Abbot in one of our empty warehouses. The last ball of a consignment of old and degraded rubber had just been removed from the building, and the rain doused the fire upon which the rest of the stock had already been burned. The market was over-supplied, and only rubber of the highest quality now fetched a worthwhile price.

Most men ran in the direction of the garrison or compound. There was nothing in the warehouse to keep them busy or entertained until the rain stopped. Others ran beyond the open space into the huts and sheds beyond, where their women waited and where drink was sold. Those working on the boats when the rain came crowded beneath their awnings and looked out at us.

The rain was early. It had been Cornelius's hope to finish burning the rubber before it came, and before Nash arrived to enquire what was happening. The man had so far spent the day with Frere, his second visit.

We were discussing this, and Abbot's fears over the closure of the quarry, when we were joined by Klein, running in from the rain with his jacket over his head, followed a moment later by Perpetua and Felicity. The women walked rather than ran and kept their hands clasped together at their waists, the flame of their conviction protected from the downpour at all costs.

Only then, watching the women, did it occur to me that they had been christened by Klein after the two saints mauled to death by wild beasts. I could only guess at the priest's sour purpose in doing this.

Klein stood in the doorway and cursed. A puddle quickly formed at his feet. It was clear by his unguarded language that he was unaware of our presence in the gloom of the building.

Cornelius had gone to the warehouse to supervise the removal of the rubber, Abbot to estimate the loss to us.

Perpetua and Felicity were the first to see us. Neither woman spoke or otherwise acknowledged us in the presence of Klein, but both stood facing us until he eventually noticed this and he too turned.

There was no avoiding the man in the Station. The crowds of worshippers at his sermons grew ever larger. He taunted and threatened them with notions beyond their understanding, and most evenings were now filled with his execrable hymns, the words of which were surely sung with little understanding of what they meant.

It was common knowledge that Nash had already attended several of these services, and that he and Klein had been seen talking in the brightly lit doorway of the tin chapel.

Klein spent a great deal of time across the river. He was negotiating with the Belgians to build a permanent mission to replace the one he had abandoned at Kirasi. It alarmed Cornelius to hear that this was now in prospect, and he had talked to me of the impossibility of locating and exhuming his daughter's body and re-burying it somewhere closer. It was beyond me to ask him what he had done so far other than make his infrequent visits to the place.

Whenever possible, he still avoided Klein, and on the few occasions he had encountered Perpetua and Felicity without the priest, he had not spoken to them about the man. They knew little of what was happening across the river. Klein told them nothing. They too were distressed by the possibility that Kirasi might now be abandoned, but neither had taken their worries to Klein for fear of being punished by him for interfering in his work.

'Ah, gentlemen,' Klein said, coming towards us. He squeezed the water from his sleeves. Piles of rotted rubber lay strewn across the warehouse floor, and he considered these as he came, careful not to touch any of them, as though they were dung and he was crossing a meadow.

'Cornelius, Mr van Klees,' he said. 'Such a waste.'

'The Company will survive,' Cornelius said.

'I daresay. But all these small losses must surely add up, and someone, no doubt, will be held accountable for them.'

'We are all accountable, Klein.'

'You'll get no argument from me on that score, my friend.'

I saw Cornelius flinch at the word.

Then Klein turned and called for the two women to join him.

They came to us, their faces slick with water. Klein motioned to them and they unclasped their hands and held them out. Rain dripped from each of their splayed fingers.

'I swear they would not have the sense to run inside and protect themselves were I not to instruct them,' Klein said.

The two women stood close to each other, and it was again clear to us that they would not address us directly, that they would not even speak to each other, unless instructed by Klein.

'I'm surprised you're still with us,' Abbot said to Klein. He objected to the supplies we were obliged to give the man under the terms of his lease on the chapel.

'Oh, the Lord's word is wherever I choose to find it, Mr Abbot. Just as yours is. Seek and ye shall find.' He laughed at the remark. He had gained weight during his time at the Station. Word among his congregation was that he was being wined and dined by our competitors so that he might erect his new mission on their side of the river and thereby make it a

229

more attractive place of employment for their own, ever-growing, God-fearing workforce. It was doubtless a tale started by Klein himself, who seemed no closer to securing permission or funding for the place no matter how many times he visited.

On one occasion recently he had been rumoured to have returned late at night drunk, unable to disembark from the boat that carried him without falling into the mud of the bank and then being unable to rise again. The boatman had sent for Perpetua and Felicity, and the two women had sat with Klein and tended to him until dawn, when others of his flock had arrived and carried him to his bed without anyone else having seen him.

'Will you abandon Kirasi completely?' Cornelius asked him. I saw what an effort this was for him.

'Perhaps. The place is falling down anyway. Any new Jerusalem needs to be built here, on the river, closer to the affairs and the hearts of men.'

'Jerusalem,' Cornelius repeated softly.

'Are you concerned for your bastard child's grave? You surprise me, Mr van Klees, you truly do. Leave the child be; she's where she belongs. It was a short and unhappy existence, nothing more. Why do you insist on turning it into the stick with which to constantly beat yourself?'

'It was a simple question,' Cornelius said. He signalled to me to reassure me that he would not rise to the man's goading.

'Ah, is that all it was,' Klein said. 'Then there is nothing I can tell you.' He paused and looked directly at Cornelius. 'Your woman, on the other hand, were you to ask me about that so-called "wife" you once professed to have, then perhaps I might have been able to tell you something more enlightening.'

I saw the alarm come into Cornelius's eyes, like a sudden flash of passing light reflected there.

'He knows nothing,' I said to him.

'Oh?' Klein said. 'Then ask Perpetua here. Ask her if she didn't only a week ago encounter a group of those poor unfortunate women from Port Elys on their way to the colony at Ososo, all degraded and worn out and cast away from the place. Ask her. Or perhaps you believe she too will only lie to you.' He fluttered his hands as though to suggest disinterest, and then he nodded at Perpetua to speak.

'I saw them,' she said. She spoke directly to Cornelius.

Port Elys was renowned for its brothels, for the women it attracted when there was nowhere else left for them to go. It was where, all those years ago, Klein had sent the mother of Cornelius's child. Ososo was the largest leper colony on the river.

'Was Evangeline among them?'

'Ha! Evangeline,' Klein said.

'That was her name.'

'It was what you called her, van Klees, nothing more. And you called her it because it felt better to you that way, because it was better than calling her what she was.'

Cornelius kept his eyes on Perpetua as Klein spoke.

The woman shook her head.

'Then what?'

'There was another woman there, a woman suffering greatly, who asked me if you were still here. She said she had long ago met Evangeline, and that she had asked after you. She had asked this woman to find out if you were still here.'

'If you still existed to haunt her as you once existed to blight her life,' Klein shouted.

'If you were still here,' Perpetua repeated.

'Did you tell her I was?' Cornelius asked her.

'Of course she did. The truth is air, light and warmth to these women.'

Klein grabbed Perpetua by the arm and pulled her back to him. 'Tell him what you told her.'

'I told her that you were still here, that the woman's child still lay at Kirasi, and that you still visited there.'

'Thank you,' Cornelius said.

'Thank you for what?' Klein said. 'She told it all to a woman on her way to Ososo. Do you imagine she was going to be cured there and return to resume her calling at Port Elys, meet this *wife* of yours and tell her the good news? How long do you think they last at Ososo? What, six months, twelve? That's it, my friend – your small and flimsy piece of news has been extinguished.'

Cornelius continued to look at Perpetua. Her eyes averted from Klein seemed to deny what he said and I saw what slender hope Cornelius took from this.

'How long is it?' Klein said, diverting Cornelius from the woman.

'Nine years,' Cornelius said.

'Nine years in Port Elys on her back. How do you imagine a woman can live for so long like that? Or perhaps the passing years are of no consequence to her, not now, not now that she is damned to an eternity of suffering. Perhaps it is only that knowledge which allows her to live with herself and what she has become.' He paused, hoping for some response from Cornelius, and when none came, he went on: 'And never forget this, van Klees, she is there because of her liaison with you, *you*, and for no other reason. You blame me for sending her, for banishing her, but she knew as well as I did, as you did then and do still, that there was no other road open to her. You think the death of her sickly child, your so-called daughter, upset the balance of her mind, but that is only another excuse you make for youself so that you might live with the consequences of your actions.'

I hoped Perpetua might say something more to give Cornelius hope or to divert Klein's provocations from him, even at risk to herself, but she said nothing. I regretted that she had not trusted Cornelius sufficiently to visit him privately with the news, instead of first giving it to Klein to sharpen to this point.

Abbot, who had so far remained silent, said that he thought Cornelius and Klein were behaving disgracefully. Neither man acknowledged him.

Klein pushed Perpetua back to where Felicity waited, her part played.

I began to wonder if her story hadn't been an elaborate lie, one she had been forced into telling by Klein to further antagonize Cornelius.

The rain, which streamed into the building all around us, gradually slowed and then ceased. Men reappeared in the compound outside and resumed their work on the boats. The mound of blackened debris stood like a small black pyramid at the centre of the yard. Cornelius had ordered the balls of rubber to be destroyed out of sight of the compound, but the men entrusted to this had halved their effort by building the fire where its remains now stood.

Klein left us, beckoning Perpetua and Felicity to him as he went.

Abbot, embarrassed to be left alone with Cornelius and myself after what had happened, made a further cold remark about how Cornelius had behaved, and he too went back outside, waiting only until Klein and the women had gone from view before stepping out into the mud.

'Are you all right?' I asked Cornelius.

'Her name is Evangeline,' he said.

'I know,' I told him.

He looked out beyond the flooded compound and the river, a look so hard that he might have believed that if he held the gaze for long enough he would have seen the lost and distant woman looking back at him.

There was nothing more I could say to him, nothing that might reassure or calm him, and certainly nothing that would not now force him to further expose and uselessly re-examine his grief.

I left him where he stood and went to examine the sodden mound of the fire.

21

The following four mornings, Nash rose before any of us and began his interrogation of Frere. We were again told to stay away from the garrison and the gaol while this took place. Even though allowed otherwise, I made no attempt to visit Frere as Nash began his assault upon him.

Each afternoon, Nash returned to his quarters, saw no-one, and spent several hours there transcribing the notes he had taken. It was in all our interests, he repeatedly insisted, that the fullest account possible be kept of these proceedings. He was accomplished in shorthand and promised us that an accurate record was being made of everything that passed between himself and Frere. We would none of us see this record, of course, but we were asked to believe in its integrity.

On the second morning of this questioning, Abbot arrived at the quarry to discover a sealed package on his desk marked confidential. He opened it to find a copy of the quarry's working accounts over the previous eighteen months. Whole swathes of figures had been underlined and circled and dotted with question marks like trees on a map. This was accompanied by a letter from Nash insisting that from that day forward, work in the place be suspended indefinitely. He was acting on orders; no-one was accusing Abbot of mismanagement or falsification.

Abbot spent several hours reading from these accounts and comparing them with his own. The tallies differed endlessly and he was at a loss to understand how these new figures had been calculated, and by whom, and to what end. Some of the pages were signed in verification with the names of shipping agents in Impoko and Stanleyville, our line of dispatch; the Board of the defunct Railway Company had submitted its records of quarry labour used and ballast supplied; other concerns sent in their own reports. For eighteen months, it seemed, others had been at work on these contradictory tallies, and Abbot was stunned by the blow. He insisted to anyone who would listen that he had recorded accurately and honestly all the rock blasted and removed, all the wages for the labour supplied.

He waited until the evening and sought Nash out, taking Fletcher with him to confront the man.

Nash affected surprise at the furore he had caused. He listened to Abbot's outrage and then repeated that neither he nor the directors were accusing Abbot of malpractice, merely pointing out that grave discrepancies existed between labour and cost expended and benefits achieved. What good, he said, was a week of a man's labour, when all there was to show for that labour was a pile of rubble of no use to anyone? It was an unassailable argument where effort and achievement, cost and profitability were all part of the same miserable, deflated equation.

Fletcher said little in Abbot's defence, merely nodding in confirmation or agreement when called upon by Abbot to do so. Nash remained calm throughout. He had been given no other choice but to suspend work at the quarry. It was part of his reason for being there. And yes, he had known from the moment of his own briefing by the Board in London that this drastic course of action was needed and would be taken.

But Abbot continued to rage like a spoilt child. He insisted on re-submitting his own accounts to the Company, and Nash told him he was at perfect liberty to do so, but that he ought to be aware of how this might affect his chances of future employment by the directors. Abbot stopped shouting at this. He was a man who had raced screaming to the edge of a cliff only to find himself with neither the voice nor the energy to take those final steps over its rim. He gathered up his ledgers and left Nash and Fletcher alone.

Fletcher told me afterwards that he had asked Nash about his own position at the Station and that he had learned all he needed to know by Nash's first evasive answer. Nash, he said, was a man who liked to control the pace and direction of the race, and was considerably less certain of himself when issues were forced beyond that control. He told me it was something I would do well to remember.

Having spent the late afternoons writing up his reports, Nash would then feel himself at liberty to wander among us, watching and assessing us as we worked, calculating the web of connections between us, and between ourselves and Frere, and all the time insisting that these encounters were nothing more than coincidental, men socializing, men relaxing after the rigours of their day's labour.

It was clear to us that whatever was happening between himself and Frere, the questioning was proceeding to Nash's satisfaction.

He joined in our discussions and complaints. He

shared our meals and asked us about our lives and pasts and the families we had left behind us. He showed us pictures of his own mother and father and of the fiancée he hoped soon to marry. By 'soon' he meant five years, and he hoped the woman would come out to him when he was settled here. He alone staked his belief in the woman's devotion and patience.

This suggestion that he saw his own future in the place – Naiyasha and Tanaland were the places he mentioned – surprised us; we had imagined him returning to London when he was done with us, imagined only ourselves wandering aimlessly into the void of his absence and recommendations. He would become a gentleman farmer, he said, and a Colonial administrator. The coming years, the new century, would see a need for men like him.

Abbot surprised me by sitting late into the night with the man; I saw how quickly he had learned to tack into those same favourable passing winds, and listening to his feigned interest in everything Nash now said was as painful as listening to the secrets of any pathetic man.

Before leaving him, I asked Nash how long he thought his interrogation of Frere would last, and instead of telling me it was none of my business, as I had expected, he said casually that he would not be seeing Frere for three or four days. He saw my surprise at this, and said he needed time to reflect on what he had already been told. He would say no more.

'Go and see him,' he said off-handedly, turning back to Abbot, to the bottle and glasses which stood between them. 'I assure you, he will complain of no mistreatment from me.'

Outside, I heard their shared laughter. I wondered at the speed of Abbot's change of heart, at what reassuring glimpses of his own future he yet hoped to secure.

*   *   *

I encountered Bone standing on a high bank over-looking the swollen river. Small islands raced down-river, whole trees with their families of apes and flocks of roosting birds intact.

It was mid-morning, a time when I would have expected him to be occupied at the garrison.

He looked up at my approach, but made no effort to leave. I sensed his resentment at something before he spoke.

'Nash?' I said.

He spat into the water beneath him. His few teeth were darker than ever, and when he chewed or opened his mouth, his whole face took on a faintly imbecilic look.

' "Make the most of what little time remains to you here, Sergeant Bone," ' he said.

'You, too,' I said.

Without warning, he drew out his pistol and fired at a passing branch upon which sat a solitary bird. The shot missed, and the branch and bird were soon out of range.

'Have you been present at his questioning?' I asked him.

'Guarding him, you mean? I offered, but he said he needed no guard. Heard most of it, though. He couldn't keep me from sitting outside, not in the garrison. He said he might take Frere back to the compound with him, but I soon put him right on that one. Said he had authorization, but didn't have it with him. I told him the only "authorization" I needed to see was the letter telling him to send Frere down to the coast to be hanged.'

'What did he say to that?' I did my best not to sound too interested, but he saw through this.

'Wouldn't you like to know,' he said.

I offered him my tobacco pouch and he took a handful from it and stuffed it in his pocket.

'You seem convinced it's what's going to happen,' I said.

'Not really. Put it another way – you're the only one left with half an idea it *won't* happen.' He laughed at his cleverness, but whereas in the past he might have continued to play to this small advantage, he said nothing more and turned back to look out over the river. If it had been anyone other than Bone, I would have described his mood as contemplative.

'He told me he knew I'd taken money,' he said.

'From me?'

'From anybody I could get it from. He said I'd "misappropriated" supplies, whatever that means, and that I'd neglected my duties here.'

'He's swinging his stick at all of us,' I said.

'He had my bloody contract with him. "Three months, Sergeant Bone, three months." He wanted to know what kind of real work I considered myself capable of.' He fired his pistol again, but this time only at the passing water.

'Will you go back to the coast? Home?'

He shrugged, unwilling even to consider all he was about to lose.

'And in the middle of all this there's him and Frere like a pair of bloody lords sitting together in their club.'

'Oh?'

'You'd think he'd come out here to pin a medal on the man instead of fit him up for a rope.'

'They're both educated, civilized men,' I said coldly, hoping to suggest some sympathy for his position, some false alliance between us.

'Aren't we all?' he said. 'Not educated, but civilized.

We're all civilized.' He turned to me for the first time. 'You must feel a bit left out of it, you and Frere being such friends, and all.'

'Not really.'

He laughed. ' "Not really." Who are you fooling? You'd pay a shilling a word to know what passed between them.'

'Once, perhaps.'

'No – now. Don't worry. It won't cost you that much.'

'I imagine Nash must find it hard work,' I said.

'Nothing of the sort. Every question he asks, Frere answers. The pair of them are at it for hours on end.'

'Questions about what?'

'About everything, about all this, this place, about you lot, about me.' He slapped himself on the chest.

'And Frere answers him willingly?'

'Tells him everything. Can't tell him enough. What you think, reckon he's seen a chance to save himself?'

I doubted this. That would amount to salvation – something it was beyond Nash to offer, and even further beyond Frere to accept.

'Spent all the first morning talking about that useless hole in the ground, what happened there. Then about the wharves, about trade there, about the rubber, about them across the river.'

'But nothing about Frere leaving us?'

'Oh, all that came later. Where he went, why he went, what he saw, what he did.' He stopped abruptly.

'And did you overhear all that, too?'

He considered this for a moment before shaking his head. 'It's where Nash left off. He's not stupid. He wants everything else first before Frere finally tells him and then falls dumb on him.'

I saw the sense in what he suggested.

'So you think he's building up to asking him what he did?'

'About the girl he killed.'

'Is *alleged* to have killed.'

'Still can't bring yourself to even think it of him, can you? You'd believe it of me, but not him. And what if it was more than killing her he had a hand in, what then, what else wouldn't you force yourself to face up to?'

I remained silent. He, too, said nothing for several minutes.

A steamer passed us going upriver, its stern paddle working hard against the current, churning up a spray of dirty water and making hardly any progress. Men at the prow fended off the larger pieces of floating vegetation with poles. I saw the master standing in the wheel-house, his face fixed ahead of him. It was a foolish journey to attempt so soon after the rain.

'He's going nowhere fast,' Bone said, taking pleasure in the vessel's struggle. He aimed his pistol at the man and said, 'Bang.'

'Do you imagine Nash is aware that you can overhear him with Frere?' I said.

'He knows everything else. He doesn't strike me as a man who ever left anything to chance in his life.'

So, presumably, he knew that Bone would in turn repeat what he had heard.

'Must worry you,' he said.

'What must?'

'Knowing that when the time comes, Frere's going to talk about what he did in exactly the same way he's been talking about everything here.'

'If you say so.'

'If I say so. Face it – he's desperate for it, aching to tell Nash everything that happened.'

'So why should *I* find that worrying?'

242

'Because he's ready and willing to do it for Nash and he never would for you, his so-called friend. He'll tell the man with the rope, but not the man who might have helped him away from it all.'

'You overestimate my powers.'

'I know. But don't lie and tell me it isn't what you once thought you'd do. You think he keeps it all separate, all away from us by telling that stuffed shirt and not the rest of us?'

'I imagine it's what Frere wants, what he believes, and that he has his reasons for doing it.' It was a weightless answer.

'Then he's wrong. This is all going to come crashing down whatever Nash gets to hear or not hear. Frere's going to tell him everything and then get handed over to the clever niggers and they're going to hang him. He'll be theirs, a present from us to them, something to let them know we think they'll be as good at running the place as we were. We all know different, but that's not going to be said, is it? A million of them for every one of us.' He looked into his dirt-encrusted palm as though every part of this simple understanding lay revealed to him there. 'Nash is just here to wrap him up and hand him over,' he said.

The boat at the centre of the river abandoned its struggle and turned in an awkward curve towards the far shore. The current on our side bit into the bank and scoured it away. The slanting piles of our damaged jetty had been lost several days ago. Traders were beginning to complain that others among our moorings were unsafe.

'Fletcher tell you about our attack?' Bone said.

'Attack?'

'One of my men. Clayton. Shot in the bloody head. Arrow. Nigger sitting up a tree. Fired straight down at

243

him.' He pressed a finger down the side of his face and into his neck.

'Where? Why?'

'About half a mile inland. Been to see some woman or other. Never heard a thing. Just shot from above. Inch to one side and it would have been through his skull. As it is, he's going to have a six-inch scar and mumble his words for the rest of his life. Fletcher not tell you?'

'I haven't seen him recently,' I lied.

'Happened two days ago. Perhaps he doesn't think it's important, not with everything else that's going on.'

I wondered if he was going to make more of this, but he seemed unconcerned by the event.

'Do you know why he was attacked?'

'Who knows. Most of their crops have gone. Perhaps they're just getting brave, perhaps that's it.'

'I didn't realize anyone hereabouts was hostile towards us.'

'One day they aren't, next day they are.'

'Perhaps Clayton did something to upset whoever attacked him.'

'I wouldn't put it past him. He's one for the women. And he's not choosy.' He grinned at the suggestion.

'Was anything done to try and apprehend the man responsible?'

'What's the point? He was long gone by the time Clayton got back to us with his face all cut up and the arrow still sticking in his neck. This long.' He stretched his thumb and forefinger to indicate the dart.

'Do you still have it?' I asked him.

'Clayton does. Why?'

'Frere might be able to identify it.'

'Him? What good is he to any of us now? Forget

it. The next nigger Clayton sees and there's nobody looking, he'll be the one who fired it.'

'That would be unadvisable,' I said.

He turned and laughed at me in disbelief.

'I mean it,' I said.

'So what?' He looked away to watch the distant boat approach the far shore. A large number of other vessels had already gathered there. A small white cloud hung above a boat off-loading crushed talcum.

Finally, Bone rose from where he sat.

'Anything you want me to pass on to Frere?' he said.

I shook my head.

'Thought not. Not much left for any of us to say to him, is there? Suppose he might as well get used to that.'

He left me, whistling loudly as he went from the open ground into the trees. He still held his pistol, and now he pointed it ahead of him as he walked.

Beneath me, the river undermined an overhang, and I watched as a length of the bank was cut away, roots and soil falling into the current, darkening it briefly, and obscuring even further the restless boundary between the earth and the water.

I finally went to see Frere. I waited until mid-afternoon, knowing that Nash, if he too had been to the gaol, would have finished his questioning by then.

I was surprised to see Frere outside, at the centre of the garrison yard with Bone. The two men stood close in conversation. Frere was the first to see me, over Bone's shoulder, but he made no acknowledgement; instead, he pulled Bone closer to him and continued talking, and only as I approached to within a few feet of them did Bone finally turn to face me. He leaned closer to Frere's ear and whispered something to him, at which Frere nodded in agreement. Frere then took out a handful of coins and tipped these into the pocket Bone held open for him. Seeing this transaction, and the hurried exchange which preceded it, there was no doubt in my mind that my arrival was welcomed by neither man.

After pocketing the money, Bone made a great play of holding out his hand to Frere and shaking Frere's own for longer than was necessary. The energy was all Bone's.

Following this, he held out his other, disfigured hand to me, as though I too played some unknowing part in their conspiracy, but as I raised my own hand, more in surprise than with intent, Bone laughed and took back his own. He considered me for a moment and then walked away. Several of his men, the wounded Clayton among them, sat in the garrison doorway.

'Were you paying him for news?' I asked Frere, giving him his answer, and avoiding any embarrassment between us when he refused to tell me more directly what he had paid for.

'For what he tells me. I don't work too hard to separate the "news" from the rumours and sundry tale-telling. It helps me to stand a little more steadily at the calm centre of things and imagine I still have some control over what's happening.'

'He's selling it in both directions,' I said.

'I know. I think you underestimate our Sergeant, James.'

'Oh?'

'Truly. I envy him the simple, straightforward way he has of looking at things.' He rubbed his thumb and forefinger together.

'He considers himself first and foremost, and anyone else hardly ever,' I said.

'Precisely. You and I, James, we step back to take in the whole canvas; Bone, however, goes directly to the small, poorly painted figure in the bottom corner, sees himself, and disregards everything else.'

'I don't see how that could be thought of as enviable.'

He walked ahead of me. We resumed unheard at the centre of the space. The voices of Bone and his men came to us distorted through the heat.

'You know, of course, that Nash has been to see me and started his work.'

'We all—'

'And that it is his policy to start from a distance and circle me in ever-decreasing circles, that he resists all my attempts to draw him into me more quickly.'

'Is that what you want?'

'Not necessarily. I merely object to having to comply to his own timetable, to make everything fit so neatly into his own plan of events.' He smiled. 'Almost as though his report were already written and I were merely adding my initials to each printed page.'

'So you still see that broader picture, then?'

'I saw it the instant I came round and saw Hammad's men staring down at me and felt my hands and feet tied.'

'I'm sorry,' I said. 'Did Bone tell you about Nash closing the quarry?'

'I imagine Abbot will soon find some new purpose in life.'

I told him about the understanding which now seemed to exist between the two men.

Afterwards, when he had made his own assessment of what was happening at the quarry, he said, 'Nash has a great deal more to do here than prepare me for dispatch to the coast.'

A month ago, a week even, I might have felt an

impulse to deny what he said, but standing with him there, I said nothing, and this appeared to relax him, knowing that I had begun to accept the unacceptable.

'Did Bone tell you about his man who was attacked?' I said.

'No. Attacked how?'

I told him what Bone had told me the previous day. He was concerned by the news, treating it as though it were not an isolated incident of revenge, but rather something he had been anticipating. He asked me if there had been any reports of other attacks. I said I hadn't heard of any, and he told me to ask the traders and boatmen if they had encountered anything similar. I promised him I would.

I had with me several nine-month-old newspapers I had acquired from an indigo trader earlier that morning, and I gave them to him. Like the rest of us, he had long since learned to live out of step with the world, but he thanked me for them as though they contained that morning's news and it was all good.

It had not been my purpose for visiting him, but I had a sudden desire to ask him if he wanted me to let Caroline know what was happening to him. I would not relate the matter in all its speculative detail, of course, but I might at least suggest something of his situation to her. My last letter to her, written ten days after his disappearance, would still be a month away from her, and I gained some reassurance from seeing how this dislocation worked in reverse. He would be hanged and buried and his grave overgrown and she might still be writing to me to ask me about our specimen-collecting adventures together. I felt a sudden chill at the awful task which lay ahead of me.

I was diverted from all this by Frere remarking aloud on something he read. I half-listened to him and half-answered his questions as he went on talking to me. After several minutes of this, he stopped, folded the papers and pushed them under his arm. I walked with him further from the watching men.

'In three days' time, Nash intends to quiz me on my disappearance – my desertion and dereliction of duty – and my crime.' He raised his hand to prevent me from speaking. 'Until then I must live in this limbo. I am prepared to accommodate him and adhere to his plan. It is how he works. I understand that. And in understanding that, I consider myself to have some small advantage over him. It is not what another man might consider to be an advantage – I am still condemned – and it may be a very short-lived advantage – he will learn all he needs to know in a single hour of quizzing me – but, nevertheless, it is how I choose to see it: an advantage. Put crudely, I know something he does not; I know something it is his duty to learn, and that one question and its answer define his whole being. I know he has interests elsewhere, and that he involves himself in those wherever possible, now here and soon elsewhere, but at the very centre of him lies what I must tell him and what he must learn. Do you understand what I'm telling you, James?'

I nodded.

'And you do not need to tell me how fragile and possibly worthless that power is, how illusory and deceptive it may yet prove to be. It will not save me; it will not redeem me; it will not remove me from Nash's blessed plan. But while I possess it, it is all I possess. Do you understand that, too?'

I told him I did.

He had raised his voice to tell me all this, and a fleck of blood had appeared at the side of his mouth. He touched this gently with his fingertip, studied it briefly and then wiped his lips with his palm. Whatever illness afflicted his gums and tongue, remained. I remarked on it, but he said he was still treating it, though with little effect.

He had told me what he wanted to tell me and I felt a great relief at having heard him after so long being refused and denied by him. After all that time, I felt as I had felt being in his company during our first months together.

Then, as though he had earlier read my dark thoughts, he said, 'Do you hear from Caroline at all?'

'Nothing. Nothing since all this . . .'

'I suppose that is to be expected.'

'Nor have I written anything concerning any of this to her,' I said, knowing that this was his true question.

'I'm grateful,' he said. 'I spend most of my time when Nash is absent composing long letters of my own. I hoped you might take charge of them and ensure—'

'Of course,' I said.

Then he took a deep breath and said, 'I think of her often.' But no more, as though those five words were to convey to me a whole day's conversation filled with remembering and longing – a thousand words, a hundred thousand, where the same few, simple things were to be said over and over again in their variant forms, just as they were said over and over again in all good conversations made endless by excitement and savoured by each participant.

'I know you do,' I told him, and I too could say no more.

We remained silent after that, walking absently towards the garrison wall. It was as we reached this that we heard shouting behind us and saw Bone gesticulating in our direction from the shade of the buildings.

'I've strayed too far,' Frere said. He embraced me and thanked me again for the newspapers. 'Please, let me return alone. Tell Cornelius to avail himself of anything of mine that Nash has not already taken as evidence.'

It was beyond me to tell him that Cornelius would have cared little for the offer, that for most of the time he now kept himself apart from us as the nightfall of his own future descended around him.

'He sends his best wishes,' I said.

'Tell him his medicines are working.'

I saw how each of these small gestures and remarks was a gesture or remark of detachment. More blood had appeared at the corner of his mouth, but this time he made no attempt to remove it.

I left him by the gate in the garrison wall and he returned to the gaol. I watched to see if Bone might once again approach him, but Frere entered the building alone and was lost to me the instant he stepped from the light into its impenetrable shade.

22

The following day I was distracted from my work by the sound of gunfire coming from upriver, and I went outside to investigate. Fletcher and Cornelius had heard it too and had left their own work. The shooting continued. Cornelius suggested that the commotion was coming from the quarry, and Fletcher ran to fetch a rifle. He returned with two, and offered the second to me. But I refused it, and the weapon was taken by Cornelius. Fletcher told me that if I insisted on being unarmed, then there was no point in me accompanying them. He ran ahead of us out of the compound. It was beyond Cornelius to run any distance, and so he and I followed at a slower pace.

There was a break in the shooting as we went, but it resumed as we left the river and passed into the trees beyond. There was by then little doubt that the noise was coming from the quarry.

It was three days since Nash had ordered the digging to cease. I did not know for certain what had happened since then, but I assumed Abbot would have dispersed the diggers and concentrated on completing his accounts of the place and preparing a Statement of Closure for the Company.

Cornelius was quickly out of breath and we frequently stopped for him to rest. There were now longer periods when the shooting fell intermittently silent. There was no real pattern to the noise, but amid it we could now hear an occasional human yell or scream.

We emerged from the forest onto the broad track which led from the workings to the river. Ahead of us, Fletcher crouched behind a mound of the salvaged pipes. He motioned for us to join him, looking hard at Cornelius, who gasped for air, and whose face was red and slick with sweat. Fletcher took the rifle from him and gave it back to me. More for Cornelius's sake than his, I took it without argument.

I asked him if he had identified the source of the shooting, and as though in answer to this, a fusillade rang out ahead of us.

'Whatever it is, they're *our* rifles,' he said. He searched over the top of our cover and then slowly rose. Emboldened by the weapon I held, I rose beside him.

Ahead of us lay the rim of the quarry. A group of men stood there and these were the shooters. A short distance away stood the overseer's hut and another man stood beside this. I recognized Abbot. I started to raise my hand to him, but Fletcher grabbed my arm and forced it down.

'They're Bone's men,' he said. He, too, looked to where Abbot stood apart from the riflemen. 'The bloody idiot,' he said.

'What?'

Cornelius rose beside me and stood looking at the quarry. He wiped his face, but this had little effect on the wetness that constantly formed there. Fletcher told him to stay where he was and to keep anyone else who arrived with him. He was still holding my arm, and he pulled me alongside him as we approached the riflemen.

Mid-way between our cover and the men, he called out to them. I pulled myself free of him. At first no-one heard him, but then a single man turned and pointed.

'Hold up your rifle,' Fletcher told me.

I copied him.

He called out again, identifying himself.

I did the same.

Several others turned in our direction. Some pointed their weapons at us, but then saw who we were and lowered them. Others among them continued to aim and fire away from us, but as we approached closer to them I saw that they were not shooting at specific targets, merely firing out over the void of the quarry. Some of them held their rifles in the air and fired.

I looked for Bone among them, but he was not present.

As we approached the quarry rim, Abbot left the shelter of the hut and came towards us. He was holding a pistol, but I saw by the way his hand shook that he was unlikely to have fired it. It was the first time I had ever seen him with a weapon. I imagine he looked at me in much the same way.

Fletcher called for the shooters to stop. There was a strong smell of powder and the sooty haze of shooting all around us.

'They went crazy, went wild,' Abbot said. 'No reason, no reason at all. They would have attacked us. I had to do something, they went wild, no reason at all.'

One of the men continued firing into the quarry until Fletcher stopped him by knocking the rifle from his hands. The man resented this and made his feelings clear to us.

'Who went wild?' Fletcher said.

'Them, they did, the workers.' Abbot gestured with his pistol towards the quarry rim.

Fletcher went closer to it and looked down into the workings below. He indicated for me to join him.

Beneath us, in a group on the quarry floor, pressed to the sheer face above which we stood, were several hundred of the workers, barely distinguishable from the mounds of rock and rubble amid which they tried to hide and shield themselves.

Abbot came to us, but was careful to remain further back from the edge.

'Who sent for the garrison?' Fletcher asked him.

'I brought them with me in case of just such an eventuality.'

'What eventuality?'

'When I told them that work here was being stopped. It was as though they didn't believe me. They started to complain that it was all they had, that their crops had failed, that they needed the quarry money. I told them it had nothing to do with me, but they wouldn't listen to reason. They were going to smash everything up, I know they were. They wanted blood, they would have killed me.'

'And let me guess,' Fletcher said. 'You waited until they were all down there before making your announcement from somewhere you considered yourself safe.'

'I considered it prudent to keep myself at some distance from them, yes. Look at them, you can see what they're like, you know what they are.'

I looked back down at the terrified men, the bravest of whom were then emerging from the quarry wall to stand further out now that the shooting had stopped. I looked elsewhere in the workings to see if there were any more. Individual figures emerged and congregated together. I saw where one man, possibly wounded, was helped to his feet by several others.

Fletcher told the riflemen to move back from the edge. He told Abbot to return to the hut and to retrieve whatever he needed to take back with him to the Station. Abbot told several of the riflemen to help him, and they went reluctantly.

'Why no Bone?' I said to Fletcher.

'I imagine Bone has enough dirt on his Company-owned hands without getting involved in any of this.'

We stood for several minutes longer looking down at the men below us. If the man I had watched being helped had been wounded, then it did not prevent him from walking. Fletcher called down to them to ask if anyone was hurt, and a chorus of complaints rose up to us.

Abbot returned with the men carrying his packages. Fletcher told them all to go back through the trees. He told Cornelius to accompany them, and then he and I waited at the rim as we were left alone.

The men beneath us had fallen largely silent. They had formed into groups, and most were now sitting. A solitary man called up to us, indicating the steep path which led up the quarry face. Fletcher motioned for him to come up.

'I know him,' he told me, as the man finally climbed to the rim and approached us.

He spoke to us in broken English, complaining that Abbot had allowed them all to complete four hours' work before announcing that the quarry was to close, flanked by the riflemen as he did so. They had started shooting at the first murmur of complaint from the workers. Many of them had not been paid for their past month's work and Abbot had also announced that there was now little chance of this happening.

'He means no chance whatsoever,' Fletcher told him.

The man knew this. He left us and made his way back down to his silent companions below.

'Abbot,' Fletcher said, and shook his head.

The men below rose and gathered slowly around the solitary emissary, like filings shaping themselves to an irresistible magnet.

I watched them closely, expecting some new uproar at what they were being told. But there was nothing, and when the man had finished speaking, those surrounding him withdrew and scattered. Their anger, it seemed, had turned to resignation in an instant.

Fletcher left the rim and I followed him back to the Station.

At the edge of the trees he turned and looked back at the quarry. The first of the workers had already climbed the walls and had gathered there, more shapes than men, and they all watched us go. Others struggled up through the mud to join them. Some pointed at us; others wandered aimlessly amid the abandoned machinery; and a group of them went to the empty shed and beat upon its tin door until it buckled and fell open.

I asked Fletcher if he thought they might follow us, but he simply shrugged. I walked close beside him until we re-entered the trees. Once inside them, he occasionally paused, raised a finger to his lips and turned slowly to search in a full, close circle around us, and though I did not say it, I sensed that we were observed – if not by the quarry men, then by some silent, watching others – along the whole of our route.

*   *   *

Two days later, I was interrupted by a single perfunctory rap on my door, followed immediately by Amon coming into the room.

'Please, come in,' I said.

He looked at me, barely able to contain whatever it was he had come to tell me. There was never anything unprepared, unrehearsed about a visit by Amon.

'I interrupt you,' he said.

'Of course you do.' In truth, I had been doing little other than embellishing my finished charts, more often than not filling them far beyond their requirements. For all the good I did, I might just as well have been Ptolemy drawing his spouting whales on interminable, unfathomable oceans, or drawing his never-seen elephants according to the descriptions of others on his thousand-square-mile blanks of jungle or desert or plain.

Amon came to the desk and looked over my shoulder, turning his head from side to side to better understand what he saw.

'The Ma'ata,' he said eventually.

'Possibly,' I said. I was in no mood for his strategies.

'A very profitable river, the Ma'ata,' he said. 'The people there are very trusting. They jump out of the forest and into our boats.'

'I'm sure they do,' I said.

He lifted a corner of the map to study the one which lay beneath it – the one upon which I had spent hours in the night trying to determine the course of Frere's wanderings away from us – and I slammed my hand down on his so that he might look no further.

He considered my reaction for a moment before withdrawing his hand, touching it to his lips as though to kiss away some pain, and then folding his arms across his chest.

'Is there something I can do for you?' I said.

'You? For me?'

'I assumed you were here on behalf of your lord and master.'

'I have come in advance of him,' he said, and he straightened slightly in recognition of the duty he performed.

'We're honoured,' I said. 'Once again, Hammad deigns to visit us here.'

He shook his head at the remark.

'What did he send you ahead to tell us?'

'Nothing. Merely to forewarn you of his arrival and to give you time to prepare yourselves.'

'Prepare ourselves for what?'

'For his—'

'Arrival. You said.'

'Your manner is both puzzling and offensive,' he said.

I refused to be drawn. If Hammad *was* coming, then anything else Amon had been told to impart to us, he would tell us well before the slaver's appearance. He was a bell rung in summons, and that was all.

One of the first tales I had heard of Hammad on coming here was that, upon reading a biography of Alexander the Great, he had stood outside the walls of Sokolo on the edge of the Sahara, had looked out over the expanse there and had wept. Just as Alexander had wept, gazing down from his mountain top and realizing there were no new worlds left for him to conquer. Cornelius had told me the story, adding that Hammad had wept because he knew he could not maintain his routes of supply over so vast and inhospitable an area on his slave-gathering forays. That, and the fact that the desert was so sparsely populated, and its people so evasive and fearsome, that attempting to enslave them would cost him too dear while others elsewhere continued to behave more compliantly, or were at least more easily and cheaply subdued.

Another story told to me by Cornelius concerned Hammad and the punishment he meted out to a garrison of slaves awaiting auction in Kabinda thirty years ago, some of whom had freed themselves from their chains and had attempted to escape. Several of the men were quickly captured and killed where they were found, but others – the number varied from a handful to a hundred – escaped. Seething at this, and wanting to quash all further attempt at revolt, Hammad had assembled his human cargo in its entirety and ringed them with armed men. He had then announced to all these gathered slaves that in Ancient Rome it had been the habit of the emperors to punish a defeated army by killing one in every ten of its beaten survivors. This, he said, as calmly as though he were announcing the arrival of a ship or the departure of a caravan the following morning, was what he now intended to do with those men who had not attempted to escape, but who might, encouraged by the success of the others, have considered making the attempt in the future. There was a great outcry at this and several of the chained men were shot where they sat on the ground. Hammad explained how the act of decimation worked, and said the only problem now was where to start counting from. It would be far too simple, he said, too predictable, to begin at the end of one row of men, count along it and then switch to another. Far too simple. Instead, he would bring in a priest, who would consider the eyes of each of the hundreds of men, and if he saw evil there, or resentment, or even anger, then that man would be chosen.

The upshot of the story was that in excess of fifty men were delivered to Hammad by his tame priest and these men were killed, one by one, in full view of the others, by being beheaded.

I was diverted from these thoughts by Amon who, having picked up a bottle of mapping ink, then dropped it, careful not to spill any of the liquid on my maps or desk, but for the bottle to spill only onto the floor. He considered this spreading stain for a moment before drawing his foot over it.

'I came,' he said, 'because Hammad is here to see Mr Nash. He has evidence he feels he needs to present to him.'

'The torn pages,' I said.

He studied the sole of his boot, but with no concern for the stain there or on the floor. 'Perhaps. I don't know. Whatever it is, he felt that he might be of great assistance in the enquiry. Apart from which—' He stopped abruptly, conscious, perhaps, of having exceeded his duties.

'What?'

He looked back at the open doorway. From there he was able to see directly across the compound to the river. There was no sign of Hammad. A low mist lay over the river, belying the motion of the water beneath it.

'Tell me,' I said. I picked up the empty bottle and stood it on the table.

'There have been communications with Stanleyville and the coast.'

'Concerning Frere?'

'Frere? No, concerning Hammad.'

'Communications saying what?'

'Informing him of the changes taking place, offering him—' He stopped again.

'Offering him a position in some new government, some new legislature, what? Are the Belgians selling us out again?'

'The word is that Hammad will become Minister for the Interior.' He said the words slowly, rising to their capitals.

I concealed my surprise at the notion.

'And so, naturally, he wishes to do all he can to assist Nash with his enquiry,' I said.

'Don't we all? A great crime has been committed. Who among us would wish to see such a crime go unpunished?'

'Perhaps Hammad could also become Minister for Law and Order. Perhaps he might one day even be crowned emperor.'

I saw by the way Amon considered these remarks that the same had already been suggested to him, perhaps by Hammad himself.

'And what will that mean?' I said. 'Minister for the Interior?'

'Mean?'

'What will his duties and responsibilities be?'

It was something he had not considered. My own assessment was that Hammad would continue to operate exactly as before, but that now all his operations would be cloaked in legitimacy, that he might even be shielded and aided by his new power and authority.

'More importantly,' I said, 'what will all these grandiose changes mean for *you*? Where will *you* stand when the emperor is crowned?'

'Me? I am his right-hand man.'

'A hand can be chopped off.'

'My services . . . I am indispensable to Hammad.'

You are his monkey on a rope now, I thought, and

you will be his monkey on a rope in his new court. Or perhaps once garlanded and crowned with all this new power, Hammad might wish to sever himself from those parts of his past trailing and shadowing him into his new life, into his new reign. I suggested none of this to Amon. I didn't need to; I saw that he too was making those same silent assessments.

'When is he expected?' I said.

'Noon.'

It was not yet ten o'clock.

We spent the remainder of the morning together, and I tried to determine what Hammad was going to reveal to Nash regarding Frere.

'He'll tell Nash nothing Frere himself will not readily admit to,' I said.

'He knows that. He knows your Mr Frere is an honourable man, a man who succumbed, perhaps in a moment of delirium or madness, to a grave error of judgement. Or perhaps a man who imagined that he could do what he did and that he would afterwards be neither apprehended nor punished for it. Perhaps he believed that living in such a corrupt and lawless place . . . Or, perhaps, as you say, he is already condemned by his own confession. However, I imagine the testimony of others might have an even greater weight in these proceeedings – in Mr Nash's investigation – than the confession of a man whom some might argue had lost the balance of his mind, a man who might not have known what he was doing, what he imagined he had done. There are some very clever lawyers, English lawyers, down on the coast. I am surprised your own employers have not appointed someone to act in his defence.'

The thought had long since occurred to me – as it must have done to the others, and to Frere himself –

but I refused to reveal my feelings on the matter to Amon. Everything that was said to him would undoubtedly be repeated to Hammad on their return journey together.

Approaching midday, there was a growing commotion in the compound and at the jetties, and Hammad's steamer was closely watched throughout its short crossing. It was a powerful vessel and the strong current diverted it little as it came. I saw that it had been festooned with bunting and flags, and the master sounded his whistle every few seconds throughout the crossing. I knew that Hammad would not come without some further, louder announcement of his arrival, but I saw something more in all this noise and colour and flapping of flags: I saw a man already celebrating his endless good fortune, already flexing the first new muscle of his coming authority.

Amon insisted we went down to the river to be present when Hammad docked.

As I locked the door on my charts, he asked me not to repeat to Hammad anything he had told me. I told him I would say nothing, and in that simple exchange I saw that he was already preparing his own strategy of withdrawal from the man.

Neither Cornelius nor Fletcher came to the river. Only Abbot arrived, uncertain what was happening, why the crowd of traders and natives had appeared.

We saw Hammad emerge from his cabin to stand at the prow of the steamer as it slowed and manoeuvred towards the shore. He gave no indication of having seen us, looking instead to either side of us and to the men who gathered around us.

'He was hoping Mr Nash would be here to greet him.'

'Were you meant to have told Nash?'

'I shall say he was busy with Frere and needed to prepare himself before the two of them met.'

As usual, Hammad had used the opportunity of crossing the river to bring trade goods with him, and his men leaped into the shallows and began unloading these long before Hammad himself disembarked.

Amon went immediately to him and made his excuses for Nash. Hammad walked quickly into the compound, causing Amon to run to keep up with him.

And then Hammad saw me and altered his course.

'I appreciate your presence,' he said. 'No doubt Amon has told you everything.'

'That you wish to present your evidence to Nash, yes.'

'Not *my* evidence, Mr Frasier, for I was not present to see anything.'

'The pages,' I said.

'Them? What do they prove? The ramblings of a madman.'

'Perhaps. You still took them.'

'Stole them, yes.' He laughed.

Amon, I saw, stood well beyond his reach.

'You seem tired,' Hammad said to me.

'I'm busy, working hard.'

'Of course.' He continued to look around us.

The few boats at our wharves were empty and waiting for loads which promised to come, but never did. Men from the quarry now squatted in makeshift shelters erected against most of our buildings. The compound remained rutted and pocked with its dried mud, and the black pile of burned rubber still stood beside the warehouse.

'Of course,' Hammad repeated. He said something to Amon in Arabic and the agent ran back to the steamer on an errand.

'The man has such a tongue,' Hammad said, as much to himself as to me, glancing over his shoulder at the running figure.

'He's told me nothing,' I said, knowing immediately it was the wrong thing to have said.

'Of course he didn't. What does he know?'

'We do hear of these things,' I said.

'Of course you do.'

Amon ran along the wharf and climbed aboard the steamer.

He reappeared a few minutes later accompanied by another man. At first this second man seemed reluctant to come with him, having occasionally to be held by Amon as they returned to us. The man wore only a loincloth, and a rag fastened round his neck. His eyes were circled black, his teeth filed to points, and one of his arms and the opposing leg were painted white.

Hammad considered him as he came.

Amon stopped at his usual distance from Hammad and the man stood close beside him.

I recognized him then. He was the feather-gatherer. He had grown flabby during his time with Hammad, his cheeks and chins bloated by recent good living. He seemed embarrassed to be considered by me, and in the presence of Hammad he trembled where he stood.

'I told him to appear as he appeared to Frere on the day he saved your friend's life and was so cruelly rewarded for the act,' Hammad said. 'Otherwise he would have presented himself to Nash scrubbed clean and wearing a linen suit.'

'Did he take much persuading?' I said.

Hammad laughed at this. 'He is a remarkably compliant man.'

'I can imagine.'

'Then can you also imagine what he has to say to

Mr Nash, how valuable his testimony will prove to be?'

Men from the steamer threw bundles of tobacco leaf from the boat to the jetty, and seeing them roll together there I could think of nothing other than those fifty severed heads. Hammad saw that my attention had wandered from him, and he, too, turned to look. He called for the men throwing the bundles to be more careful with them. He beckoned the feather-gatherer towards him, and the man came with his arms half raised, as though expecting to be struck.

'Imagine the distress of Mr Frere at being discovered by such a heathen,' Hammad said. He put his arm round the man's shoulders and kissed him on the side of his head, immediately afterwards wiping a sleeve across his mouth.

23

That night, Nash changed his instructions and told us that none of us was to attempt to visit Frere until he had finished his questioning. I protested at this, but mine was a lone voice; apart from Cornelius, a fortnight earlier, none of the others had visited Frere; as far as they were concerned, the sooner he was removed from among us to face a proper trial, the better. I told Nash that he had no right to prevent us from seeing Frere, and he stopped my pleading by saying he had every right. I was defeated largely by the silence of the others. I looked to Cornelius for some support, but he avoided me. He held a glass to his mouth, from which he barely drank, but beyond which he saw little.

He had become even more withdrawn of late, and I expected daily to be told by him of his own plans for departure. I imagined he would travel as far as the coast and then settle, probably working as a shipping agent for one of the growing concerns there. Perhaps his Company pension might even allow him to etablish himself as an independent trader or agent. Each time I raised the subject he avoided answering me directly, allowing me instead to indulge this fantasy of another man's secure and comfortable prospects. It had even occurred to me to ask him if he might accompany Frere to the coast – if that was where he was to be sent – and see that he was treated fairly there.

When Nash had left us I berated the others for not having opposed him. They refused even to argue the point.

'He's tying up all the loose ends now, that's all,' Abbot said. 'He finally got everything he needed from Hammad and his painted savage.'

'He has yet to interview any of *us* properly,' I said.

'You mean you haven't been summoned by him?' Fletcher asked.

'No. Have you?'

'Of course. Several times.'

'We all have,' Abbot said, warming to the subject. 'All very private and confidential, of course. He assured us of that.'

'Perhaps he's saving you until last,' Cornelius said. It was the first time he had spoken in an hour. He drained his glass, clenched his cheeks at the rawness of the spirit and turned to face me. 'Perhaps you're the neat red ribbon he needs to tie round everything.'

'Ridiculous,' I said. 'I know nothing more or less than any of the rest of you.'

'You fool yourself more than you fool us,' Cornelius said.

'You were the one who accompanied Frere on all his so-called expeditions,' Abbot said. 'You were the one he shared all his confidences with.'

'What confidences?'

'You were the one who knew him best, knew what he was trying to do here, knew what he wanted. If anybody saw what was happening, it was you.'

'Saw what?'

'Leave it,' Fletcher said. 'Nothing that's said here will

269

make the slightest difference now to what happens to Frere. Nothing's made the slightest difference since the day Nash stepped out of the trees and puffed out his chest at us. Leave it. They've got Frere and that's all they need. Leave it.'

'They?'

'Oh, for Christ's sake,' Fletcher said.

'Abbot's right,' Cornelius said to me. 'He'll leave you till last because by then he'll know everything there is to know about whatever crime Frere committed. He knows it all already. You saw him earlier. He was a man starting to close the book. Hammad will have seen to that.'

'Cleared his way, so to speak,' Abbot said, and laughed coldly.

'Has he interviewed you, too?' I said to Fletcher.

He nodded.

'And me,' Cornelius added.

'What did he ask you? What did he want to know?'

'What do you think?'

'And you told him everything there was to know about Frere?'

'According to Nash,' Abbot said, 'all Frere's little expeditions away from here were uncalled for and against Company policy. Looks like he was doing it all for himself; hardly anything to do with the Company's commercial interests at all.'

'And so he knows I accompanied him.'

'And that you were breaking the rules, too,' Cornelius said. 'But don't worry, I imagine he'll be rubbing down the edges of the facts before submitting them.'

'Meaning?'

'Meaning he'll want from you what he couldn't get from any of us. You and Frere spent a great deal of time together. A great deal of time away from us, from here.'

'Almost as though you were in league together,' Abbot said.

'Shut up, Abbot,' Fletcher said.

'That's what Nash believes.'

Fletcher turned to me. 'He believes Frere might have told you something about what he intended doing before he did it. And if that's the case, then it proves intent. He wasn't sick or lost or out of his mind when he left us. You above all others knew how single-minded he was when he wanted something. That's why he came out here – not to serve the Company; to serve himself.'

No-one spoke for several minutes, each of us alone.

'Nash hasn't said anything about wanting to interview me,' I said eventually.

'He will,' Cornelius said, his tone less harsh. 'Or perhaps he'll only want to see you to tell you what he knows, and what, presumably, he believes you to already know. He's hardly building a case for the defence, don't forget.'

'And anything *I* told him might have done that?'

'Anything you told him would only have dug the hole deeper for Frere,' Fletcher said. 'Listen to yourself. You behave as though the man could do no wrong. Well, he has done, and he knows he has, and he did it deliberately and he's confessed to the fact. I doubt Nash could believe his luck when he realized how little he'd have to do to prove his case. It's why he behaves as he does. He's leaving you till last because he neither needs nor wants to hear you pleading on Frere's behalf. Everybody else here has told him the same story. And they've told him the truth about what happened, about what Frere was like, what he did, about his ambitions.'

'And that, above all else – that ambition – is what has condemned him,' I said.

'Shut up,' Cornelius told me. 'He was involved in the killing of a child. And he might or might not have indulged some other passion. That's what condemned him. We all have, or all had, ambition, yet none of us did what he did. If anything, you should consider yourself lucky that Nash hasn't interviewed you. Every time you open your mouth you halve the effort he himself needs to make.'

I felt stunned by all this. Cornelius handed me his bottle and an empty glass. I filled and drained the glass.

A further silence followed. It was no longer raining, and we heard the noise made by the small apes scrambling across the roof.

'He runs circles round us,' Abbot said eventually.

'We do that ourselves,' Cornelius said.

'He'll come for your charts before too long,' Abbot said.

'My charts? What do you mean?'

'He has the authority. He spent two hours last night telling me which of my accounts he wanted to see, which ones he might take away with him.'

'And so you've no doubt been busy filling in all the blank spaces and amending all the wrong sums,' Fletcher said.

'I sat up all night. Where's the harm?'

'What will he want my maps for?' I said.

No-one answered me.

'They only show him what's already there,' I insisted.

'He'll want whatever you mapped in connection with your wanderings with Frere,' Fletcher said.

There were at least thirty of these.

'Are there many?' Cornelius said, interrupting my thoughts.

'A dozen or so.'

'He'll know,' he said.

'Know what?'

'Know if you're keeping anything from him. Frere will have told him everything.'

The half-drawn map of Frere's final journey remained weighted and covered on my desk.

'Be careful what you do,' Cornelius said.

'I'll be as careful as Abbot,' I said.

Abbot took offence at this and left us.

I myself left soon afterwards.

Crossing the compound, I saw Nash and Klein standing together in the light cast from the chapel doorway. The small building was brilliantly lit in the darkness, and they stood in this light as though it were a liquid and they were bathing in it. Other members of Klein's congregation stood around them. The two men spoke loudly. There was a great deal of laughter at what was being said. I searched for Perpetua or Felicity, but could see neither woman. By then, Klein had been with us almost a month, and the latest rumour was that he was finally close to concluding a deal which would allow him to begin work on his new mission on the far shore, and that Nash was instrumental in helping this to happen. I could imagine all that Klein might have told the man – not about Frere, necessarily, but about the rest of us, what we had become, what we had allowed ourselves to become, and how we now compared with those on the far side.

They saw me watching them and fell silent for a moment. Then Klein beckoned to me and called for me to join them. My first instinct was to walk away, pretend I hadn't heard, but instead I went. It surprised and unsettled me to see Klein and Nash on such friendly terms. I did not remember having seen Nash laugh before, other than at one of his own remarks.

Everyone turned to look at me as I came into the

lighted ground out of the darkness, and most nodded in silent agreement at something Klein said, but which I did not catch. He then told these others to go, which they did. Several of the younger women approached him and he drew crosses on their foreheads and kissed them before they went.

'You have no doubt been discussing my instructions,' Nash said to me.

'Among other things.'

'I doubt that.'

'Poor Mr Frere,' Klein said, unable to tolerate his exclusion from our exchange.

'You sound as though he's already been tried and found guilty and had sentence passed on him.' I looked hard at Nash as I said it, but he gave nothing away in his response.

'Father Klein has been telling me about van Klees's unfortunate "wife" and child,' he said.

'I daresay they contravene Company policy, too,' I said.

'Of course,' he said. 'But it is of little or no consequence now. Company policy or not, it was still disgraceful behaviour. Abandoning the woman like that, whatever she was, and whatever she ultimately returned to be, and then remaining deliberately oblivious to his responsibilities to his proven child. Neglecting the child even unto the grave.'

Klein smiled as he listened to all this.

'And you got all this from him,' I said.

'I put everything I know to van Klees himself and he denies nothing.'

'Cornelius,' I said. 'Not Frere.'

'Ah, yes, but so . . . so symptomatic of how degraded and uncaring you have all become.' He held up his hands. 'Please, please, it is only a personal judgement.'

'But one that will find its way into your report. You listen to men like him – ' I pointed at Klein, still without facing him ' – and you choose what you choose to believe.'

'I listen to you all,' Nash said.

'You still pick and choose and dress things up to suit your purpose,' I said. It was a clumsy way of expressing what I wanted to say and I regretted the words; I wondered if I had drunk more of Cornelius's brandy than I had realized.

'I understand your anger,' Nash said.

'Mr Frasier is a very angry man,' Klein said.

'But it is anger occasioned by frustration and dis-illusionment,' Nash said.

If he had hoped to provoke me to a further out-burst with the words, then he was disappointed. I felt suddenly unsteady on my feet. I coughed and a bitter taste filled my mouth.

'Are you unwell?' Nash said.

'How convenient,' Klein added.

I turned to the man, but the sudden motion made my head swim. He said something else to me, which I did not hear. The bright light of the chapel blinded me. I heard a noise from within, and without speaking to either man, I went inside.

The light there was even brighter; dozens of lanterns had been lit around the walls and on the bars of the pulpit. I shielded my eyes to look. At first I saw nothing, and then a slight motion attracted my atten-tion. I saw Perpetua and Felicity standing against the far wall. I went towards them, but as I approached I realized that what I had seen were not the women, but only their outfits, empty and hanging there. Then one of the women called out for me to leave. I stumbled to the end of the aisle, searching for the voice. By then,

Klein and Nash had come into the doorway behind me. Klein called to me, urging me on, laughter drowning his words. My head continued to spin. I resumed coughing and then started to retch. Again I heard one of the women call out to me, and I stumbled forward, clutching at the seats and scattering them as I went, until I finally arrived at the front of the small space. There, on the floor ahead of me, half hidden by the banner which Klein had draped from his altar, lay Perpetua and Felicity, naked and prostrated, neither woman attempting to rise as I approached them, both of them with their faces turned to watch me with fear in their wide eyes, their cheeks and palms pressed to the boards. They were telling me to go back, not to look, to close my eyes. I stopped where I stood, trying to steady myself, and I looked down at them, at their naked backs and buttocks and tried hard to understand what I was seeing. Klein called again to me. He told me to look hard at what I saw. He was by then alone in the doorway, his outline molten in the bright light. I looked again at the women, and as though the motion of turning along with understanding was too great for me to bear, I felt my legs buckle and fold beneath me and I fell onto them, unable to prevent myself, unable even to throw out my arms to protect myself. The last thing I heard was their screaming as they scrabbled to free themselves from beneath me, my fall broken by their naked bodies.

PART FOUR

24

I woke to the sound of voices and to someone wiping a cloth across my brow.

'He's coming round.' It was Cornelius's voice. The wiping continued.

I had some difficulty opening my eyes, but when I finally managed this and was able to focus, I saw that I was in my bed. Cornelius sat beside me. Fletcher stood at the foot of the bed, in conversation with the deformed boy. Upon hearing Cornelius, he looked across at me, gave the boy some final instruction and told him to leave us. My vision remained fractured. My face ran with sweat. I felt beneath my sheets; someone had undressed me. There was an odour of sickness in the room, of medicines and vomit. Cornelius wrung out a cloth into an enamel bowl.

I tried to push myself upright, but was unable to, and my head spun at even that small effort. I started to retch and Cornelius pushed the bowl beneath my chin. Nothing materialized and my throat felt sore from the effort.

'I collapsed,' I said, my voice a dry whisper.

'We know. Nash sent for us. We found you in the empty chapel.'

I struggled to remember what had happened, what I had seen.

'Too much drink,' I said. 'Last night.'

'Last night? That was three days ago. You've been delirious and barely conscious for all that time.'

I shook my head. 'Last night. Klein and Nash at the chapel.'

'It's painful for you to speak. You were sick. River fever, Fletcher reckons. I agree with him. We've been treating you. We sent to the Belgians for whatever they had. That was the boy's errand.' He indicated the bottles and jars arranged on my bedside table.

'Three days?' I said. I tried hard to recall if anything of the time remained with me. Nothing came.

'Nash said you went inside with Klein. He left the two of you together. He saw Klein later, and the man said something to raise Nash's suspicions. He went back to the chapel, and there you were, on the floor in the darkness. You must have gone inside, passed out, fallen and hit your head.'

'Klein was there,' I whispered.

'Whatever.'

'Frere?' I said.

'Still in the gaol. Nash has finished with him. Now we're just waiting.'

'For what?'

'For what we all expected. He's being sent to Stanley-ville to stand trial there. The Belgians are relinquishing some of their judicial powers.'

I felt the last of what little strength I still possessed drain from me. Cornelius lowered my head onto my pillow. I turned into it and felt its wetness.

I slept for several hours longer.

When I next woke, it was dark. Fletcher had gone, and Cornelius sat alone at the foot of the bed, asleep, a book face-down in his lap. I watched him, making no sound. I tried to remember everything that had been said earlier and it all came back to me. I felt the remaining tremor of my limbs. I took one of my hands from beneath the sheets and held it to my face. It, too, shook, and the skin was discoloured and gathered. The veins stood out along my inner arm. In the bowl beside my bed lay several phials. The same smell of sickness pervaded the room. I held my palm to my face and smelled it even stronger there.

The motion alerted Cornelius, and he sat upright to look at me.

'I feel better,' I said.

'You were ranting and raving for two days,' he said.

'Is the worst over?' My voice remained dry and cracked.

'Possibly.' He rubbed a hand over his face.

'And Frere,' I said. 'Is it all over?'

'It seems so.'

'Has anyone been to see him?'

He looked down at the book still balanced in his lap. 'Speke's Journal,' he said. ' "Speke, we must send you there again." '

It was the distant past. It was an unknown landscape filled with promise, hope and wealth turned to mud and holes, and stripped of all it once possessed worth having.

As before, I tried to raise myself in my bed, but again the effort was too great for me.

'It's almost two in the morning,' Cornelius said.

I felt a ravenous hunger, but knew I would be unable to eat. A metallic taste filled my mouth; my breath was sour.

'Go to your bed,' I told him. I watched him rise and go.

For a long while afterwards I lay awake, looking around me in the dull glow of my lantern, trying to make some sense of what had happened, knowing only that the long-gathering storm had finally arrived and blown itself out in our midst and that I had remained oblivious to its final coming and the power spent upon us. The book lay on my bed where Cornelius had left it and I kicked it to the floor.

The next time I woke it was to find Nash sitting beside me. It was daylight and the shutters at my window had been folded back to let in the sun. He held a board across his lap and was writing as I half opened my eyes to look at him. He looked up immediately and waited for me to speak.

I asked him the time.

It was one in the afternoon. He had arrived mid-morning to find Cornelius asleep at the foot of the bed.

'I changed your sheets,' he said. 'You needed washing. Some of your dressings . . .'

My limbs and chest were no longer bathed with sweat.

'My dressings?'

'Your joints, knees, wrists; there were sores.'

I lifted the sheets to look at the bandages.

'You saw Klein follow me into the chapel,' I said.

'I left him. I came only as far as the doorway. He told me to go.'

'He was with me when I collapsed. He lied about finding me later.'

'I believe you. I trust the man no more than you do.'

'Did he tell you what happened, what I found in the chapel?'

He shook his head. 'Just that the two of you had spoken and that he had left you.'

282

I said nothing about the two women.

He brought a glass of water to me.

'I took the liberty of gathering together some of your charts,' he said. He avoided looking at me as he spoke.

'For the Company or as evidence?'

'Both, I imagine.' He returned to his seat.

I spilled most of the water over my chin and chest. My hands were still not steady.

'Cornelius is convinced of your recovery,' he said.

'Is that why you came?'

'What do you mean?'

'To interview me about Frere.'

'My work with Nicholas Frere is over. I finished two days ago.'

'Over?'

'As I knew it would be. He kept nothing from me. You know him for the man he is.' He seemed weary of the task completed. He looked away from me, through the window to the locust trees covered in jasmine, the scent of which was added to the room's other odours.

'But there are things I could tell you in his favour, things which need to be considered,' I said.

He shook his head at the suggestion. 'No, there aren't.'

'You interviewed all the others.'

'Background. Circumstantial events. Something to gain a flavour of the man.'

'I know him better than any of them.'

'I never doubted that.'

'I shall insist on you taking a deposition.'

'Insist?' He closed the book in which he had been writing. 'And what if I were to tell you that one of Frere's own conditions for telling me everything himself was that I was not to question you?'

'You're lying.'

'I am many things, Mr Frasier, but never a liar.'

'He wouldn't do that.' But my voice lacked all conviction. It was precisely the kind of thing Frere would do.

'Why wouldn't he? He told me all about his attachment to your sister.'

'Why would he tell you that? It has no bearing on any of this.'

'I know that. He told me to convince me that I should comply with his wishes. He wanted you to have no involvement whatsoever in what happened following the desertion of his responsibilities here.'

'And presumably you now know what that was.'

He nodded once. 'I do.'

'And?'

'And I know that you – that you all – remain ignorant of the details, that Frere kept everything from you, that he built his moat well. Surely, you of all people can understand his reasoning in the matter.'

'Will *you* tell me what happened?'

'There will be a full report in good time.'

'Was a child killed?'

He paused, considering. 'There was.'

'A girl?'

'A girl.' He rose and went to the window, standing with his back to me. 'If it is any consolation to you, I believe Frere was as much a victim of circumstance as he was a protagonist, not wholly willing, shall I say, in his involvement. Please, I can tell you no more at present. Arrangements are still being made. My report, though completed, has yet to be submitted to the authorities.'

'In London?'

'In Stanleyville. Please, save your breath and your strength. You all knew what would happen. Be grateful that this awful responsibility fell to another man and not to any of you.'

'He'll hang,' I said, the words little more than mouthed.

'It is almost certain that he will be sentenced to death, yes.'

'For who he is and what he represents, rather than for the crime itself.'

'Neither you nor I can possibly say that.'

'No, but only because we continue to deceive ourselves.'

He returned to sit beside me. 'The humpback wanted to bring a gree-gree man to shake his stick at you. Naturally, we refused him. He holds you in high regard. Would you deny him his birthright?'

'Meaning what?'

'Meaning he may one day become a court official, a lawyer, a judge even.'

I stopped myself from laughing at this.

'See?' Nash said. 'He brought the gree-gree man and Fletcher kicked them out. The man was an albino, blackened with walnut juice and anointed with powder of cloves. You could smell him a mile away. He was in the room before Fletcher knew what was happening.' He breathed deeply.

'You could have let him perform,' I said. 'For the boy's sake if not my own.'

'But that would have implied belief, Mr Frasier, and whatever else we may be prepared to relinquish here . . .'

'Is the boy still in the Station?'

'He comes and goes.'

'And when will Frere go?' I said.

'Ten days. A steamer is on its way.'

I was about to ask him how long ago this had been

arranged when, without warning, the door opened and a man appeared in the doorway. It was the albino witch doctor. He was washed clean of all his colouring and did nothing other than stand in the doorway and consider me. Neither Nash nor I spoke to the man. He began to chant in a low murmur, and from the pouch at his waist he took out a small carved figure. He came to the bed and laid this beside me. It was of the crudest kind, and with no indication, other than a piece of cloth tied around it, of what it was intended to represent. I could only assume that the doll was me. He looked at us both with his half-closed eyes and then he went. Nash closed the door behind him. I took the doll and pushed it beneath my pillow.

'Which of my charts did you take?' I asked him when he came back to me.

'Those I imagine you might have had some difficulty accounting for under the terms of your employment. No-one will see them.' Another of his deals with Frere in which I faded to nothing.

I struggled for a direction in which I might now turn.

'And you?' I said eventually.

'Me?'

'Will you return to Stanleyville with Frere?'

'Unfortunately, yes. Believe me, he is no trophy. It had been my original intention to continue upriver, perhaps even to cross to the east. However, all that is now beyond me. Two days ago, news reached us of a revolt at Kayasa. The Station Manager and his clerk were killed over a dispute concerning wages paid in cloth instead of the promised food. There has been considerable unrest elsewhere, too. Gathering Stations are being threatened all along the river, and though no-one has yet suggested as much, I suspect all these supposedly isolated incidents are being orchestrated for the purpose of creating that unrest.'

'Orchestrated by whom?'

He shrugged.

'Hammad?' I said.

He smiled. 'Would it surprise you to learn that Klein is with him now? You'd be surprised how much respectability the construction of a mission or a chapel might stamp upon a host of other, considerably less worthy enterprises.'

'He left me lying there,' I said.

'So you say.'

'My word against his.'

'There were no other witnesses.' He had seen the two women.

'No.'

He rose, ready to leave.

'What did Frere say about her?'

'Who?'

'My sister. Caroline.'

He paused before speaking. 'He said that he loved her, that he had never loved anyone before her, and that the hardest part of what he now had to endure was the knowledge that he had brought shame on her, that he had disgraced himself and that she would now feel only disgust and contempt for him as long as she lived.'

'She loved him, too,' I said.

'Hence his conviction. He tried occasionally to pretend otherwise – that she did not love him as he loved her – but he could not.'

'She would have forgiven him,' I said.

'Forgive me, but you are as little convinced of that as he was. Perhaps when you are in full possession of the facts . . .'

'He asked me to communicate nothing to her until all

this was over. I see now that what he really meant was that I was to wait until he was dead.'

'Knowing him as I now do, I imagine that was his meaning,' he said.

And thus we retreated from the blood and flesh of the matter into the cold and sterile language of its understanding.

He went again to the doorway. He seemed reluctant to leave me, and I saw how long those remaining ten days were now likely to be, for him as well as for Frere. He no longer had any purpose among us and wished to detach himself from us, not to endure what we had yet to endure, not to be drawn into the wasteland of that longer waiting, into that emptiness of the future in which we were all now condemned to wander like blind men in unfamiliar places.

He neither turned nor spoke to me as he left.

I waited in the hope that the gree-gree man might return, but he never came.

25

I went outside for the first time two days later. I had imagined myself sufficiently recovered and strong enough to resume my part in the slow life of the place, but even the simple act of crossing the compound exhausted me, forcing me to pause every few steps, and then to rest on an empty case before reaching the water's edge.

I was surprised to see all our wharves and jetties empty, with not even a single small boat tied up there. The river had fallen during my illness, and I had anticipated a back-log of traffic, but other than a pair of fishing boats unloading their meagre catch directly onto the bank, there was nothing.

Other men and women congregated in the shallows and beside the path leading to the quarry. I recognized the dismissed workers among them. They watched me sitting on the case, just as they had watched my painful journey from my room, but no-one approached me.

A canoe left the main channel of the fallen river and came to where I sat. I shielded my eyes and recognized the old boatman and the boy. The boy leaped out and splashed in his usual ungainly fashion towards me. He asked me how I was feeling. The old man looked up at us, but made no attempt to join us.

The boy told me that Hammad had been visiting all the nearby villages and settlements, nailing up posters and calling for everyone to come and read them. He took a piece of folded paper from his pocket and gave it to me. The writing was in no language I understood. The boy took it back and translated for me. A new nation was being born, a nation governed by its own people. A census was being taken and land was being surveyed. Everyone was exhorted to rejoice in these coming changes and to participate in them. That was all. I asked him if Hammad's name appeared anywhere on the announcement, but it did not.

He and the old man intended leaving, he said. He wanted to go to the coast and live in one of the new cities there. They were towns calling themselves cities. I asked him what the old man would do. Live somewhere on the river until he died, he said. He pushed the announcement back into his pocket and took out several coins. He insisted that I took these and I asked him why. They were the coins I had thrown into the canoe the last time I had crossed the river. The old man had refused to retrieve them and they had laid untouched in the water there until I was spotted. I told him I felt ashamed at what I'd done.

I asked him if he'd seen or heard anything of the unrest along the river. At first he was unwilling to answer me, hoping to avoid the question by shrugging his deformed shoulders, but when I insisted, he said that many of the villages along the Lomami had recently been abandoned for no good reason, and that only the previous day smoke had been seen pouring into the sky above the trees surrounding the Kirasi mission.

As we spoke there was a commotion among the fishermen and women. I looked down and saw several of the men pointing into the water a short distance away. I thought at first that a crocodile or hippopotamus had been spotted, but when I looked more closely I saw that it was a corpse in the water that had attracted their attention. Then a further shout went up, and following that, another. There was more than one corpse – five or six, all floating together, all travelling in the same slow current. From where I sat, these were nothing more than indistinct shapes rising and falling at the surface of the water. I considered it unlikely that so many bodies would have been carried so closely together, and that a mistake had been made in their identification.

The old man in his canoe remained apart from the fishermen, watching as the body which had been spotted first was retrieved by a man throwing a rope from the shore.

I followed all this as closely as I could. My vision was beginning to blur, and I depended on the boy to tell me what was happening. He told me that the first body had been secured and was being pulled ashore, and that the others – he was certain there were five more – were following it.

This first corpse was laid out and a rope was found tied to its ankle – the rope to which the remaining bodies were attached. One of these was missing both its arms, another both its legs from the knees down.

Slaves, the boy said.

I made some facetious remark about the new nation and its people, but he remained oblivious to whatever connection I hoped to suggest. The women washed the bodies and started their wailing.

A short while later, attracted by all the noise,

Cornelius arrived. He was surprised to find me out of my bed. He told the boy to leave us, and he went without speaking, first to look more closely at the laid-out corpses, and then back to the canoe and the old man.

I told Cornelius about the proclamation. He said they had also appeared in the Station and nailed to the trees along all our trails. I told him Nash had been to see me, but he knew that, too, having contrived to leave the man alone with me. He told me he had just come from the garrison, where he had gone in the hope of seeing Frere, but that Frere had refused to see him.

'What did you expect?' I asked him. We had forsaken Frere in unequal measure, but however we might now prefer to see it, we had forsaken him all the same.

He watched the men and the women and the corpses in the mud without speaking.

Afterwards he helped me back to my room, turning away from me at the door as I made my way inside.

26

The next morning, Cornelius came to me as I washed myself. He took off my dressings and replaced them. The sores on my joints had still not healed, and it was impossible to avoid the stink of the bandages. He suggested that I went no further than my veranda, and that if there was anyone I wished to see, then he would send them to me.

The only person I truly wanted to see was Frere, but I knew that the journey to the garrison was beyond me. I asked Cornelius to tell Nash I would like to see him.

Later, I watched Bone walk out of the trees carrying his rifle and with an animal slung over his shoulder. He saw me and came to me. The creature over his shoulder was a small deer, already gutted and missing its feet and head, the pearly joints of its bones protruding from the skin.

'Shot it,' he said, holding up his rifle.

'Are you going to cook it?'

'Sell it. They're buying anything they can.'

'Who are?'

He motioned in the direction of the sheds and shelters out of sight along the river.

The small carcass can have weighed no more than ten or twelve pounds.

'Is Frere still in the gaol?' I said.

'Been there with nobody near him since Nash finished with him.'

'Has he asked for me?'

'You?'

'I mean, does he know I've been ill and unable to visit him?'

He shrugged. 'I imagine so.'

'Will you tell him for me? Tell him that but for my illness I would have been to see him.'

He held out his hand for payment. He no longer made any attempt at subterfuge. I gave him what he asked.

'He'll have known anyhow,' he said. 'Not long now until he's gone.'

'Seven days.'

'If you say so. They had thirty more bodies wash up at Makura, all of them roped together like ours. What do you reckon, boat sink?'

'I don't know.' I knew the figure was likely to be an exaggeration.

'Or perhaps somebody tried to take what wasn't rightly theirs, and these poor beggars got caught in the middle.'

'Your compassion does you justice,' I said.

'Not mine. I'm just grateful they washed up further downriver.' A detail of his men had been sent by Fletcher to bury the bodies washed up the previous day.

I smelled the blood of the small deer. Flies swarmed over the severed neck.

'What will you get for it?' I asked him.

He dropped the meat at his feet and prodded it with his boot. 'Who cares?' he said.

We were both distracted by the arrival of a small boat, from which Klein and Abbot disembarked together in close conversation.

'Where have they been?' I asked Bone.

He shook his head, unconcerned.

I watched as the two men came from the river towards Abbot's office. Abbot saw me with Bone. He spoke to Klein, who also turned to look at us. The priest paused to consider me, but then resumed his journey.

I looked back to the river, hoping to see either Perpetua or Felicity, but they were not there. I had seen neither woman since the night of my collapse in the chapel. I asked Bone if he had seen them. I tried to make the remark sound casual, its answer not worth paying for, but he shook his head without even considering its worth.

Klein and Abbot continued to Abbot's office and went inside.

Bone rose and left me. He retrieved the carcass and swung it from side to side in an attempt to rid it of its flies. The insects followed their feast like a waving scarf.

I had intended spending the remainder of the day examining my charts in the hope of discovering precisely what had been taken by Nash and what remained, but seeing Klein and Abbot together had intrigued me, and so instead of returning to my desk, I followed them to Abbot's office.

The two men stood on either side of his desk. Mounds of his own files and ledgers all around the room indicated where another of Nash's inventories had been carried out. A single large chart lay unrolled and weighted on the desk.

I entered without knocking, and Abbot, who had been speaking, fell silent at seeing me. He was clearly excited about something, and he looked back and forth between Klein and myself as I approached them.

'You need a seat,' Klein said to me. 'You clearly remain unwell.' He smoked a cigar and its smoke marbled the warm air of the room. 'Abbot, get Mr Frasier a seat.'

Abbot remained where he stood.

'A seat,' Klein repeated. He stepped to one side, took hold of the ledger-filled chair beside him and tipped its contents to the floor. 'This one. Here.' He wiped the chair with his sleeve and offered it to me. I was unable to refuse.

'Apparently, I'm in your debt for finding me in the chapel,' I said to him.

'I left you where you lay for an hour. One hour, that's all. Did you want to be discovered with those disgusting women?'

'What?' Abbot said to Klein. 'You knew he'd collapsed there and you left him?'

Klein alarmed him further by kicking a pile of ledgers away from where he stood.

'It doesn't matter,' I said to Abbot.

'But you almost died.'

'Is that true?' Klein said to me, smiling. 'Did you almost die, Mr Frasier?'

'He did,' Abbot insisted, as though he believed Klein's mocking tone suggested he did not believe me.

'Perhaps if you had,' Klein said to me, leaning over so that his face was close to mine, 'perhaps if you had, then perhaps Nash might have been persuaded to change your clothes for those of our doomed Mr Frere, and your corpse could have been taken to Stanleyville in place of him. Imagine how convenient that might have been for all concerned.'

'What?' Abbot said, still unable to grasp the nature of the man's hostility towards me. 'What are you saying?'

Klein kept his eyes on me. I waved the tobacco smoke away from my face.

'But fortunately you recovered,' he said. 'You burned and you recovered. Another little hero.'

'What's he talking about?' Abbot said to me. He started to come round the desk towards us, but Klein held a hand to his chest and stopped him.

'What are you doing?' Abbot said, affronted by the gesture.

'Doing? What do you imagine I am doing, Mr Abbot? I am merely suggesting to you that we resume our business here, that we ignore this side-show – ' he pointed to me ' – and carry on. Did I hurt you? I'm so sorry.'

Abbot brushed at his chest.

'I apologize. I am a man of the cloth. I meant you no harm. Here, let me.' He too wiped a hand over Abbot's chest. Abbot withdrew immediately and returned to the far side of the desk.

Klein waited a moment, ensuring he was once again in control of the situation, and that Abbot and I both understood this, before going on.

'You join us on a momentous occasion,' he said to me. 'These plans and drawings are the blueprint for my new mission. Everything is agreed. Tell him, Mr Abbot.'

Abbot lowered his gaze to the plans, but said nothing.

'Mr Abbot is too modest,' Klein said. 'Without his assistance, I would have been unable to proceed.'

'I simply—' Abbot said.

'Without Mr Abbot and all the assistance he has been able to offer me, my plans might not even have

297

been thought worthy of consideration in the first instance. Perhaps I shall insist on a statue being erected in honour of his endeavours. Imagine that – a statue to a humble clerk.'

'Labour. I offered . . .' Abbot said.

'A labour-force of a size and at a price a poor man such as myself would never have believed possible.'

'The men from the quarry,' I said, wanting to end this painful performance. 'You sold them to him cheaply?'

'Oh, not to me personally,' Klein said. He drew deeply on the cigar and released its smoke in a slow plume between us. 'To my new benefactors across the river. To those men with a vision of the future in which accommodation is made for the Lord's work, and in which—'

'What about the mission at Kirasi?' I said.

'You didn't hear? Of course not, you were ill. There was a fire. Such a pity.'

'You had it burned, you mean.'

'A very unfortunate fire, after which the place was overrun by savages. I believe there may have been some fighting, some loss of life even, one never knows with these people, so much screaming and chest-beating.'

'Does Cornelius know this?'

'Van Klees? I imagine so. Why? What concern do you imagine it is of his? *This* is what should concern us now.' He slapped both palms onto the outline of his church. '*This, this* is where we should turn our gaze.'

I stopped listening to him.

'He's right,' Abbot said.

I saw from a map at the corner of the chart that the new mission stood closer to Hammad's home than to the river or the Belgian Station.

'It will employ men for a year,' Abbot said, as though still hoping to persuade me of something I had so far failed to grasp. 'All the excavated stone from the quarry. Don't you see – nothing undertaken there will be wasted. This is a perfect solution.' He began to point out the features of the plan.

Klein played no part in this; instead, he continued watching me, merely nodding in mocking agreement with everything Abbot said.

When I could stand this no longer, I rose from my seat and said to Klein, 'Perpetua and Felicity.'

'What of them?'

'Where are they?'

'I've scarcely seen them since their act of debased sacrilege on the night you became ill.'

'They were doing what you had commanded them to do. Why?'

'Commanded? You were ill, Mr Frasier, delirious. Ask anyone. Ask Abbot here.'

'What?' Abbot said, only then distracted from his litany of excuses and self-justification.

'Are they still here?' I said to Klein.

'Who knows? Perhaps their work for the Lord is finished. Perhaps He has looked down on them and told them to rest, that they have done enough for Him. Or perhaps the new mission demands new servants to do His work. Who knows?' He fell silent after that, waiting for me to leave. I saw the slender cane he carried hanging on the back of Abbot's door. I wanted to take it and break it into pieces and throw it at his feet.

He saw where I looked, and said, 'It's merely a cane, Mr Frasier. Even Jesus had his staff.' He spat the stub of burning cigar onto the papers at his feet and then watched as they began to smoulder.

*   *   *

Nash eventually came to see me as darkness fell. It had been my intention to talk to him about Frere, but I asked him instead what he knew of the arrangement between Abbot and Klein. He was reluctant to discuss the matter. I saw the figures in Abbot's ledgers juggled into their face-saving columns on the back-breaking work of others. Nash seemed tired, unwilling to prolong any of the small conflicts which had forever existed between us, conflicts born of conflict, in which the distinction between allegiance and responsibility had long since been lost. He dressed my sores and helped me to my bed. He asked me about my illness, but in a way which did not so much indicate concern for me, as suggest to me that he was a man preparing himself for his own coming suffering.

'I saw no reason not to sanction the use of the quarry labour-force,' he said eventually. 'Abbot will act in some supervisory role while the thing is being constructed.'

'Is there so little for him to do here?'

Earlier, there had been unverified and scarcely believable reports of what sounded to be an approaching flotilla of traders, and our wharves had been made ready for them. But the vessels had passed us by without any signal to us. Some of our canoes put out to them, but returned empty.

Afterwards, there was no talk of what had happened.

Several hours later, a dozen porters and guides arrived from Lado with a cargo of Egyptian blue glass, gum and amber. And with news of what had happened to Dhanis and his thousands of mutineers ransacking the country.

Fletcher and Cornelius went to inspect the trade goods and told the men who carried them to take them elsewhere. The glass, Fletcher said, was plunder, and the guides carried rifles which, in all likelihood, had come from Dhanis's insurgents. The traders complained at being treated like this, insisting Cornelius accept the cargo. Fletcher sent for Bone and his men, and following an uncomfortable stand-off lasting most of the day, the traders left us. One man took out a dozen of the precious glass bowls and smashed them at the centre of the compound.

Nash told me he had spent much of the day gathering together and packing his belongings, awaiting his own departure a week hence. I wondered at his caution, and it occurred to me later that he might have lied to us about the steamer coming for Frere and himself, and that the vessel would arrive earlier, under cover of darkness perhaps, and that he and Frere would be gone from us before we knew it.

'He was asking after you,' he said upon my mentioning Frere.

'I want to see him. Before he goes.'

'He knows that. He asked me to arrange it.'

'I doubt I can walk that far,' I said.

'I can bring him here to you.'

'He'll probably offer to be tied and hobbled,' I said.

'He did.'

We both fell silent at this, acknowledging our shared responsibilities towards the man, responsibilities now as destructive as they had once been sustaining.

The night around us lay brooding and largely silent, and he remarked on this, saying it was not what he had expected. I remembered my own thwarted expectations. I remembered the game I had played with my sisters of the endlessly beating drums, the roaring beasts and the strangled screams which would forever rent the jungle darkness.

'Will he tell me what he told you?' I asked him eventually.

'I imagine that is the purpose of him wanting to see you before he goes.'

'He may just wish to say goodbye. Will you stay with him at Stanleyville?'

'A day or two, perhaps. A week.'

'But not until the end?'

'No, not until then.'

'If you were given the choice would you stay?'

He thought about this. 'No.'

I had earlier considered asking permission to go with him and Frere and to wait with Frere while he was tried and while I recuperated, but I knew the request would only raise higher his guard against me, and that any other, lesser concessions might also be lost.

'The Company will most likely appoint someone through one of their agents there,' he said.

'To present his case fairly?'

'To see that all the proprieties are observed; to ensure that everything is done in the correct manner.'

'Is it true about Hammad?' I said.

'That he has his expectations? Yes.' He looked around at my now empty walls. 'We don't know the tiniest part of it, you or I,' he said. 'Not the tiniest part.'

It was the first time I had heard him talk with such resignation or uncertainty, and I saw that he too had finally been betrayed by his expectations. His last few days among us were nothing more to him than a void to be crossed, something worthy of endurance only because it was within sight of whatever lay ahead of him.

'I've made a list of all the maps I took from your office,' he said. 'I'm obliged to let you see it so that you

302

can confirm what I've taken in connection with the trial.'

I had not yet investigated the missing charts; there seemed little point in knowing. All that mattered was that I had plotted Frere's wanderings and now he possessed that map. What was the map of our shining blue lake against that?

'I ought to have destroyed them all before you arrived,' I said.

'You would have confessed to it.'

'Or Frere would.'

'What do you imagine you would have been hiding from me? Burning them would have made no sense. You had no idea.'

I said nothing to disabuse him of this – of everything that had passed through my mind when it became clear to me that Frere had chosen not to include me on his final journey – and he left me soon after.

I woke the following morning and knew that the worst of my fever had passed and that my strength would now slowly return. I felt weary, as though after a long journey or struggle. I woke from a dream in which Frere and I had been together on the *Alpha*. I knew I had called out, but whether in the dream or in waking, I was uncertain, and the instant I woke I listened intently, as though for some faint echo of this cry. My door and shutters were open. Fires burned in the compound outside and the usual restless figures – as though dreaming men themselves – passed ceaselessly among these.

In my dream I had been standing with Frere at the prow of the *Alpha*. The vessel had been diverted and we stood becalmed in the roadstead off Badagry. The impassable surf stretched in an unbroken white line a hundred yards from us, and the water rolled and burst on the barely submerged reef there. Canoes came and went from us through the few narrow openings. We were there for five days, and each night we stood on the deck to watch the impressive display of rockets fired from the shore into the night sky. We tried to determine the function of these fireworks, but could not, knowing only that they were not fired in celebration.

While we waited, we heard from an official brave enough to venture out to us that a week earlier a vessel had foundered on the reef, lodged there and been battered to torn planking and lengths of rope over the three days she had taken to break up. With the exception of seven men who abandoned the ship soon after she struck, the remaining crew of twenty had all perished on the reef, which was notorious for its patrolling sharks.

I had seen all this – the sea, the surf, the calmer water and the land beyond, in my dream. And I had seen too the caught ship and the men on its battered deck running back and forth in their useless attempts to save themselves, eventually one by one throwing themselves into the water and the waiting sharks, creatures so voracious in this dreamed assault that they leaped wholly out of the ocean to seize the falling and jumping men before those fish waiting submerged could launch their own attacks. I recalled how Frere had applauded these leaps, standing with his telescope and notebook, in which he wrote and sketched the day's dramas. He had already tried to photograph the disintegrating ship, but knew that little would be revealed at such a distance. He spoke with rising admiration for the creatures. For him, the doomed crew were nothing more than the vital part of some experiment.

In my dream, the whole of the surrounding ocean

turned red with the blood of the savaged men, and the sharks came in even greater numbers, it seemed, merely to indulge themselves in the pleasure of swimming through this blood. I saw creatures here and there carrying torn limbs; I saw men scrambling along the reef to where they believed they might be safe only to have the sharks become birds and seize them where they crawled; I heard the screams of men in the water attacked from below by a dozen of the creatures at once; I saw men themselves thrown clear of the water by sharks twice their length.

And throughout all this, Frere, beside me at the rail, had become more and more excited, almost yelling with joy at the spectacle before us, applauding some particularly dramatic or entertaining effort on the part of the men or the fish. Some of these men, seeing us anchored so close, grasped at the salvation we offered and swam towards us through this bloody feast, and some, I saw, even managed to clear the immediate carnage before they were seized and drawn back into it.

Others among the *Alpha*'s crew stood alongside us and chorused Frere in his cheering. I was entirely alone in the disgust and revulsion I felt at the spectacle, and I had woken from the nightmare at the sight of a man almost reaching one of the *Alpha*'s ropes, but who, even as he reached out to grab it, was seized by two of the sharks, shadows beneath him all the way as he came, one for each leg, and slowly drawn beneath the water in their grinning maws, his waving arms and screaming mouth long visible to us as he was taken down and torn to pieces, and as the calm, clear water above him turned red with his blood.

It was then, seeing him finally consumed and his suffering ended, that I woke, pushing away my tangled sheets as though they too were waves from which I needed to escape.

The dream was as vivid to me in its waking aftermath as it had been while I slept, and my wet brow and shaking hands registered the last of its passing tremors.

I sat for several minutes until I grew calmer. I had seen nothing of what I dreamed, and yet it seemed more real to me then, in those first waking moments, than the empty room in which I found myself and the restless figures outside.

I closed my eyes, but nothing of the sunlit ocean remained.

In the distance I heard the chapel harmonium being played, and I remembered then that it was Sunday, still a day of obligation and devotion amid a waste of days where no other beacon was ever now in sight. The instrument suffered in that humidity, and its mournful, discordant melody sounded like nothing more than the breathless crying of a child, lost notes providing the briefest clicks of silence into which all this surrounding melancholy, dreamed and real, now ebbed.

27

'Do you still imagine that even the smallest part of all this has been left to chance? Is that what you want to believe?'

Frere walked beside me across the garrison yard, pausing every few paces to allow for my slowness. We came to a balk of cut timber and sat on it. He had asked me about the arrival of the steamer sent to take him to Stanleyville, and I had tried to make my answer reassuringly vague – 'A week, perhaps,' – but he told me again not to make the effort on his behalf. He knew better than any of us that the vessel was due to reach us in three days, and that after that he would be as lost to us as he was already lost to himself.

He laid a hand on my arm.

'I had hoped one of us might accompany you,' I said. His grip tightened.

'I cannot imagine Nash took to that idea. I am a dish best served unaccompanied by any sauce of outrage or pickle of extenuating circumstances. Forgive me. I know this apparent flippancy offends you. Perhaps I'm just a man laughing in the face of—' He stopped abruptly. Not because he did not want to say the word 'Death', but because he did not want me, sitting there beside him, to have to consider it. I saw what final weight this confession to me lifted from his shoulders.

Neither of us spoke for a few moments. We looked out together over the empty parade ground. Women pounded grain somewhere beyond the wall, and the double rhythm of their drumming came to us like a heartbeat.

'I had been sick for ten days,' he said unexpectedly. He took back his hand.

I looked at him, but he had already half turned himself away from me.

'What was it?' I asked him.

'It makes no difference. The symptoms of these things are invariably the same. Who knows? Perhaps yellow fever, perhaps dysentery. I took what medicines I had. Imagine your own recent suffering.'

'But you were alone and lost, unsought.'

'I was never lost. I had gone to the confluence of the Lomami and Pitiri for a purpose.'

'To hopefully witness an act of cannibalism?'

'To witness it at the very least.'

'Then what? Are you saying you hoped to go further – to *participate* in it?'

'I can't answer you honestly, though I suspect that was always my unconfessed and uncertain intention. You might say circumstances made that decision easier for me to make. I suppose you – particularly you, James – might even say I was conspired against in my enthusiasm, my need to know. As you know, it has always been the abnormalities and not the divinities of men that have fascinated me.'

'What circumstances?'

'When I woke one morning I found I was in the company of three men. I imagined at first they were

308

there to strip me of my belongings. This was on the banks of the Pitiri.'

'Where you were eventually found.'

'Where I was eventually found. I recognized them immediately by their markings and their stature: they were Aruwimi, renowned for their cannibalism, a long way from their usual haunts, but Aruwimi savages all the same. I tried my best to communicate with them, but other than acknowledge my presence, they made no attempt to approach me closer or to take anything from me. One of them even gave me clear water to drink. I offered him what little I had with me, but nothing I possessed was of any interest to him. I believe he communicated something of my plight to the others, neither of whom made the slightest advance on me. Perhaps if I had been more in control of my senses, then I would have feared them more.

'All three men were naked and with their faces painted red, and all were anointed with rancid tallow: black lines around their eyes and mouths. They came and went in and out of the forest, but always returned to the same place, and it occurred to me then that they were waiting for something or someone, a rendezvous.

'As I recovered further and felt something of my strength returning, I tried to communicate more with them. The two hitherto silent ones started to approach me. They brought me fruit. They caught fish in the river which they ate raw. One of them caught a small snake, which he skinned alive and then chopped up and ate while each of its cut lengths was still flexing in spasms in his hands. He approached me with a small piece and I ate it. I chewed it as little as I could – my mouth was raw even then – and after swallowing it I swear I could feel its movement, its dying throes in my stomach. I vomited shortly afterwards, so I imagine I lost most of what I had eaten.' He raised a hand to his throat at the memory.

'Did it never occur to you that these men might have considered you a prize catch and that they were waiting to decide what they might do with you?'

'At first I believed it possible. But they could easily have killed me where I slept. Or perhaps it is true what is said about white flesh being repulsive to them. I don't know. My impression was still that they were waiting for someone. Why, otherwise, would they stay so close to the river? And why would one or other of them be endlessly watching for the arrival of a boat? No, I was only an unwelcome interloper, a chance find.

'After three, possibly four, days of this, I sensed a growing excitement among them, a new urgency. Now all three of them stood at the water's edge and searched. I tried, of course, to ask them who or what they were expecting, but either they did not understand me or they refused to tell me; I suspect the latter. And in all that time they constantly re-applied their paints, attending meticulously to each other's faces.'

'And did someone come?'

'A canoe. Late one afternoon.' He cleared his throat, still a painful thing for him.

It was plain to me that he did not want my interruptions, that what he was telling me set an unstoppable pace of its own.

'A canoe. In which sat the feather-gatherer with small bundles of his wares. Some cages of live birds, but mostly their snapped-off wings and tails and heads to save space. At first I thought the man was alone, and that perhaps these three others either had their own hidden birds and feathers to trade with him, or were collecting something from him.'

His pause now was a long one.

'And then I saw that there was another bundle on the floor of his canoe. The man was alarmed by my unexpected presence and at first he refused to come to the shore. But the others shouted some reassurance to him and eventually he came. It seemed to me that the four men were already acquainted. The boatman showed no sign of fearing the cannibals, and remained more wary of me than of them. I tried to speak to him, to determine if he too was Aruwimi, but he dashed at me and struck me with the club he carried. He, too, was as naked as they were. I thought at first one of my three reluctant companions might defend me or tell him to stop, particularly as I had imagined they had shown some solicitude towards me.'

'And did they?'

'No. They watched him as he continued to beat me and they laughed at what he did and called out to him, encouraging him to even greater violence. I passed out after several minutes of this – there were often long delays between the blows while he circled me – and when I came round I saw that the four men were sitting together and that they had lit a fire on the high part of the bank. I lay still and quiet, watching them. They smoked and drank from gourds the feather-gatherer gave to them. By then – I reckoned it to be early evening – he too was painted red. Whatever it was they drank must have been potent, for I saw that they were often retching and sick, and that they did this where they sat, making no effort to move back to the river or away from the fire.'

'Another of their liquors,' I said.

'I imagined so at first. But I realized afterwards that what they were doing was purging themselves, that it was some part of their ritual, and it occurred to me, despite my beating, how fortunate a position I so

311

suddenly found myself in, that I was witnessing the very thing I had set out to find.'

'They were going to eat human flesh? Whose? Did it not even cross your mind that you were—'

'The bundle in the boat was the body of a small girl.'

'A girl.'

'Or at least I imagined it was a body, that she was already dead, but when the feather-gatherer returned to retrieve what lay there, I saw that the child was still alive, that she was trussed and gagged and paralysed with fear and by the understanding of what was happening to her.

'I must have made some involuntary noise at seeing her, because at the same moment she was uncovered, the three others turned to me. I raised my arms to cover my head, but this caused them only to laugh. No-one came to me. Instead, they occupied themselves by smothering the mound of their fire with leaves. This caused the few remaining flames to produce an immense amount of smoke, which drifted low over the river and through the trees, and which hung in a dense pall above us, a low roof beneath which we sat. Only where it floated across the water did this show any sign of clearing. I remember choking on it as it blew around me before rising. They laughed at this, too, and I saw that they were damping down the blaze to contain and increase its inner heat.

'The feather-gatherer picked up the girl by a rope which ran the length of her curved back, tied between her neck and her ankles, as though he were lifting a small suitcase from the canoe. She struggled at being picked up like this, but she was so securely bound that it had little effect. He brought her closer to the fire and threw her down there. I imagined her age to be seven or eight, but it was difficult to be certain because of how she was tied and contorted. I knew that she was still a young child by the thinness of her limbs. She was considerably paler than any of the men, another tribe completely.' He paused again and took several deep breaths.

'The feather-gatherer told Hammad she was his daughter,' I said.

'I know. Nash told me. An interesting sequence, wouldn't you say: the feather-gatherer told Hammad, who told Nash, who told me.'

'Is it true? Was she his child?'

'I doubt it. I imagine she was someone he had taken in a raid and kept alive solely because he believed he might sell her.'

'Do you believe Hammad told the man to say she was his daughter?'

'It would certainly add weight to the case against me.'

'But why? What does Hammad hope to gain by it?'

He turned to look at me for the first time since he'd started talking. 'A year ago, I might have said your naïvety did you credit, James.'

I acknowledged this in silence.

He waited.

'Go on,' I said.

'The man who had dropped her by the fire removed her gag and she screamed. I knew by her voice that I was close in my guess of her age. This screaming only served to increase the pleasure of the four men. They were still smoking and drinking and vomiting, and occasionally one of them threw up on the girl, or emptied some of their milky liquor over her. You can imagine how this also added to their pleasure. They were beyond control of themselves, literally out of their senses with their stimulants and purges, and for the

313

first time I began to fear for my own safety. I knew that my pistol was still in my satchel and that it remained loaded. I felt its outline against the wet canvas, convincing myself that if one of them did come to me with the intention of doing me harm, then I would at least be able to shoot either him or myself. If they could treat a small child in such a way and derive such great pleasure from it, then I was in no doubt what they might afterwards do to me. I pushed myself upright until, though still sitting, I was supported between the high roots of the tree beneath which I sat.

'Then they began to pull the leaves from the fire, inspecting the ashes beneath, encouraged by what they saw there. They took branches and spread these glowing embers over a wide area. The girl resumed her screaming at seeing this, and having let her continue for several minutes, the feather-gatherer then went to her and kicked her violently in the face, concussing her briefly and silencing her.

'When she came round her nose and mouth were bleeding and she began to sob convulsively. This seemed to offend the men less than her screaming and she was allowed to go on while they attended to their fire. I could see that they were close to being ready, that they had driven themselves to the pitch of their excitement.

'Throughout all this, I found myself mesmerized by what I was seeing. Do you see, I was perhaps the first Englishman to witness this ritual from start to finish? Perhaps I even contributed to their excitement, to whatever perverse pleasure they took in what they were doing. Imagine that, James, I was participating – not willingly, perhaps, and with no true understanding of the part I played – but I was *there*, I was *watching*, I *wanted* to watch, I *wanted* them to go on doing what

314

they did. It was what I had gone in search of, what I had found.'

'No!' I shouted, unable to stop myself. 'No, it wasn't; not that. You were ill, you were unable to be anywhere *except* where you were, unable to do anything *except* witness whatever they performed in front of you. You were no part of it, no *part* of it.'

He allowed me to finish before going on. Everything I said he had known I would say.

'But what did I imagine I was doing there in the first instance?' he asked. 'How did I imagine I was going to find what I went in search of and yet remain detached from what I saw?'

I shook my head in despair at his reasoning. 'Go on,' I said.

'They dragged her closer to the fire and started to untie her ropes. They released her feet first, and the girl, perhaps imagining she might still escape her fate, attempted to run from them, dashing only a few yards before stumbling and falling and being caught and dragged back to them.

'Then, with her hands and neck untied, they passed her from man to man, prodding and squeezing her like the meat she was to them. The feather-gatherer pretended to bite into her arm and then collapsed with the laughter this occasioned. Another of them kicked her feet from under her and then stood with his foot on her back, pressing her small naked body to the ground as though she were some trophy he had just acquired. They played with her like this for a further hour.

'I tried several times to intervene – though this amounted to nothing more than shouting out to let them know that I was still watching them – but this had no effect on them other than to cause them to shout

315

back at me and taunt me, helpless as I was to divert them from their course. One of them even brought the child close to me and swung her from side to side by holding her arms and lifting her off the ground. She cried out at the pain of this, and the man holding her made it clear to me that *I* was the cause of that pain, that my attempt to intervene had prolonged the child's suffering. I covered my eyes to let him know I understood him, and he dropped her beside me and she landed awkwardly across my legs. She was again crying almost continuously. I felt her grab my leg and then be pulled from me, her head striking the ground as she was dragged away.

'Back at the embers, another of the men, the man who had previously attended to me, gave a cry and I saw that this was a signal to begin. They gathered together. One of them took a long blade from among the bird-cages in the canoe. The girl was held by two of the men now, each holding an arm and a leg and stretching her until her limbs were pulled straight, and presenting her to the man with the blade. She fell silent at her first sight of this and began gasping, convulsing with fear. I imagined he would plunge it into her heart, or perhaps slit her throat and that she would be killed quickly. But he did neither of these things, and instead he started a drunken dance around the stretched child, jabbing at her so that only the very tip of the blade pierced her, opening up wounds, and then drawing the edge of the blade back and forth over her, scoring lines into her back and chest and thighs, and again drawing blood while doing her no mortal harm. I screamed at them again, but they paid me no mind.

'And just when I imagined there were no new horrors for the child to endure, that she would soon be insensible from her wounds and oblivious to what must now happen to her, the two men holding her took her closer to the fire and raised her until she was directly above the glowing ashes. Smoke rose off her hair, and her screams grew shriller and shriller and more animal than human. And then I watched as the men released their hold on the girl's legs and these fell into the embers themselves, disturbing them and causing her to try to kick herself free, almost as though she were running through the fire in an effort to be free of it before it consumed her. But she was still held by her arms, and for every feeble effort she made to escape, so the two men pulled her back. The smell of scorching flesh filled the air. Her feet were firmly inside the embers, and I wondered how much longer, how many more of those endless seconds, she would remain conscious before her suffering became too great for her.

'And then, just as I was about to call out again, she fell silent, and I thanked whatever cruel god was looking over her that her ordeal was over. I remained silent. I could not imagine how she had persevered for so long. But then, just as I anticipated that the four men might now drop her corpse into the embers, one of them threw a container of water over her face and revived her slightly. It seems they were not to be denied even a minute of their pleasure.

'And having burned her legs, they grabbed her by her blackened knees and held her upside down over the flames so that she scrambled now with her arms to lift herself free. It was more than I could bear to see. What little remained of her hair burned quickly. Her face was only inches from the embers and she pushed through these with both hands in an effort to keep herself above them. The smell of her burning flesh grew even greater, and it was no longer possible to make out any of the punctures or lines on her scorched body.

'And then, because all this had lasted too long, and because I had again remembered my pistol, I took it from my satchel and pointed it towards them, shouting for them to turn and look at me, to see what I was doing, but even though I attracted their attention this time, they were all by then so greatly excited by what was happening, that none of them took the slightest notice of me other than to glance across to where I sat. Perhaps they calculated their chances of being hit, or missed, and perhaps they had found my pistol and unloaded it. I no longer cared. And then, just as I picked out the feather-gatherer as my target, the two men holding the girl released their grip on her and she finally fell into the embers.

'And seeing this, I knew immediately what I must do, and I aimed at the screaming, flailing body and I fired. There was still a bullet in the pistol, and the instant I fired the girl stopped screaming and struggling and so I knew that I had struck her and killed her. The small flames and grey dust rose all around her and she quickly lost her outline in the heart of the blaze. I saw where her head lay, and the bulk of her small body, but her legs and arms were quickly covered and lost to me. There was nothing else I could do, and the pistol fell from my hand. I waited for the men to dash to me and to kill me too, but in the few seconds of consciousness which remained to me, I saw that not a single one of them moved, that they remained by the fire, and that with various gestures of dismissal they turned away from me back to the body which now cooked at its centre. That was all I saw. I passed out immediately afterwards.'

He stopped speaking, and for a few seconds the heartbeat of the drumming women filled the air, until that too fell quiet on a single beat and the overwhelming silence of the place descended upon us and laid itself over us like a shroud.

Frere sat with his eyes closed, his fingers pressed tightly into the flesh of his face, as though they too were flames and he might himself now be consumed by them. I could not imagine the depth or the extent of the darkness into which his closed eyes gazed. I considered putting my arm around his shoulders, but even that simple gesture was beyond me, and so, in yet another act of abandonment, I rose and left him where he sat.

28

I left the garrison in a daze, my mind filled with all that
Frere had just told me. At the edge of the yard I was
accosted by Bone, who emerged from the trees and
grabbed my arm, demanding to know why I had left
Frere alone and in the open. I pulled myself free of him
and pushed him in the chest, causing him to stagger
backwards, lose his balance and fall. He cursed me and
scrambled back to his feet. He retrieved the rifle he had
dropped and pointed it at me. He jabbed me in the
stomach with it and I pushed back even harder. I told
him that Frere had no intentions of going anywhere. He
turned in a full circle and peered into the trees behind
him.

I saw that something other than Frere was on his
mind. I asked him what was wrong and he told me that
another of his men had been attacked earlier that
morning, wounded in the leg by an arrow he believed
to be tipped with poison.

There had been reports of unknown men approaching the garrison yard during the night. Fires had been
started in the surrounding trees to burn off the under-
growth. I knew he was over-reacting to the situation
and told him so. I asked him where the wounded man

was and he indicated the garrison house. I told him to send the man to Cornelius, but he said the man was too scared even to venture outdoors. Then let him die here, I told him, unwilling to indulge this fantasy of attack any longer.

I left him and followed the path to the compound. Behind me, I heard him running and calling to Frere.

Upon reaching my room, I rested. The walk had exhausted me. In places the blackened ground still smouldered and I had been forced to make detours. I was determined to go in search of Nash and demand to know why, having been told the same story by Frere, he still insisted on sending him to trial for murder.

But despite my resolve, my exhaustion was greater than I realized and I fell asleep where I sat, surrounded by the last of my charts.

When I woke it was evening. I had slept for six hours.

I went outside. The deformed boy lay asleep on my step. I prodded him with my foot, and when he did not respond I kicked him harder. I told him to fetch Nash to me, but he made no attempt to rise. He rubbed his eyes and looked up at me. I saw that he was naked. He had shaved his head, and someone – he was unlikely to have done this himself – had followed the curved hump of his spine in a line of white thumbprints, extending this over his twisted shoulders and along each arm. I kicked him again and repeated the order before returning indoors.

Nash came an hour later. He entered without announcing himself and cleared a space at my desk. He seemed intoxicated. He told me immediately that he had come as a courtesy to me, and that, regardless of what I had been told, what I now understood or believed to be the truth of the matter, he would not discuss with me any of the events Frere had related.

The girl had been killed and Frere had willingly confessed to shooting her.

But my outrage at this was uncontainable and I listed reason after reason why Frere should not now be facing trial.

He listened to all this without speaking, unmoved by my protests and pleas. At one point he rose, took the bottle of brandy from beside my bed and drank from it.

When I finally fell silent, he pulled his chair closer to me and handed me the bottle.

'He killed the girl,' he said. His words were slurred. He was unshaven, with a small cut above one eye which shone wetly each time he ran his hand across it. 'It's all that matters.'

'But surely, the circumstances—'

'Tell me, if you're so concerned for the wretched child, what was her name, what was she called?'

'What does it matter what she was called?'

'Precisely.' He retrieved the bottle. 'Did he tell you that she was the feather-gatherer's youngest daughter? No? Seven years old.'

'Hammad's lie. The man—'

'And that, having come across Frere barely conscious, barely alive, on the bank of the river, the man was attempting to help him when Frere pulled out his pistol and fired at him without warning, missing him but striking the girl, who was unloading the canoe beside him.'

'Even *you* can't convince yourself of that.'

'It's the story the feather-gatherer tells.'

'Rehearsed by Hammad, who wants his show trial. What about the testimony of the others present?'

'What others? According to him, he, Frere and the girl were alone.' He raised both his hands. He knew every protest I would make.

'The burned body, then.'

'She fell into the fire when Frere shot her. Her father was fighting with Frere to prevent him from re-loading and firing again. Hammad's agent found the grieving man two days later at one of their usual rendezvous to trade the birds and feathers.'

'And the man's story was worth more to Hammad than his cargo?'

'Incalculably more.'

'Where is he now, the feather-gatherer?'

'Presumably being measured up for a suit at Hammad's expense ready for his visit to Stanleyville.'

'And after that?'

Nash shrugged. 'Ask Hammad.' He drank again from the bottle. 'If it is any consolation to you, Frere denies none of it.'

'But his own story is entirely different.'

He acknowledged this in silence. 'He killed the girl. He went in search of what he found. His journals tell the whole story.'

'The journal Hammad brought to you.'

'And others. The man was obsessed. Did he tell you that, had he not been exhausted and unwell, had he not been suffering and delirious, that he would in all likelihood have accepted the men's offer to take part in what they were doing? Imagine that – *he cannot deny*, for all the extenuating circumstances, for all that did or didn't happen, *he cannot deny* that he may have participated.'

'And so his honesty will hang him.'

'He was delirious. Who knows what he did or didn't do?' It was the last feeble echo of a broken argument.

'You do,' I said. 'And I do.'

He shook his head.

'And he does,' I added.

But his work here was finished, and nothing I said

would divert him in the slightest from the course he now followed.

'I did what I was told to come here and do,' he said eventually.

'Of course you did.'

I could see that my words stung him, but that he no longer possessed the strength or the will to persist in trying to convince me that, of everyone at the Station, I alone insisted on following this different course.

'I shall leave Stanleyville as soon as it is expedient for me to do so,' he said, as though in response to another question.

'Of course you will. Expedient. And Frere will be long dead before you even reach the sea.'

He rose at that, picked up the bottle and tipped it upside down so that what little remained of its contents splashed over the papers scattered at his feet.

I slept fitfully through that night. The colony of small apes returned and ran clattering over my roof until something scared them off two hours before dawn.

I made a small pile of my spoiled papers and took them outside to start a fire. The boy sat and watched me. I cared little for him any longer. I asked him where the old boatman was, and he said, simply, 'Gone,' nodding upriver as he spoke. He, on the other hand, would fulfil his blighted dream of travelling downriver to the growing cities there. He insisted on helping me gather up more papers and feeding them to the blaze. Those soaked in brandy burst into blue flames and floated above the dying fire. The boy took some pleasure in watching all this, and he rolled on the ground like a satisfied dog. He picked up the blackened papers and crushed them to dust in his hands. In the darkness, the white markings along his spine gave him the appearance of a serpent curving back and forth, attracted and repelled in equal measure by the blaze. I fed more to the flames than I had intended, but I was as mesmerized by them as the boy was, and once started I did not want the fire to die.

It was a clear, dry night, and the sky above me shone with the intensity of lacquer. The moon was gibbous and pale and it lay whole on the water, barely disturbed in its outline.

The compound was in darkness, but a succession of lights still showed along the far shore. It was said the Station there was now so inundated with trade that vessels were filled and unloaded through the night. They were distant, but it was possible to make out the figures of men passing among these lights. Klaxons and whistles sounded, faint and distorted over the expanse of moving water; there was no peace there.

The boy complained that the fire was burning low. I returned to my room, pulled the trunk from beneath my bed, and took from this the journals Frere had asked me to keep safe for him, those accounts of all our early wanderings together, of everything he had discovered and described. I took them all out to the boy and showed him how easily they burned if fed to the flames a page at a time. I could not bring myself to look at the writing, drawings and small paintings and maps they contained. But I knew that if I did not burn them, then someone else would, someone who had never known Frere, someone disgusted by the mention of his name.

I burned packet after packet of his precious photographs.

The boy looked more closely at the torn pages; he recognized the animals and birds, each of these identifications a small thrill for him. There were some pages he was reluctant to burn, and I stood over him to ensure that he concealed none of them and later took them away with him.

The bindings and covers of the journals burned more slowly, with a strong and acrid smell, and the boards themselves cracked and spat like burning bark. We were at least an hour in the task.

At some point before the fire died, Fletcher came out to us. He carried his pistol and wanted to know what I was doing. I told him to mind his own business. He looked from the blaze of consumed papers to the boy and said that he too had been unable to sleep. He said that earlier in the night he had seen Abbot feeding a fire of his own, tending it some distance from the compound in the hope that no-one would see him.

He left us after that.

The boy held his hands close to the dead fire. He rubbed the soot from the charred paper and boards onto his forehead and cheeks. He spat into his palms and moulded a handful of this mess into a small ball, which he smeared over his lips and teeth, and which he then sucked as though it were some sweet fruit.

Ensuring that nothing legible or identifiable remained, I left him and returned to my bed, the dawn's first light already showing above the trees.

29

Later that morning, and ensuring I was not observed, I went to see Cornelius. The noise of hymns and of Klein berating his flock rose from the chapel, the voices amplified and distorted by the tin walls and roof which could not contain the racket.

At first I thought Cornelius had fallen and that he lay unconscious on the floor, but as I knocked and entered he roused himself and rose slowly and stiffly from where he had spent the night. He wore only his trousers and boots. There were dark rings of sleepless-ness around his eyes, and his usually neatly trimmed beard and moustache had started to spread over his neck and cheeks. He mumbled an apology for his appearance and told me to sit down. He pulled at a cloth tied around his upper arm and then flexed his arm back and forth. The cloth left a dark welt.

I started to tell him what I had learned from Frere the previous day, but he remained distracted, unconcerned by what I said.

Eventually he held up his hand to silence me and moved closer to the window to better hear the singing and the voice of the priest.

'Listen to him,' he said. 'Listen.'

I stopped speaking of Frere.

'He antagonizes you deliberately,' I said. 'It's a game to him.'

'He doesn't have to antagonize me,' he said. 'His very presence, his very existence is a constant reminder of my own failings and weaknesses.' He took his crumpled jacket from the bed and put it on.

'He knows that, too,' I said. 'But what do you imagine you will ever achieve by confronting him?'

'All I want to know is the truth.'

'About your wife?'

' "Wife",' he repeated softly.

'Your child's mother,' I said.

' "Wife" will suffice. She was that in all but the eyes of the church, *his* church.'

'Can't you accept what Perpetua told you?' I said.

'And for which she was punished. Perhaps I will have to accept it, but I would much prefer to hear it from him before everything here is gone forever and we too are forgotten to the world.'

'What do you intend doing?' I asked cautiously.

He finished buttoning up his jacket before turning to me and slowly shaking his head.

'Are you going to see him?' I knew he was. 'Then let me come with you to—'

'To what? To witness fair play? Save that for Frere. You are as useless to him in that respect as I ever was to her or my daughter.'

The remark caught me unawares.

'Yes, I intend going to see him. And, if necessary, I'll pay him to find out exactly what happened to her, where she was sent, where she might still be.'

We went outside together, and no sooner had we secured his door behind him than we heard a loud scream, followed by another and then another in rapid succession. There was a short silence, followed in turn by three more screams, as evenly spaced as the first three, and leaving us in no doubt that they came from inside the chapel.

Cornelius ran ahead of me. I tried to grab him and stop him, to give us time to send for Fletcher, but he pulled himself free of me and ran panting to the chapel door, pushing it open just as a further three screams filled the air.

I ran to join him.

The chapel was full, the congregation on their feet and dancing in a common rhythm from side to side, men and women groaning aloud and shouting out. Some of them stood with their faces pressed to the corrugated walls and others lay writhing in the aisle and round the edges of the small room.

At first no-one appeared to notice our arrival and the commotion continued unabated. It was difficult to see what was happening at the front of the chapel because of this throng of shifting bodies, but Cornelius pushed through them, shouting for people to get out of his way as he went. Those he pushed aside complied without resistance, and many became silent in his wake; some even fell back into their seats, exhausted by their exertions.

I followed a short distance behind him, and as I passed into the body of the crowd, and as the men and women gave way around me, a further three screams filled the small space, echoing against the walls and low roof so that this time there was no silence between them, and so that the three were drawn out into a single, prolonged cry.

Ahead of me, Cornelius continued to push through those at the front of the crowd and emerged into the space before the altar. He called out at what he finally saw there, and the people closest to him moved away in alarm. I hurried to join him. A woman fell at my feet and shook on her back as though having a fit. I stepped over her; no-one else made any approach to her, merely moving further beyond her reach as she continued to twist and turn and bang her head and palms on the ground. Everyone in the overheated room was bathed in sweat, their faces dripping with it as though they had all been doused.

I finally arrived where Cornelius stood and saw what he saw.

There, beneath the altar, on a rack resembling a slanting cross, lay Perpetua, bound by her ankles and wrists to the upright and cross-piece in some semblance and mockery of the crucified Christ. She was naked but for a cloth fastened around her groin, and upon her head was a crown of thorns, pushed hard into her flesh so that she bled where it pierced her. I looked at all this, unable to fully comprehend what I was seeing, looked closer and saw the welts across her legs, breasts and stomach, saw where these bled in lines over her black skin.

Only then did I see that to one side of her stood Felicity, her eyes closed, her hands clasped in prayer. She was once again wearing her nun's habit, the hood of which covered most of her face. She kept her head bowed, intoning whatever useless prayer she uttered.

And at the other side of the woman on the rack stood Klein, his slender cane in his hand, held above his head, as though he had stopped mid-stroke at Cornelius's sudden intrusion. The man seemed unperturbed at his discovery. He looked hard at Cornelius, at the disgust and incredulity which filled his eyes, and he smiled, almost as though he had anticipated this interruption, as though Cornelius's arrival were part of the ritual and the punishment, and as though the ceremony and the woman's suffering were now enhanced by Cornelius bearing witness to it.

And from Cornelius, Klein looked briefly to me, and I saw a flicker of uncertainty and anger cross his face. I looked from him to the cane he held, and almost as though in response to this, reminded of the act he had interrupted, he brought it sharply down across Perpetua's breasts.

Before either Cornelius or I could respond to this, Klein swung the cane and struck her again, and then again, this time not looking where his blows landed, but instead keeping his eyes on Cornelius. The first of the blows landed across Perpetua's stomach, and the second caught her on her neck and immediately raised a welt there. Her screams were louder than before and I felt each one as though it were a blow to my own face.

Unable to tolerate any longer what was happening, Cornelius ran at Klein and pushed the man so harshly that he fell back against the wall, where he stood for a moment recovering from the blow. Cornelius turned to Perpetua. He took out a knife and cut her from the cross. I anticipated that the rest of the congregation might finally make some move against him, but instead they cleared an even wider space around us and watched us in fright. Cornelius pulled down the embroidered altar cloth and gave it to Perpetua to cover her nakedness. She trembled uncontrollably and needed his support to remain standing. Cornelius called for Felicity to help him, but the woman remained where she stood, still refusing to raise her head.

By this time, Klein had regained his composure. He ran at Cornelius and struck him across his back with his cane. Cornelius turned, grabbed the stick and snapped it easily in half. Klein backed away from him. He stabbed his finger at Perpetua and told her to remove the altar cloth, accusing her of desecration. Cornelius positioned himself between the priest and the woman. Klein called to his congregation to help him, but despite the ripple of fear his words sent through the crowd, no-one approached the altar to carry out his command.

Cornelius took the crown of thorns from Perpetua's head, causing her to cry out as each of its points was prised free of her. He gave her a handkerchief to wipe the bloody mess of her brow.

Klein exhorted the men who stood closest to him to seize Cornelius, but they too refused to obey him, looking at each other over his head and then backing away from him.

'She is *possessed*!' Klein screamed at Cornelius. 'By devils. By her own admission. This is for her own good. She will not be allowed entry into our new church until she is rid of them. It is what she wants. *Ask her. Ask her!*'

'You have no intention of taking her with you,' Cornelius said loudly. 'Nor Felicity. They know too much of you. They've seen the dirt on your hands.'

'Such eloquence, such insight,' Klein said, raising his hands in mock surprise.

Cornelius turned back to Perpetua and again wiped her brow. 'I know you understand what I'm saying,' he said to her. 'I know you won't speak, won't answer me.'

She held his hand briefly as he wiped the blood from her eyes. She still trembled beneath the gold-embroidered cloth.

'You, too,' Cornelius said to Felicity, who raised her head barely an inch in acknowledgement before lowering it again.

Then Cornelius turned back to Klein. 'You're right,' he said. 'I did want answers from you, I did want to know what happened to the child's mother and—'

'The whore!' Klein shouted. 'Say it. That was what she was when you met her and defiled her. And that is surely what she went back to being when you abandoned her with her belly already swollen.'

I saw the restraint Cornelius exercised at hearing all this. I saw his fists clenched hard by his sides.

The rest of the congregation continued to watch us in terrified awe. Klein's snapped stick at his feet had done nothing to diminish their fear of the man.

He saw them looking, pointed to Perpetua, and shouted, 'She was possessed by devils, many devils, devils that would have defiled her just as this man defiled and abandoned his own woman! There is no place in our new church and mission for women like that or men like him. Is that what you want? Is that what you truly want? To be forever surrounded by such animal evil? Is it? Or do you want to follow me and build anew in the new light of a new age?'

No-one answered him. There was considerable agreement with what he said, but no-one responded directly, preferring instead to nod their concurrence and to either bow their heads or to avert their eyes when he looked at them.

'She was a whore!' he shouted at Cornelius. 'And a bigger whore when you left her. What did you imagine – that I would take pity on her and keep her at the mission, give her work and a home there for her and her bastard child, is that what you thought? We sent her to Port Elys as soon as the child was born. Perhaps we even believed that we might save the child by removing her from her mother, and her from us. Whatever, she was a sickly child, and so who knows?'

He paused to catch his breath. 'Or perhaps she pined for her mother and that was the reason she was so sickly. Perhaps having a whore for a mother was better than having no mother at all. Perhaps she would have learned to live with the idea just as you learned to live with it. Oh, you did learn to live with what you'd done didn't you, van Klees, with the lives you'd blighted? Surely you learned to beg forgiveness of the Lord for what you'd done, and then to live with that forgiveness? No? No? What, *never*?'

Cornelius pulled at the cross until the top was lifted free of the altar and he threw it to the ground.

'One cross,' Klein said. 'Such a resurrection. And your woman, van Klees – don't imagine that we at Kirasi did not in some way benefit from her departure. Or should I say her sale?'

Cornelius looked up at this, his fists still clenched, his thumbs running back and forth over his knuckles.

Klein seized his advantage. 'Did you imagine we just gave all those poor, disappointed women away after all the mission had done for them, after all we had provided for them? The Port Elys traders knew where we were, how to reach us. They understood the quality of our goods. Tell me, is that where you hope to go in search of her? Because if it is, don't bother. Port Elys is only where they start out. No-one lasts long there. From Port Elys they are sold on to Yalata or Petit Coeur, and you know what those places are like. Perhaps you've even visited the women there. Of course you have. Rest assured, van Klees, your wretched child was better off not knowing how she came into the world, far better off. And you, too – I imagine you made your own convenient excuses which were easier to live with than the truth of the matter. I pity you, I really do. You're no different from that wretched man Frere, no different, except that he is to be called to account for his actions and you are left to live damned but unpunished with the consequences of everything *you* have done.'

I doubted if Cornelius could stand much more of this, and I stood ready to restrain him should he again attempt to reach Klein. Klein, too, I sensed, understood that he had said as much as he dare, and he turned away from Cornelius and Perpetua and raised his hands above his head and started singing, stopping briefly to shout for his congregation to join him, which they did, falteringly at first, but then with growing conviction and enthusiasm, as though they too understood that this was the only release available to them.

Cornelius attempted to get Perpetua to accompany us out of the chapel, but she resisted, and he knew not to insist. He whispered something to her which I did not hear, and she went painfully to stand beside Felicity, who held her in her arms.

'Whore,' I heard Klein say behind me, uncertain if he was referring to either of the 'nuns' or again to Cornelius's lost woman.

Seeing that neither Perpetua nor Felicity would accompany us, Cornelius moved away from them, knowing that upon our departure they would again become the targets for Klein's rage.

I told him we ought to leave, and he nodded his agreement. The singing grew ever louder as we passed back through the body of the singers to the chapel door.

Once outside, I said to him, 'He was lying about your daughter's mother.'

'Was he?' he said, and left me.

I looked back at the chapel and saw Klein come to the doorway and stand there looking out at me. Perpetua and Felicity stood on either side of him, Perpetua with her arms folded over her naked breasts.

Klein held the altar cloth, which he looked at distastefully for a moment before throwing it to the ground at his feet.

'There may still be time to save yourself,' he called to me, laughing loudly and attracting the attention of a line of passing soldiers, who stopped to consider what was happening and to gape at the near-naked woman.

30

I took the news of all these events to Frere, but he showed little interest in what I told him. I started to tell him of the contradictory stories Nash had been told, but he insisted he did not want to hear them. He asked me instead if there had been any word of the steamer, but I could tell him only that it was two days from us on a falling river.

I told him of what I had destroyed, and in a voice devoid of all conviction and emotion he said I'd done the right thing.

Looking around for anything further he might want removed and burned, I saw that a great deal had already been taken from his cell.

'Bone,' he said. 'I paid him to destroy what was left.'

'Was that wise?'

'I insisted on watching the fire through my window and paid him when he was done.' He picked up his Bible from the desk. 'I want you to take this,' he said. He paused slightly before releasing his hold on it. 'Is it tainted, do you think?'

I took the book from him. 'May I send it to Caroline?' I asked him.

He nodded. 'It was beyond me to ask it of you.'

'I *will* write to her,' I said.

'I know. I imagine you've already started and destroyed a dozen letters. Tell her *your* truths. Make no case for me other than what exists in your heart.'

'She would never have condemned you,' I said, knowing that these most distant of connections would never be severed. I took his hand in mine and felt his fingers tighten around my own, and we sat like this for several minutes, neither of us speaking or knowing how to speak, until finally his grip slackened and he withdrew from me.

'Go,' he told me. By which he meant that this was our parting, his final act of severance.

I went without complaint and he watched me from where he sat, his hands splayed on the boards of his table.

A bright light shone in on him through the open doorway and I stood to one side to see him fully bathed in its glow. His eyes were closed – though whether against the intensity of this glare or the fact of my departure, I could not tell.

At the outer doorway I paused again and secured the Bible beneath my jacket. Men and women passed back and forth across the garrison yard; Bone and his men performed some perfunctory drill; a tethered goat repeated its child-like bleat. I saw how far I had come in those few paces and seconds from the man alone and adrift at his table.

I walked into the yard and passed through the crowd there towards the river. I was accosted by several traders, but I ignored them all, knowing that if I attempted to speak I would only choke on the silence I had swallowed.

*　　　*　　　*

The following morning both Perpetua and Felicity were found hanging from the same limb of an ironwood tree a hundred yards from the compound wall. It was a low limb and the two bodies hung barely a foot from the ground. They were close together and the arm of Perpetua was extended towards Felicity as though the two women had held hands during their final moments. Both wore their nuns' habits, and around the neck of each woman was a sign saying 'Please Forgive Us'; the same three words, and each sign written in the same careful hand.

I was alerted to the discovery by Cornelius, who had himself been roused by Bone, but we knew nothing of what we were about to see until our arrival at the tree, beneath which the women still hung and twisted on their ropes. Twenty or thirty others knelt in a circle around them, praying, and occasionally falling forwards to clutch the ground in their grief.

Klein stood to one side of this crowd, his head bowed, a book of prayer closed over the fingers of his hand.

No-one turned at our approach, and Cornelius and I stood at the edge of the trees, unable to take our eyes from the bodies. I felt numbed by what I saw.

Cornelius went ahead of me, through the praying circle, until he stood beside the women, and just as he had cut Perpetua from her cross, so he took out his knife and cut her from her rope. He called for help from the crowd, but no-one rose to assist him.

He held Perpetua as she fell loose, and then laid her on the ground beneath the tree. He then did the same for Felicity, laying her close beside Perpetua and folding their arms across their chests. He pulled their long skirts straight and brushed the leaves and dirt from their shoulders. Then he cut the messages from around their necks and took them to where Klein stood. He tore the boards into pieces and threw them in the priest's face. Klein, though lifting his head to look directly at Cornelius, did nothing to protect himself, merely standing as the pieces of torn card struck him and then fell fluttering to his feet.

I wondered what Cornelius might do next, and I started moving towards him, but as I did so he turned away from the silent priest and came back to me, passing me without speaking.

A detail was sent to remove and bury the two bodies, at which Klein himself insisted on officiating.

I watched this later in the day and saw the two younger women chosen by Klein to become his new helpers, the black-and-white outfits already worn by these grateful, excited novices.

I left the graveyard at the first of the hymns.

Late in the afternoon, the deformed boy ran terrified into the compound and lay on the ground screaming until Fletcher went out to him and shook him into silence. He called the boy our bird of ill omen and told him to leave. But the boy refused to go, and afterwards Fletcher and Cornelius took it in turns to question him until he screamed again and told them of what he had seen.

31

The following two days were spent in an emptiness of waiting. No-one approached Frere, and nor was he seen outside his cell.

The only activity of those days, it seemed, was the removal of our quarry workers across the river in preparation for their work on Klein's new mission. All around us there was unrest and rumour of unrest, and, closer to our hearts, averted glances, sudden silences, and old hatreds burnished to new points.

A still and earthy atmosphere descended on the place; weeds and grasses grew where men had recently plied their trades; the river fell and its lesser channels were quickly clotted with drifted growth.

On the first morning a succession of canoes passed us by, each filled with standing men, their faces painted with antimony to resemble skulls. They made no attempt to approach us or to divert to the Belgians, merely standing and watching us as they went silently by.

The second day, a native worker was carried into the compound who had been stung over his whole body while attempting to secure a wild bees' nest. He was attended by four women, and he died in agony where he was laid. The women beseeched us to help him, but there was nothing we could do for him. Fletcher took out a bottle of spirit so that the man might become intoxicated beyond the reach of his pain, but even that seemed a cruel joke to play on him. When he was dead the four women carried him away again, leaving behind a patch of dirt rubbed bare by his thrashing about, and several of his faeces, alive with worms.

Fires burned along the river as our workers dismantled and destroyed their makeshift homes. An explosion at the quarry excited no-one.

We lived among each other like ghosts through those days and nights of overheated uncertainty, and I surely cannot have been alone in believing that the world beyond our close and encroaching view of it had at last ceased to exist, that it had finally changed beyond all recognition and understanding, beyond all we had ever known of it.

And at the appointed hour – the time only Nash still truly believed the steamer bound for Stanleyville would arrive – Frere was brought under guard from the gaol to the compound and made to await the vessel's arrival there. Bone and four of his men came with Frere, Bone walking ahead of him, and the others forming themselves into a square around their charge, this unaccustomed formality an echo of Frere's delivery to us a month earlier. They were joined by Nash, who came to the water's edge only when his prisoner had arrived there, and when the rest of the compound had been cleared.

Seeing what was happening, and knowing that Nash would not now alter his plans to allow for the late arrival of the steamer, I gathered together Cornelius, Fletcher and Abbot, and the four of us stood and watched the proceedings from a distance. Frere saw us, understood our purpose there, and turned away from us. Bone's men congregated in a group, and Nash insisted on them returning to their positions around Frere.

It was then late in the afternoon, and clear enough to everyone except Nash that the steamer would not arrive until the following morning at the earliest.

Both Fletcher and I tried to reason with him, but he insisted we were wrong, that we were men who now lived our whole lives in the expectation of delay and disappointment, men who had grown too attached – too *attuned* – to the formless existences we had so long lived. I started to argue with him, saying that I was thinking only of Frere and the time he would be forced to stand waiting, on display to anyone who passed by, and then afterwards waiting through the darkness, but my pleas made no impression on the man, and eventually Fletcher pulled me away. Nash called out after us that he accepted full responsibility for what happened. The militia men would wait with him, he shouted. He himself would remain armed.

We waited like that for two hours beyond nightfall. A man was sent to stand watch three miles down-river and told to fire a signal at the first sign of the boat.

Bone and his men, tired of standing, now sat and lay on the ground around Frere. Complaining of an ache in his legs, Abbot brought out chairs for us, and took two of these to Nash and Frere, placing them side by side overlooking the river. Bone and his men repositioned themselves accordingly.

I had expected to see Frere taken with some of his belongings, a change of clothing perhaps, clothes for his trial, a final satchel of his papers or letters, but he carried nothing, and he and Nash sat like strangers at a railway station awaiting their long-overdue train.

By then it must have been apparent even to Nash that the vessel would not come. What did arrive, however, catching us all unawares, and adding a further degree of uncertainty to the situation, was a vessel from the far shore, and we all watched as it crossed the river towards us.

I watched with dismay as Amon emerged from the cabin and leaped from the prow. He was followed by Proctor and eight more men, all armed. Others remained where they stood in the vessel's wheel-house and on its deck, and I imagined that Hammad might be among them, watching us unobserved, our every movement reported to him, there to set his final seal on his own involvement in the matter, to confirm that the train of events set in motion by him all those weeks earlier was at last aimed unstoppably towards its conclusion, there to wash his hands of us, and to applaud himself and all that now awaited him.

Amon paused beside Nash and Frere, but spoke to neither of them. He told Proctor to position his men mid-way between our two parties and then came on alone to where we waited. He extended his hand to both Cornelius and myself, but neither of us returned the gesture. He asked us what Nash thought he was doing, allowing his prisoner to remain so exposed. I refrained from asking him why he had come to us with so many armed men.

We discussed the late arrival of the steamer, and he told us there were a dozen suitable vessels waiting idle at their own wharves, but that these had not been offered to Nash for fear of the Belgians appearing to be anything other than impartial observers in the affair. I laughed at this and he smiled at me, at his own greater

understanding of the politics of the situation. I asked
him then why he was there.

'To offer assistance,' he said, indicating Proctor and
his men. 'To ensure the whole operation proceeds
smoothly.'

'And to protect Hammad's investment,' Fletcher said
to him.

'Perhaps. Who knows? You and I, Mr Fletcher, we are
such little men in these affairs.'

I had said all I wanted to say to the man at our last
encounter and did not want to again become tangled
in his deceits and dismissals. I told him he had no
jurisdiction on this side of the river and asked him to
leave.

'Jurisdiction?' he said, savouring the word and all it
implied. He looked around us, at our empty wharves
and at the scattered buildings already lost to view in
the darkness.

He left us after that and returned to Proctor. He told
the armed men to join Bone's guard on either side of
Nash and Frere.

Fletcher wondered aloud what the man was up to,
what he feared concerning the handing over of Frere,
or, worse, what he was there to provoke. He left us
briefly and returned with a rifle.

An hour later there was a false alarm. Someone
downriver started beating a drum and we all imagined
this was a signal sent by our look-out. Torches were lit
along the bank and the wharves. Everyone strained to
look and listen for anything approaching, but nothing
came to us out of the darkness. It was by then almost
midnight, and the river, though illuminated along its
surface by the broken outline of the moon, flowed
swiftly into the blackness of the trees beyond.

Fires were lit around Nash and Frere, and some

among the guards took out bottles. I called for Bone to prevent his men from becoming drunk, but his only response was to approach one of the men, take the bottle from him and drink from it himself. The shifting light of the fires showed Nash and Frere at the centre of all this, distanced by their silence and stillness from everything that was taking place around them. I saw how disappointingly different all this was from what Nash had planned for and anticipated. His own belongings had long since been taken from his quarters and stacked on one of the jetties.

I anticipated that Amon might return to me, but he never came. Presumably, he had already calculated the exact point and line of his own departure and path away from Hammad.

Eventually, the drumming downriver ceased, and just as I prepared myself to wait through the remainder of the night, I was alerted to the arrival of others at the far side of the compound. At first I could not make out these newcomers, counting them only by the lights they carried, and then I heard their singing voices and knew that Klein had come and brought with him his congregation so that he and they might witness and delight in Frere's final humiliation.

Both Bone and Proctor commanded their men to keep this crowd away, but Klein himself told the men and women with him to stay back and to arrange themselves into an orderly half-circle behind the seated men. I could not believe that the man and his followers had come so late in the night and with so little warning to us.

Klein approached Nash, and Nash rose from beside Frere and told the priest to keep his distance. Klein raised his hands in submission. He remained where he stood, talking to Nash, and occasionally shouting abuse at Frere. Frere responded to none of this. Behind Klein, his congregation sang one hymn after another. And when they had exhausted their meagre repertoire, they started again, the same few songs over and over. Both Bone and Proctor called for them to shut up, but, despite faltering briefly at these commands, they continued.

I was now more convinced than ever that the time had come to insist that Nash made other arrangements for guarding his prisoner, certain that with so many unexpected spectators and participants he would have little choice but to agree with me. I put all this to Cornelius and Fletcher, but neither man was anxious to intervene. Cornelius, I saw, kept his eyes fixed on Klein and would not be distracted from the man. Fletcher rested the rifle across his lap, his hand on the bolt.

Nash then moved closer to Klein and ordered him to return to his congregation. Amon, I noticed, stood a short distance from the two men and watched them closely. I saw that he was deriving great satisfaction from the night's events, and I began to wonder again why he had come if not to participate in them in some way.

There were times when the congregation fell silent for minutes on end, regaining their breath and preparing themselves for their next outburst. The singers still held lights, candles, lanterns, burning torches, and these rose and fell in the darkness amid their bodies like the lights of a town seen from afar.

I heard Nash shout at Klein to get the singers to withdraw, and Klein shout back that he, Nash, was the one making a public spectacle of Frere. I saw that Klein carried another of his slender canes and that he slashed this back and forth through the air ahead of him as he

347

spoke. The watching soldiers laughed at the two men and shouted their drunken encouragement to one or other of them. Neither Bone nor Proctor attempted to intervene and restore order to the situation.

I looked to Frere and saw that he still sat with his back to all of this, but that now he held his hands firmly over his ears and was slowly shaking his head from side to side as though to deny the existence of everyone around him. He leaned forward slightly until his elbows rested on his knees. And then he folded his head into his chest and held one arm over the back of his head, the other over his eyes. I saw how intolerable all this had become to him, and even as I watched him, silently calculating what I might now conceivably do to lessen his suffering and remove him from the centre of the men around him – men who seemed themselves to be almost oblivious to his presence – Klein pushed past Nash and began beating him across his back and head with his cane. Nash attempted to restrain him, but Klein pushed him away and caused him to fall. Nash rose and pulled out his pistol, standing off from Klein and pointing it. Beside me, Fletcher took his rifle in both hands and slowly aimed it towards the three men. Klein went on beating Frere where he sat, and the singing of the congregation grew even louder, so that I could no longer hear if Frere cried out at each of the blows. The soldiers continued their cheering and shouting, and just as it seemed that Proctor was about to intervene and pull the priest away from Frere, I saw Amon approach him and prevent him from doing so.

By now, Klein had worked himself into an uncontrollable rage and he struck out ever more vigorously at Frere, little concerned where his blows fell, so long as each of them landed somewhere on his unresisting target.

I told Fletcher to fire above the heads of the men, which he did, but the shot had little effect other than to cause each of the participants to pause briefly before resuming, and for a further hesitant ripple to run through the singing crowd. I told him to fire again, but he refused, saying the effect would be the same.

Then Cornelius rose beside me and said, 'Put a bullet through his head. What difference will it make? Do it now and spare him everything he has yet to come. This is just the start of it all.'

It took me a moment to realize he was talking about Frere.

Fletcher considered what Cornelius said, but kept his rifle pointed into the air.

In a break in the singing I heard Klein's grunts and Frere's muffled cries. Nash shouted again and moved even closer to the priest, his pistol pointed directly at his head. But either Klein remained oblivious to this or he did not believe that the man would shoot, for he went on slashing at Frere.

Throughout all this, I could not understand why Frere did not rise from his chair and defend himself.

'Do it,' Cornelius said again. 'Do it.' And before either Fletcher or I fully understood what was happening, he pulled the rifle from Fletcher, pointed it towards Frere and Klein, and fired. His whole body shook uncontrollably, as governed by rage as Klein was, and the weapon trembled in his hands. He drew back the bolt and fired again, and this time, primed by the first explosion, everyone fell silent at the shot and looked anxiously around them to see where the bullet might have struck.

I looked hard at Frere: he remained in his seat with his arms around his head, but so convinced was I that he was about to unfold himself and then fall to the ground that I did not at first see Klein falter in one of his blows and stand frozen for an instant, turning my eyes from Frere to the priest only as Klein dropped his cane, half-turned to look in our direction and then fell onto his knees and then his face, unable even to put out his arms to protect himself.

The men standing closest to all this cried out. Some of the soldiers took up and aimed their own weapons, some towards Klein's congregation, others at us.

A scream rose from amid the hymn-singers, followed by others until it seemed that every single one of the men and women there was screaming. They disbanded and started running in all directions.

Nash stood with his own pistol still extended, and at first it must have seemed to those standing near by that he himself had fired and killed the priest, and several of the militiamen, including Bone and Proctor, ran towards him, their own weapons raised. But Nash ignored them and the wailing crowd, and turned instead to where Cornelius stood beside me with the rifle raised, and looking from the fallen Klein to Frere and then to Cornelius, he swung his pistol and fired without warning. Cornelius cried out, took a steadying step backwards, and in the same instant fired involuntarily towards where Nash stood.

Fletcher and I, alarmed that others might now start shooting in the confusion, threw ourselves to the ground. Cornelius fell backwards beside us and I saw that he had been struck in the face. His hands clawed at the ground for a few seconds and then he lay still. I shouted for everyone to stop shooting.

I looked at Nash, who stood unhurt over the body of the priest, and I waited a few moments longer before rising and walking to where Cornelius lay. He had been struck in the forehead by Nash and his eyes remained open and fixed. Abbot knelt over him, pressed his ear to Cornelius's mouth and then shook his head in disbelief.

Over at the river, Nash returned to Frere and sat beside him. I doubted if either man was fully aware of what had just happened. The pistol fell from Nash's hand and he looked down at it briefly before raising his eyes back to Frere.

Amon and Proctor approached Klein's body. Amon tapped it with his foot several times and then withdrew, satisfied that the priest was dead. He motioned for Proctor to follow him, and after Proctor had called for his men, he and they returned to the waiting boat.

Women from among the congregation ran to Klein, flung themselves over his body and continued their wailing, covering the corpse from head to foot, almost as though they believed their living warmth and fanatic beseeching might somehow resurrect the dead man, inconsolable in their grief and flailing their arms and beating their fists against their own faces and chests. Most had by then thrown off whatever garments they wore and were now pressed naked over Klein, the mass of their bodies red in the light of the fires, and they seemed to me, seeing them at that distance and still struggling to understand everything that had just happened, like scavengers in a frenzy of bloody feeding over a recent kill.

Nash, I saw, had helped Frere upright and had taken his arms from around his head.

Beside me, Fletcher laid his jacket over Cornelius's face and pulled Abbot to his feet.

And out on the water, Amon's steamer drew slowly clear of the shore and moved ever faster into the quickening flow of the middle channel, visible to us only by the lamps it still showed, and I watched it as it went, until even those few dim lights were one by one extinguished and lost and the vessel disappeared completely into the utter and impenetrable darkness of the night.

THE END